From the desk of
Jacki Simmons

Stripped

http://www.melodramapublishing.com

Stripped
Copyright © 2006 by Jacki Simmons

For information address:
Melodrama Publishing
P. O. Box 522
Bellport, New York 11713-0522
646-879-6315

Web address: www.melodramapublishing.com
e-mail: melodramapub@aol.com
author's email address: **msvisualeyes@yahoo.com**
Library of Congress Control Number: 2006934899
ISBN 1-934157-00-7
First Edition

This novel is a work of fiction. Any resemblances to actual events, real people, living or dead, organizations, establishments, locales are products of the author's imagination. Other names, characters, places, and incidents are used fictitiously.

10 9 8 7 6 5 4 3 2 1
First Paperback Edition

Stripped

Acknowledgements

John 16:24 "Ask and you will receive, and your joy will be complete." I have asked, and I have indeed received. The darkest times in my life, You were there, even if I didn't know it. I owe my all and everything to you and yet you've never asked for anything but my love and faith. And they *still* doubt You.

I want to thank my mother, Wanda, without whom, nothing I've ever done would be possible. No human on earth knows me better than you. They call me mad now and then but only you know there's a method to my madness. You've never tried to change who I am, and you've never made me apologize for being me. You have gone above and beyond the call of duty when it comes to being my mother.

To my brothers, first I want to thank you guys for putting up with me as I finished this book. Then I want to thank you for keeping me sane. I used to complain that I wished I was an only child and then I looked back and realized that all my happiest memories were with you. I love you kids.

To Dad, they say everything happens for a reason. Our checkered past has only paved the way for a stronger future. I love you. And I'll see you Tuesday.

To Ed, thank you for treating me as if I were one of your own and not a "step."

To my girls, Kimma, Jazz and Dre: I love you girls more than you will ever know. Thank you for being there when I needed you, for finishing my sentences, for calling at one in the morning just to see what I was doing, and for letting me be me no matter what the situation. I couldn't ask for better sister friends and I'm blessed to have you all in my life.

To the people that have helped me get this far: Tah and Lazy, who made me what I am and help me bring out my inner bitch, I love you two. Stay exactly as you are. Change is for the bus, remember that. Marc Etienne and Rachel Wiemerskirch, who first helped me express myself through writing and then Ehrlich and Baslaw and Masso who always believed I could make it here; my Taino Towers family for staying on me and making sure I kept walking tall: to Uncle Arthur for loving me and the fam regardless; to Monica for being my buddy and for helping me max out those Cingular text messages (air five from across the country), to Jason for not being pissed at me when I didn't call, to my other Jason for making it worth my while to be in school everyday when I was *this* close to saying f*** it, to Kevin for picking up where Jason left off, to Tony for making me laugh (do you believe me now nigga?), to Tera for just being that bitch, to my original crew, Angela, Amber, Jennifer, Shanice, Taheerah, Aquellah, Toni and Rhoviea, we were all destined for greatness. Hopefully we all make it there at the same time. To the *other* crew, I'm on my New York ish, you know how it goes. I could never forget about any of you. *Winks*

To Batman: I guess here is the part where I admit you were right. So what? You *still* ain't that nice. Anyway, I'm not sure the definition for 'friend' quite covers exactly what you've been this past year. Webster says a lot of things about what friend can be but the bond shared cannot be summed up merely with words. Every time you cursed me out, started a sentence with "*Gonna lay down my sword and shield…*" or gave me the Three Mm speech, I knew it was done out of love. Every debate that started at ten and ended at seven the next morning was worth it. Every laugh, cry, or pissed moment has been the solidification of a powerful union. I know we're both busy and we don't get to speak as often as we should but you are still and always will be my nigga.

Big ups to my C2C family, for holding me down throughout the past year. You all are a major part of my success and this is for you. (Big ups to Trish, the very first person to ever lay eyes on Stripped. You've been an inspiration from day one. You, and what can only be described as a bomb ass pen, have kept me going for longer than you know. Write on, sis.)

To Nailah Jackson for being the best test reader/literary advisor a broad could ask for. You da man!

To Malik for showing me the ins and outs before I stepped foot in the deep pool that is the literary world.

Special thanks to Lacey for opening her doors and giving me a chance when no one else would. I'm forever in your debt for giving me a shot and proving to the world that age ain't nothin but a number.

(Shoutouts to my BRU Crew: Big Ron, Lil' Ron, 'Zo, XMan, Vice, Peso, Big D, Junie, Steph, Frannie and Tracey. Special shouts to the *night shift* J Ellen, Hector, Jessie, Joe, DeVaughn and Melissa. Even though ya'll are ALL goin' straight to hell for what ya'll put me through these past few months, I gotta love you anyway. Thanx for makin me feel at home despite…well, you know.)

I had to save the very best for last: to my Mikey, what I wanna say I can't really fit on this page and as you would say "*that's bad business*." Gift, blessing, good luck charm, whatever you wanna call it, that's what you are to me. I feel lucky when I wake up and think about you. I don't remember a time with you that didn't involve happiness, a laugh or a smile and that's just fine by me. xoxo

I'm just as imperfect as a pair of jeans off the Gap clearance rack, so please forgive me if you were not mentioned. It does not mean that I love you any less, only that I'm still suffering from that chronic case of CRS (Can't Remember Sh*t.) Odilo o amilo.

Prologue

Trina ain't hardly the baddest bitch.

Trust me, the diamond princess ain't have a damn thing on La Perla. She, no matter how many songs she writes, will never be me. She claims that shit; I lived that shit. And then some.

Furs kept me warm. Diamonds weighed me down. My ass got permanent jet lag from all the trips I was taking. Parking lot full of cars, safe full of money, cabinets full of liquor. The finest men in the world beat my door down trying to get a taste. All I had to do was smile to get whatever I wanted.

I can still smell the blaze they used to hit with me; the champagne that flowed for me is still on my lips. I'm still smiling thinking about how fun those parties were. I had been a good girl my whole life, and when I finally broke out of my shell, I was ready to give 'em hell.

They say life has a way of making you live it. No truer words have ever been spoken. At the peak, at the very top, the height of my fame, something happened. It's called life. Just when I thought it couldn't get any better, it went and got worse.

I don't blame anyone else but myself. Too busy ballin' outta control to notice what was going on with the real world. I thought I was slick, thought I could outsmart life, but the Good Lord looked me in the eye and like

Biggie, said, "You dead wrong." By the time my high came down, I was out of it, left and right. The queen had to give up her crown and go back to stomping grapes with the rest of the kingdom.

I've come a long way in the past few months. No doubt I've still got a long way to go. I'll never get over it but I can try and move on. I've buried my demons and made peace with my past. If anyone didn't like it, they could kiss my honey-brown ass.

I'm not proud of any of it. But I did what I had to do to survive. I heard a funny statement the other day. Something like, "It's a cold world out there, and if you ain't under the umbrella, you gonna get rained on."

Lord knows I was soakin' wet.

I

How You Like Me Now?

Caiza Bell ran her hands over her hips, savoring the feeling coming from below her. She couldn't remember the last time she had enjoyed so much pleasure. It hadn't really been that long, but in her mind, it had been more than enough time to forget how good this made her feel. A smile curled her mouth, and she bit her bottom lip, loving every minute. She looked down and smiled wider, blushing and feeling like a little girl. Her mind went back to her first time.

She had just slipped on her new Jimmy Choo slingbacks.

"This is what it feels like to go to heaven," she murmured, not wanting to destroy the groove. Caiza's reflection mimicked her every move as she poured her curvy body into the hugging wrap dress. She brushed her teeth and applied her makeup. Pouting and kissing her lips, Caiza let the pin out of her hair. Her dark brown curls cascaded down around her shoulders as she took one last look in the mirror. "Honey, you are too damn fine for words." She flipped her hair over her shoulder and turned off the light. The phone rang.

"Hello?"

"Are you on your way?"

Caiza rolled her eyes. "Did I sleep with you last night? I will be as soon as you hang up."

"Oh no, don't trip. I ain't the one everybody waitin' on."

Caiza looked in the mirror again. "Everyone's there already?"

"Well, not everyone. Jacey should be here any minute now, but besides that, yeah, we waitin' on you. So hurry it up."

"Bye, Myeisha."

"Bye."

Caiza glided over to her dresser and clipped in her earrings, dropped her cell phone in her clutch and took one final look in the mirror. She was snatching her car keys off the vanity table when she noticed the nail polish on her index finger was chipped. She rifled through the large assortment of polishes until she found the Moroccan Mix and the clear overcoat. Her watch agreed that it was time to go. There was a whimpering sound from Sparkle, her four-year-old Golden Retriever.

"Now behave, puppy. I don't want to have to come home and kick your butt."

Sparkle scratched behind her ear, showing how uninterested she was in the threat. Caiza patted her on the head before making a mad dash for the front door. She grabbed a shawl out of the hall closet and locked up behind her.

It was Thanksgiving, her first day off in months. She took another glance at her watch. Six-fifteen. Caiza hated to be late. She prided herself on being on time everywhere she went. It made her look good and besides, she got to survey the scene. Climbing into her car, she started it up and began the short ride to 37th Street.

Midtown traffic was no joke on any night in New York, which was another one of the reasons she left early. Stopping at a red light, she opened the bottle of Moroccan Mix and delicately applied it to her damaged finger. The light changed as she blew on her wet nail. Guiding her car with her wrist, she carefully replaced the cap of the polish. She took her eyes off the road for just an instant to lift the clear polish.

It was a lovely fall evening, the kind of night when people came out just to admire the beautiful weather. As Caiza drove along at a comfortable pace, she let her mind wander. Caiza would rather stay home on the holidays. She hated Jacey's family with a passion. Both their families always spent the holidays together. Jacey was big on family and after this much time she knew how to paint on the face. Unlike her divorced mother and father, Jacey's parents were still together, and he had two brothers and two sisters.

They were a swindler, a madam, an ex-con, a wifebeater and wannabe pimp, a high school dropout with multiple children and a jewel thief, respectively. Jacey was the only one who had done anything positive with his life. His real estate business had been up and skyrocketing in the past few years, which accounted for their comfortable lifestyle.

Caiza had all but stopped paying any attention to the road, so when the Mercedes in front of her stopped suddenly and flicked on its hazards, she slammed right into his trunk. She was instantly jarred back to reality when she pitched forward and hit her head on the steering wheel.

"Shit!" Caiza cursed, holding her hand to her head. Quickly, she sealed the bottle of polish and threw it on the seat next to her. Looking out the front window she cursed again, opening her car door. The man slammed his car door and began to walk toward her, arms outstretched.

"Yo, shorty, you ain't see me stop?" He was one of those rowdy-looking men, like he had no problem rocking her jaw in the middle of the street. He was sporting long dreadlocks, a white tee under a Celtics jersey, dark blue jeans and Timberlands. *Mr. Cheeks wannabe bastard,* she thought. "Look at my shit!"

The damage wasn't serious, but it was bad enough. She could understand why he was pissed. The left light had been knocked out, and there was a sizeable dent in the bumper. The paint had been stripped away in the center.

Caiza knew she had to throw on the persuasion and she had to do it quickly. That's all she needed was the police on her ass. "I am so sorry. This is my fault. I wasn't paying attention." She shook her hips as she went to survey the dent. Checking out his bumper, she bent over at the waist and pretended to be interested. Straightening, she looked at her own fender. She pulled her phone out of her clutch. "Let me give you my information."

Dreadlock licked his lips and checked her out, doing a bad job of pretending that he wasn't. He pulled out his cell. "Yeah, you do that." Caiza turned around when she heard the car behind her lean on his horn. The two of them were becoming a traffic jam.

"Hey, get out of the street, lady!"

Caiza cut her eyes wickedly at the driver, but made her way back to her own car. Dreadlock, who was now on his cell phone, turned back to his Benz and double-parked, out of the way.

"Damnit," Caiza muttered as she maneuvered behind Dreadlock. She made the call to All State. After they exchanged information, and he had gone off to handle his business, she flipped her phone open again. Looking down at her watch, she bit her bottom lip, angry that she was going to be late.

"Hello?"

"Jace, it's me."

"Baby, where you at? Everybody's here waiting on you."

"I know. I had an accident on 40th Street. I need you to come pick me up."

"What happened?" he asked.

"Nothing much—a little fender bender."

"For real?" His voice picked up concern. "Are you alright?"

Caiza stamped her foot. "I'm fine. I just wanna get to dinner."

"Alright. Stay right where you are. Where are you?"

"Fortieth and Eighth."

"I'll be there in ten minutes." He hung up.

Jacey immediately took control once he got there. He had a tow truck take her car to his auto body shop, and he drove the rest of the way in his BMW. Caiza loved how cool he was the whole time. He hadn't even broken a sweat.

Once on the elevator, Caiza took a thirty-second power nap while leaned against the silver banister. When she popped her eyes back open she looked to her left. Jacey looked good, she noticed. He smelled even better. She hoped that he would be up for a couple of rounds later on that night. Watching his face, calm and collected, made Caiza forget she was in a bad mood.

Caiza shook her hair out of her face, and Jacey took a look at her. "What happened up there? You've got a cut."

She touched her head. Sure enough, there was a little blood on her fingers. "Oh, damnit, I hit my head on the steering wheel. Is it bad?"

He shook his head and pulled a handkerchief out of his pocket. He touched it to her forehead. "Well, it's gonna need a bandage. And it might leave a little scar. You're not hurting anywhere else, are you?"

She held the handkerchief to her forehead. She could feel a headache coming on. "I'm not hurt, baby. I'm okay."

His answer was to pull her closer to his side.

"Thanks for coming to get me."

He kissed her. "Ain't no thang, baby," he said. The elevator made it to their floor. As it opened, they were welcomed by warmth. Flowing from the ceiling were soft champagne-colored curtains. The room was dimly lit and from behind the curtain, a horde of smells hit her at once. Jacey moved one of the curtains aside and led her in the room.

"Well it's about time," a voice called. Myeisha Brown was Caiza's best friend. They had known each other most of junior high and had become tighter than tight in high school. That night, she had wrapped her to-die-for body into a floor-length black dress with a slit up the thigh that gave off a view of her thigh-high leather boots.

Caiza hugged her best friend, whispering into her ear, "Did you come straight from the club?"

"Nah, but I gotta work as soon as I leave up outta here."

Caiza's mother caught her eye, and Caiza smiled a big old fake one when she saw her. She didn't know her aunts and uncles would be there tonight, or her favorite cousin, Shane. Shane waved from across the room where she was already on her fourth champagne.

"Caiza, you look lovely. Are you putting on weight, honey?" her mother, DeLiza, asked after thoroughly up and downing her.

She rolled her eyes and accepted her kiss.

"Jacey told us you were in an accident. Are you alright?"

"I'm fine mother. I'm just a little hungry is all."

DeLiza, satisfied that she had at least spoken to her child, went to find something to complain about. Caiza took a minute to drape her shawl over one of the couches and take in the scene. The hardwood floors were glowing on account of the scented candles flickering in every corner.

There were gaps in the curtained walls near the windows, where the last rays of the sun could be seen making way for the night sky. On one side of the room was the lounge area, mostly couches and longue chairs and comfy throw pillows, the center dance floor, and on the other side was the dining area.

The two families sat down to eat after Jacey's father, Milton, said a long prayer that had everyone peeking at their wrists. Caiza peeped at her watch and found he'd been talking for ten minutes. When he finally said

"Amen," they all almost jumped for the food.

It was a typical Thanksgiving. DeLiza and Rashanna, Jacey's mother, had worked together and produced platters of mashed potatoes, candied yams, greens, macaroni and cheese, biscuits, gravy, cranberry sauce, yellow rice, red rice, potato salad, two stuffings and of course, a huge turkey. For dessert, there was cherry pie, sweet potato pie, pumpkin pie—Jacey had a slice of each because he claimed he couldn't tell the difference— cheesecake, and Rashanna brought along homemade vanilla ice cream.

After dinner, a few of them went outside to get some air or have a smoke. Music was turned on, and the older members of both families got up to "cut some rug." Caiza sat back and laughed as she watched Milton and her uncle Chuck attempt the Cha Cha Slide.

She stood at last and joined, taking their hands and schooling them. Jacey scooped her away when "Step In The Name Of Love" began to play. R. Kelly flowed through the speakers and got everyone off their feet. They ended up playing the record three times before everyone took a breather. Caiza was relaxing and catching her breath when Jacey stood up to say something.

"I want to thank everybody for coming on short notice. Usually, we plan far in advance, but I know we had a bit of a problem with the invitations," he said, eyeing Myeisha. She smiled and hid her face behind a plate of pie. Jacey smiled back and continued.

"Everybody who knows Caiza and me knows how long we've been together—five years and still going." That made everyone clap. Caiza blushed from her seat next to him. He touched her shoulder, casually putting the other hand in his pocket. Jacey directed his next words at her. "I just want to say that every day with you has been a miracle. I've never met anyone like you before, and I'm sure I never will again. You make me happy and that's all I've ever asked for. And I want you to keep making me happy."

Jacey bent down on his left knee. He pulled a small black box from his pocket and opened it in front of her. "Will you marry me, Caiza?"

Caiza thought her heart was going to stop. She felt herself blushing harder and just knew all eyes were on her. She couldn't breathe for only an instant, and everyone in the room held their breath with her. She began to blink rapidly, and her head started to feel light. Then Caiza caught

Myeisha's eye. Myeisha made a "go on" gesture with her hands. She nodded and took a deep breath, and the feeling passed.

"Yes," she whispered. There was a collective sigh of relief from everyone in attendance. Jacey beamed like the bright sun after a long rainstorm. He put the ring on her finger. Smiling the way only a happy man can, Jacey lifted her out of the chair and into his arms.

"You need to stop wavin' that thing around before I snatch it off ya hand," said Denise. Denise and Caiza had worked together since they were hired at the same time. They had become pretty close in their five years and often spent the long hours joking with each other. Today was no different.

Caiza giggled before sitting down. The long weekend was over, and it was back to work. She had been playing with Denise all day, flashing her hand in her face whenever she had the chance. "I'm sorry girl. I can't help it. Isn't this the most gorgeous thing you have ever seen?"

Denise took her hand and examined the ring closely. "It really is pretty. How big is it?"

"Four carats."

"Hmm. If I had me a man who could afford a four, then he'd have to spring for a six."

Caiza laughed as she began to file some paperwork in front of her. "That's exactly why you don't have a man, now isn't it?"

"You know what, bitch? You ain't cute. You ain't even cute." Denise smiled and turned away as her desk phone began to ring. Caiza's own phone rang right after.

"Good morning, Ester and Scarowitz, how may I help you?"

"This is Donna Glover. I'm Justin Mercer's agent. I'm confirming his twelve o'clock appointment for this afternoon with Mr. Sapling."

Caiza flipped through her appointment book as if she didn't know who he was. Justin Mercer, known in the rap community as Bulldog, was one of her favorite rappers. He just happened to be a client with the firm for which she worked. Whenever she saw him, her heart skipped a beat. He was too fine for words. But he was way out of her league.

"Yes, Ms. Glover. Mr. Smith will be expecting him."

"Thank you." She hung up.

They arrived exactly one hour later. Bulldog was never late for his appointments with his lawyer. He felt it was bad for business and bad for his image.

Caiza opened the record book. "Good afternoon, Mr. Mercer, Ms. Glover," she said politely. "Please sign here."

Donna signed first, her flourishing script taking up two lines. Bulldog took the pen from her. Caiza winked at Denise as she stood to show them into their lawyer's office. "Follow me please." Bulldog did follow her, his eyes roaming up her body.

"That's new?" he said, nodding at her hand.

"Yes."

"Who's the lucky man?"

She smiled. "His name is Jacey."

He nodded again, a toothpick dangling from his lips. "Jacey. Jacey White? That nigga that be sellin' apartments and shit, right?"

That's not how she would have put it, but she nodded anyway.

"He's a good nigga. Sold me a nice crib down on 22nd Street. Congratulations."

She blushed. "Thank you." She opened his lawyer's door and showed them inside. As soon as she shut the door, she tried not to squeal and hop-skipped down the hallway back to her desk.

She sighed, rubbing the picture of Jacey on her desk. "Girl, if I wasn't getting married, I'd rape him."

Denise held up her hand with a pencil sticking out of it. "You mind sayin' that a little louder into the microphone please?"

"What?"

"'Cuz when they arrest ya ass, best believe I'm getting the reward!"

"You should see the rock on her hand. Shit, girl, that bitch is laced," Trina said. Trina owned the Nubian Designs hair salon on 135th Street. She knew what went on in the hood before it happened. At that moment, she was leading the discussion on Caiza.

Myeisha lifted her head as Kristina finished rinsing the chemicals out of her hair. "I was there. You know she got it goin' on."

"Please. She ain't shit. She livin' off that nigga, you hear me?" Kristina pushed My's head back in the sink. She squeezed some shampoo onto her scalp.

"No she's not. You just hatin' 'cuz you ain't got no man." My wasn't about to let anybody play her girl.

"That's funny. I had your man last night."

"Oh no you didn't," Adeena, who was busy rolling someone's hair, said, laughing.

Trina moaned to herself. "Shit, I know what I would do if I had five minutes with that fine-ass nigga. I'd turn his ass out, you hear me?"

The girls laughed. Myeisha was getting uncomfortable. Kristina put a towel around her head and led her to the styling chair. "Y'all betta stop that. You know he loves that girl."

"And if I had him, he'd love me too," Adeena replied. That brought another round of laughs.

"I heard he ain't that hard to get into bed."

"He's a man. Only man it's hard to get in bed wit' is the dead ones or the gay ones."

The resident gay stylist, Peaches, raised his blow dryer. "Objection, bitches. I'd go for a piece of his sweet ass in a heartbeat, okay?"

My had to smile at that. Peaches was flaming and didn't care who knew it. He didn't have a problem coming on to someone else's man and had gotten into quite a few scraps over it.

"What you think, My?" Kristina asked above her head. "How long you think *that* is gon' last?"

My didn't like the way she said *that,* but left it alone. "Come on now. You know that's my girl. I ain't tryna dog her like y'all."

Trina spoke up waving her hot comb wildly. "Ain't nobody tryna dog her. I just wanna know what he see in her that he don't see in me."

"I know what he don't see," mumbled Peaches.

"Speak up, baby."

"I said I know what he don't see. Homegirl keep all her shit tight. That nigga don't want you with your cottage-cheese ass."

Adeena snorted loudly and covered her mouth; Kristina giggled and pretended she hadn't heard. Trina didn't appreciate being laughed at. She combed a strand of her customer's hair, pouting. "Whatever. I bet she can't do him like I can."

Adeena smiled. "I guess you ain't never gon' find out, right?"

Trina threw a brush at her, rolling her eyes.

Jacey and Caiza's engagement was the new flame on the ghetto gossip circuit. Jacey may have had money and status, but they remembered when he was the scrawny project kid back in the day. Now that he was engaged, it seemed like things were going crazy between his groupies.

He had girls fighting over him every minute of the day, and in all honesty, he loved it. He figured girls only fought over true ballers. He was wrong there. Girls fought over *anybody* with money and status. It didn't hurt that he looked good either. In the back of her mind, Trina was already forming a plan. That uppity bitch better watch her back.

"And not a single scratch. Nobody'll ever know you banged up a Benz," Alphonse joked. He had been doing Caiza's repairs ever since she learned to drive. He rotated her tires, changed her oil, and winterized her car, pretty much everything and anything she needed. He claimed he gave her a discount because she was so pretty, but she really knew it was because Jacey would whip his ass if he didn't.

"Thank you so much, Al. I've gotta hand it to you. She looks brand new."

He nodded and wiped his hands on a grease rag. "So where were you running off to that you got all banged up?"

She waved her hands excitedly. "It was Thanksgiving. I was on my way to dinner, and I wasn't paying attention. You fixed up a baby fender bender. I tried to put the moves on him, but it didn't quite work. All State called me back within the week."

"Hmm. I'm glad it was just the car that got hurt. So what else you been up to?"

She stuck her hand out. "This."

He took her delicate fingers in his. "He proposed? Jacey playa-for-life? We are talking 'bout the same nigga, right?"

She nodded happily. "One in the same. I'm gonna make him an honest man if it kills me."

"It just might," he joked. Alphonse shook his head. "That is something else, baby girl. I remember when you first drove in here for a wash. You thought it was a self-service and you got out and soaped it down by yourself."

She laughed and covered her face at the embarrassing memory. "You had to bring that up?"

"By the time me and the guys got out there, you were ready for a rinse. I was thinkin' about hiring you."

They got a kick out of that one. When their laughter died down, he pulled her into a big hug. "I'm really proud of you. You've come a long way since then."

The hug lasted a second longer than it should have. At that moment, none other than plotting Adeena just happened to be driving by. She slowed to allow a car out of the gas station, then looked left to make sure the coast was clear. As she began to look away, her eyes caught sight of someone familiar.

She saw a man place a kiss on Caiza's cheek before she got in her car, but from her point of view, she thought she saw them kiss on the lips. Her camera phone was hot and ready as she took the shot. Adeena almost crashed in her hurry to spread the news. She sped off up the block, and Caiza never saw her.

"Hello?"

"Kris? This Adeena. Girl, you ain't *never* gon' believe who I seen kissin' up on some nigga at the gas station."

Kristina got comfortable. She was always ready for juicy gossip. "Word? Who?" A minute later her phone bleeped as Adeena sent her the picture. She gasped and squealed, dialing Trina's number faster than her fingers could move.

"Hello?"

"Girl, I got some hot shit to tell you!"

Trina put on her most sympathetic face as she rubbed Jacey's back gently.

"Look," she said softly, stroking his body and his ego, "I hate to have to be the one to tell you this. And you know I'm not the type to break up a happy home, but my conscience, baby. My conscience couldn't let me go on, looking you in the face and lying."

Jacey put his face in his hands. He had just seen undeniable proof that his girl was cheating on him. Trina called and told him she had something she needed to say to his face. He figured she was just being Trina and trying to offer up her body again, but when she said it was about Caiza, he knew he should listen. Those pictures didn't just take themselves.

He stood and paced, hands on his waist. "I spent six fuckin' grand on that ring," he shouted. "I told her I loved her in front of both our families. I asked her to marry me in front of my parents. This how she gon' do me?" Jacey had spent the better part of his twenties honing his image, but the hood part of him always lingred under the surface, ready to rear its ugly head. He kicked the sofa hard.

Trina jumped. She waited until his back was turned, then took off her sweater, revealing a rather tight shirt with a severely plunging neckline. She pushed her breasts up in her bra, then took his hand and pulled him back down on the couch.

"Hey, listen to me. It's going to be just fine. You know you can always lean on me for anything you need, right?"

She reached into his lap and unzipped his pants. Moving his boxers out of her way, she put him to her lips. "Anything you need."

2

She Ain't Nobody

Three Months Later

"Do you even have a bank account?"

"Yes, I have a bank account. I just don't use it." Caiza was on yet another one of her infamous shopping sprees at the Manhattan Mall. Caiza didn't see the need to save money as long she got whatever she needed from Jacey. After she got her check from the law firm, she saved what she needed for her tuition but that was all. "How's this look?" She held up a pink cardigan.

Myeisha posed. "That would look better on me."

Caiza put it back on the rack. "Yeah, right. You know you need to be shoppin' at Hoes R Us."

"Oh no you didn't, wit' ya skinny ass."

"That's funny. My man likes my skinny ass. But you wouldn't know what that's like, would you?"

"A'ight. I see you got jokes. Okay. Remember that shit when you need somethin'," Myeisha said, stepping on her foot.

Caiza hopped around on her good foot. "Ow! If we wasn't in public, I'd whip your ass."

Myeisha put her bags down, stretching out her arms. "Come on, baby girl. Ain't nothin' but space and opportunity."

"Don't play with me, honey. I will mop the floor with you."

"You feelin' froggy then leap, bitch."

"A'ight, that's it." Caiza dropped her things and tackled Myeisha right there in the sweater aisle at Express. They wrestled like five-year-olds, rolling about as if their ages could still be found in the single digits. A salesman interrupted them.

"Is there anything I can help you ladies with?"

He scared them both. The girls picked themselves up off the floor, smoothing their clothes and fixing their hair. Both of them grabbed their bags. The salesman had a huge grin on his face.

"We're fine, thank you."

Caiza took Myeisha's hand, and they booked it out of there, bursting into laughter when they reached the front door. "Did you see his face?"

"I know. Like he was waiting for a tittie to pop out or somethin'."

Caiza giggled wildly, turning around to see if the salesman was still looking. "This is why I love you. I can only do this with you," Myeisha said.

Caiza put her arm around Myeisha's waist as they walked on. "Aw, I love your skinny ass too."

They lunched at the food court, both ordering from Ranch 1. Myeisha watched as Caiza's mood changed. She picked over her French fries, barely touching her sandwich.

"You gon' eat yo' cornbread?" Myeisha asked.

Caiza looked up and smiled. "Yeah, eventually."

"What's the matter?"

She shook her head. "Nothing."

Myeisha put one of her hands on her hip, the rhinestones on her long fingernails glistening in the light. "Do I look stupid? Come on, tell me."

"It's this wedding, girl."

My picked up a fry and nodded. "It's getting real, ain't it?"

"It damn sure is. I mean, just a few years ago, we were in high school. And now I'm getting married. This is wild."

"I know. It's funny. I was just thinkin' about that the other day. So what's the problem?"

Caiza sipped her Coke and swirled the drink around in the paper cup.

"Do you think things are going to change?"

My shook her head. "Only if you let it. If you was fuckin' him seven days a week twice a day before, keep it up."

"Myeisha! And it's three times," she corrected.

Myeisha laughed and slapped Caiza's hand. "I ain't tryna get married."

"Why not? You think you won't be a good wife?"

Myeisha took a long sip of her Sprite before answering. "Honey, it's too many fine motherfuckers out here for me to be thinkin' about settlin' down with just one. The day I get married, I will truly be a changed woman, hear?"

"You know I hear."

They both paused as a chocolate brown Lothario passed their table. Caiza watched him walk away, unintentionally licking her lips. My pulled her head back and rolled her neck, her hand landing back on her hip. "Uh-uh, Ms. Thang. You landed your catch. You gotta save some for the rest of the fishermen."

Caiza smiled and leaned into her girlfriend. "Now, baby, just 'cuz I'm on a diet don't mean I can't look at the menu, hear that?"

Myeisha choked on her Sprite laughing so hard.

"Baby! Where you at?"

"In the kitchen."

Jacey hung his coat in the closet and breathed deeply. Baby girl was making his favorite, steak and potatoes. Nobody could make a steak like her, his mother included. He tiptoed past the kitchen and into the bathroom, stripping off his clothes and stuffing them in the hamper. He took a quick shower and tossed on a jersey and some jean shorts.

"Hey," he whispered, sneaking up behind her.

"Hi, baby. I was trying to be done before you got here."

"It's alright. Your food is worth waiting for."

"Sweet." She giggled, opening the fridge for some buttermilk. "Long day, huh?"

"Why you say?" Jacey dipped his finger in the potatoes, and she slapped his hand away.

"You never take a shower when you come home."

Jacey had a white lie ready for her. "It was rough, ma. They had the radiator up to a thousand today. It was a sweatbox in there."

Caiza nodded her head knowingly. "Oh, tell me about it. Denise and I had to open both windows just to get a breeze."

He ran his hands over her bottom as she bent to look in the stove at the steaks. Caiza didn't have a perfect body, and that's what he loved about her. She was a decent height, only making five-eight and unlike every other girl, she wasn't a caramel-skinned hourglass. She was more honey colored, with a bigger bottom than top. Whatever she didn't have, she more than made for with her backside. Licking his lips, Jacey unzipped his shorts. When Caiza stood, he turned her around and sat her up on the counter. Before she knew it, Jacey was placing kisses on her neck and face.

"Oh! Jacey, let me go. I have to finish cooking. What are you doing?"

Jacey pulled her hand toward the bulge in his boxers. "Dinner can't wait?"

Caiza bit her lip when she felt that. The potatoes were pretty much done; she had already turned them off. The steaks had fifteen minutes to go, and he was looking so good…

"That's what I thought." Jacey pulled off her sweatpants and slid in her forcefully. Caiza gasped sharply and wrapped her legs around his body, pulling him deeper inside. Whispering "I love you" into his ear, she bit his neck and scratched him. Jacey pushed in and out of her harder, then lifted her off the counter completely. He came and she followed, then he set her back down on the counter, kissing her face as he pulled her pants back up.

"You're nasty," she whispered.

"But you like it though."

"You know I do." She slid down off the counter and turned off the stove, and made their paltes, then went back to the kitchen for something to drink.

"I was thinking," she said when she came back. Caiza set down a pitcher of iced tea.

Jacey sat down after pulling her chair out. "About?"

"About hyphenating my name. Caiza Bell-White." She gestured with both hands, as if she could see her name on a marquee.

Jacey stood up to get the salt. He stood next to her and repeated her motions. "Baby, that'd be cool if my last name was Atlantic or Air. Not White."

She giggled and kissed him as he bent over next to her. "Okay.

No hyphen."

"Thank you."

When he leaned over to kiss her, Caiza could have sworn she saw a mark on his neck. She didn't remember putting it there, but they were having a nice evening. Why rock the boat?

Caiza was on top of the world. She made it a point of showing off her new ring to anyone who would look. The only person who had to ruin it for her was her mother.

"You're too young to be married," were the first words out of her mouth.

"And what exactly is too young, ma?" Caiza asked, hanging Jacey's freshly washed shirts in the closet.

"You should wait, you're only in your early twenties. You're still a baby. You don't know anything about life."

Caiza stopped hanging clothes. "How're you going to tell me what I do and don't know about life? I'm an adult now. I'm old enough to make my own decisions."

"I don't know why you need to be so stubborn. I didn't marry your father until I was twenty-eight. And then we didn't have you until I was thirty."

Caiza folded a bunch of panties and placed them in her dresser. "Yes, and then you ran daddy into the ground until he divorced you nine years later."

Her mother gasped. "Caiza Bell! How dare you?"

Caiza stuck the phone between her shoulder and her ear as she folded a pair of boxers. "It's about time you got the truth from somewhere."

"Oh. So you want to talk truth? Here's truth. Since you're so content on making a mess out of your life, don't come crying to me when everything falls apart." She hung up in Caiza's ear.

Caiza placed the house phone back on the charger, frustrated. Her mother was so good at making her life a living hell. She didn't have to say much, but when she did, her words struck like a bolt of lightning. One flash and the target was destroyed. Today was no different. She and Jacey had been engaged for three months, and her mother's attitude toward her relationship was colder than the winter weather. Caiza went to the fridge for a beer.

DeLiza Bell was a bitter woman whose sole purpose in life was to make everyone around her as miserable as she was. She claimed her parents forced her into a shotgun wedding, but shortly after she married Cameron, she miscarried. Cameron was the only person there to console her. They tried again, and two years later, their one and only child, Caiza, was born.

Post partum hit DeLiza hard, and she fell into a deep depression. It was years later that she would be diagnosed and treated, but the damage had been done. Cameron cheated on her often to give her an excuse to throw him out. He left gladly, and the only real reminders of Caiza's childhood were the child support checks her mother received once a month.

Her father worked in advertising and had a hefty sum of money under his belt. Caiza didn't mind the money; it was his absence that bothered her. The last time she had seen him, skorts were still in style. She loved her father but she wished he were more than a check.

In the meantime DeLiza tried to win Caiza over to her side by throwing an eighteen-year pity party. DeLiza was a brilliant, beautiful woman, but she thought it was her right to be catered to after the way she lived. Instead of using her smarts or her talents, she served as a maid for all the years Caiza was alive. She figured if she could tell her all the stories of how hard she struggled when Caiza was young, she could get her sympathy vote.

Caiza saw right through the scam. Her mother was a freeloading bitch who used everyone to her advantage, no matter how it hurt them in the end. She caught on to her mother's games early and refused to be a part of them. She knew why her father left and when she heard the whole story, she couldn't really blame him. She plotted her escape all through high school, and finally her glory day came. The day after graduation, she moved out.

She had landed a job answering phones at a law firm, and over the course of the last four years, had moved up through the ranks until she was the secretary of the senior partners at Ester and Scarowitz in downtown New York. She was down to her last two years of school, getting her business degree at St. John's University; she had a great man, a great place to live and a great life. She stuck her tongue out at her mother.

"Tonight, we're going to have a debate. Instead of discussing economics, we are going to discuss necessity of economics in a structured civilization."

Caiza groaned. She was hardly trying to have a debate. She hated this class. It was so boring. Maybe it was her professor. Professor Caine as he-demanded he be called-was dryer than a piece of unbuttered wheat toast. He had about as much flavor as a scoop of Metamucil and had the character of a wet noodle.

He wore corny bowties to every class and beyond that, he thought tweed blazers and corduroy pants were a fashion statement. *They're a statement alright*, Caiza thought. *A cry for help*. He had a bald spot at the center of his head with white hairs sticking out at odd angles, giving the impression that he was a modern-day Albert Einstein.

The debate took up the rest of the class, and even flowed over five minutes into her management class. Professor Ruby was much more laid back. She was cool and felt no reason to make her students endure hour's worth of useless exercises. She called herself a free spirit (translation: hippie) and wore mostly tie-dye and khakis to school.

She went barefoot in class, claiming that she was "coming closer to being one with nature each day". Caiza thought she was wildly strange, but she was cool enough. Cool or not, she reminded her students that they were there to work, not play, and she piled on the homework.

Caiza was only too happy when class was over and she could go home.

"Good night, Kye," called a classmate.

She swung her head back. "It will be soon as I get home, girl. See you Wednesday."

"Study group, eight. I'll be there. Night."

Caiza smiled when she thought about going home to Jacey. Since the engagement, everything had been perfect. She made it downstairs and pulled her scarf up around her mouth to protect her face from the strong wind whipping through the city. Finding her car hadn't been much of a problem and she turned the heat up to high once she got inside.

She picked up her phone to call and tell Jacey she was on her way home. It rang three times before going straight to voicemail. "That's strange," she said aloud. He always picked up when she called, no matter what the situation. She shrugged, started up her car and drove home.

Looking for a parking spot was like torture. After she finally found one, she ended up having to walk back three blocks back to the apartment. By the time she got there, her feet and back hurt. She'd worn high-heeled boots to class, like a dummy, and the thin coating of snow on the ground made her measure each step so she wouldn't slide and break her neck.

She made it though, without an incident. Hurrying inside Caiza snatched off her mittens and reached in her pocket for the mailbox key. YOU WON! announced Publisher's Clearing House. She rolled her eyes. "Yeah right. That would be just my luck." She didn't need the Lotto; she had Jacey. He gave her any and everything she needed.

The rest was junk mail and a few letters for Jacey, one from Ossining, another from Fishkill and still another from Dannemora. Everybody Jacey freaking knew was in prison. He took care of his locked-down homies though. She looked over his shoulder when he wrote his letters and watched as he stuffed the envelopes with money for their commissaries.

All she was interested in at the moment was her man and what he would do to warm her up. She'd been thinking about him all day and knew there would be something waiting for her as soon as she opened the door. Waiting at the door was not Jacey, but a pissed-off mass of golden fur. Sparkle was waiting and she had to pee.

Caiza was in no mood to return to the ugly weather outside but she did so. Sparkle's usual twenty-minute walk was shortened to just five, and they hurried home. Once inside, Caiza unzipped her slushy boots and left them in the foyer.

Sparkle wagged her tail, rubbing against Caiza's legs. "You hungry? Daddy didn't feed you? Come on. Jacey? Where you at, boo?" She didn't get an answer so she figured he was out with a couple of friends.

She was used to it. She didn't question him about his whereabouts. Caiza didn't feel the need to interrogate him about where he spent every hour of the day. At the moment, changing into something warmer was more important. Sparkle whimpered, staying in place by the front door.

Caiza petted her dog on the head and retrieved her books from the foyer. The house felt so empty without Jacey at home. She couldn't wait for him to return and smiled at the thought of him. Shifting her books onto her left hip, Caiza turned the knob to her bedroom door.

"Damn, daddy, keep on doin' it like that."

"You like this? You like that?"

"Yeah, daddy. Ooh, don't stop."

Trina was in their bed, on her hands and knees, legs spread apart as Jacey pounded her hard from behind.

"What's my name, girl?"

"Ooh, Jacey," she moaned loudly, damn near screaming. "Yeah, yes. Oh don't stop. Jacey, don't stop."

Caiza was frozen to the spot for longer than she should have been. A million things raced through her mind at one time. Only one thought actually made it through. With a scream, she flung her books aside, hurled herself upon the two of them, and within seconds her hands were around Trina's neck.

"I'm gonna kill you, bitch,!" she screamed. "I swear to God I'm gonna kill you!" Caiza had a death grip on Trina's throat. Jacey tried to get her off but the harder he tried the tighter the grip got.

After what seemed like hours of choking but was only a few seconds, Trina was ready to black out. She was mumbling something but her throat was closing, and it couldn't be heard. Jacey grabbed Caiza and pulled her backward hard. Trina slid off the bed, choking and spitting up as she tried to get air flowing back to her lungs. Her face was a step away from turning blue. As soon as Jacey let her go, Caiza again went at Trina like a savage.

Kicking, clawing, biting, she beat on the woman like there was no tomorrow. Jacey again tried to step in, and all he got for his troubles was a busted lip as Caiza flailed like a madwoman. Trina couldn't get a hit in as she tried to protect herself from Caiza and her fury. When she exhausted herself, Caiza backed away, crying and screaming hysterically.

"Get out!" she shouted at Trina. "Get out of my house!" Trina could barely walk as she staggered around the room, collecting her clothes. As she left the bedroom hurrying for cover, Caiza lifted her foot and kicked her in the behind.

When she heard the door slam, Caiza ran out of the room and into the kitchen. She reached for a bread knife. Jacey was just coming out of the bedroom and saw her throw it in his direction. He ducked and the knife lodged in the wall. Caiza yanked it free and went after him again.

"What are you doing? Caiza, put that down. Hey!" he shouted as she lunged at him. He caught her arms and had to violently wrestle the knife from her hands. He grabbed both her wrists and grabbed her to him so her back was against him. Then with all his might, he snatched the handle of the knife from her. When he got it free, she collapsed on the floor crying in a heap at his feet.

"How could you do this to me, Jacey? I thought you loved me? You said you loved me."

"I do love you, baby. I'm sorry." He tried to bend and help her up but she wasn't having it.

"Get away from me, you dirty shit," she hissed.

"I'm sorry, Caiza. It just happened. I'm sorry."

She looked up. "It just happened? Did you trip? Did she bend over by accident? You knew what you were doing, bastard!" Standing, she punched him hard in the chest. "How long has this been going on?"

He looked down and mumbled something.

"What?"

"I said a few months."

She was confused. "A few months? Like what is that? You proposed to me a few months ago. Have you—" She paused when she saw the look on his face. A hand went to cover her mouth. "Oh my God." She turned away from him. It made sense now. She wasn't tripping. Every thought she had brushed away had just been confirmed. The spots on his body, the muffled phone calls, the all of a sudden after-work showers, it all added up.

Angry at being caught, Jacey thought now was the time to flip it on her. "This is all your fault anyway."

She was pulling on her boots. "Don't you dare try to blame this on me. I did everything for you!"

"You started it. You cheated on me first."

"Oh, right. Please explain that one," she said, wiping her face. Going back into the bedroom, she took her Louis Vuitton luggage out of the closet and began to stuff clothes inside. She didn't even know what she was reaching for; she just threw things in the bags.

"You don't think I know about you and Alphonse?"

She stood up straight. "Me and Alphonse what?"

"You talkin about me cheatin', what about you?"

Caiza stopped folding and looked at him with the most puzzled glance on her face. "*What?* I have *never* cheated on you."

"Whatever. Youll tell me anything, right? Adeena saw you two kissing in the middle of the street."

She was genuinely confused. "Jacey, what are you talking about?"

"The day you went to get your car from the shop. Adeena saw you kiss him. She told Trina, and Trina told me."

Caiza was floored. He might as well have told her that she was adopted and her real parents were the king and queen of a Morroccan tribe. "Trina? You believed *Trina*?" she whispered pointing in the direction in which Trina had just fled. "That dirty gutter bitch? You listened to her instead of coming to me?"

"She had a picture."

Damn camera phones. Covering her wet face with a shaking hand Caiza propped her other hand on her hip and spoke slowly. "Alphonse gave me a hug. He said congratulations on your engagement. He gave me a kiss on the cheek, and I was outta there. You believed *that* dirty bitch over *me*?" Her voice cracked as she choked back a whole new wave of tears. He was even lower than she thought. Snatching her bags off the bed, she went out to the foyer and pulled on her coat.

Jacey felt like an idiot. His face was burning with embarrassment and shame as he pulled on some sweats and followed her. "Caiza, I made a mistake. I'm sorry. I really didn't mean to hurt you."

Caiza whistled once for Sparkle. She had the door open when she dropped one of her bags. She paused, looked at Jacey, and then at her hand for a long time. He took a step forward, and she took a step back. Looking down at her hand again, she pulled the ring off and placed it in his hand. "I'll be back for the rest of my things."

Sparkle peed out front. Caiza drove to 116th Street in a blind rage. Sparkle didn't understand why she was upset so she whimpered the whole ride. Parking in front of Myeisha's building, Caiza pushed the door open. She rifled through her pockets for her key. Myeisha had given her a key so she could get in whenever she needed to.

Now she couldn't find it. Of all the nights for no one to be traveling in and out of the house, it would be tonight. She got back in her car and turned the heat up as high as it would go. My worked late at the club. She wouldn't be home until well after midnight. It was just now eleven. Sparkle settled down in the backseat.

Finally, after what seemed like days but had only been an hour and a half, Myeisha's Lexus pulled up in front of the building. "California Love" was blasting through the speakers. She climbed out and went into her trunk for her duffel bag. Coming around the back of her car, she stuck her hand in her pocket for her house keys. Caiza had fallen asleep, but jumped up when Myeisha knocked on her window. "Caiza? I thought that was you. Girl, what you doin' out here?"

Caiza turned her car off, let Sparkle out and got her suitcases. "I can't come spend the night at my best friend's house?"

"You know you're always welcome, girl, but I figured you'd at least wait until I got home from work."

"Yeah, well…" she trailed off.

Myeisha let her into the building, checked her overflowing mailbox and led them in. They got on the elevator, and Caiza started doing the dance.

"You gotta pee?"

She nodded.

"How long you been out there?" My pressed her floor.

"An hour and change."

"For what? It's the dead of winter. What the hell you doin' out there?" Myeisha smiled devilishly. "Ain't you s'posed to be home snuggled up with Jacey?"

"Jacey could care less."

They stepped off the elevator, and they walked down the hall. "What's that supposed to mean?" Myeisha asked as she opened her front door and flicked on the lights. Sparkle went to the first source of heat she could find and shook herself in front of the radiator.

"If he cared, he wouldna been fuckin' Trina behind my back."

Myeisha took off her boots and hung their coats in the closet. "Trina? What are you talkin' about?"

"I came home from class tonight, and he was with Trina." Saying that made her start crying again. She sat down hard on the couch and covered her face, letting the tears fall like a baby. There were so many emotions flowing through her at once. Anger, devastation, sadness, confusion. The one that hit her hardest was betrayal.

She and Jacey had made a vow never to turn their backs on each other. He had most certainly turned his back on her. And over Trina? He took the word of some grubby hoodrat when he could have come to her and asked her about it. But that was a typical male, she thought. Thinking with his little head instead of the big one.

Caiza used the bathroom and after washing her hands, cleaned up her face. She looked a mess. Her eyes were red rimmed and bloodshot. Her face was puffy, and her cheeks were tearstained. After she splashed some warm water across her face she went back into the living room.

Myeisha had taken the suitcases into her bedroom and put out a white tee for her to sleep in. Caiza took a bath and changed into it, wrapping her hair and climbing into the bed next to the one friend she felt she had left in the world. Myeisha gave her a big hug.

"You okay?"

Caiza shook her head and sniffled.

"I know, baby. Don't worry about it right now. We'll deal with it tomorrow." Myeisha kissed her forehead and turned off her lamp.

The next day, Caiza took off from work and went home to pack the rest of her things. Myeisha wasn't busy until the evening so she offered to do her laundry while Caiza was busy packing. Caiza prayed to God Jacey wasn't there, and it seemed her prayers were answered.

She managed to get about eighty percent of her possessions into her car before she heard the front door open. "Shit," Caiza muttered. She abandoned folding and packing neatly and began tossing clothes, books and shoes into the boxes recklessly. She heard Jacey's heavy boots coming toward the bedroom. She hurried and tossed things into the boxes faster. He opened the door and leaned against the doorframe, watching her.

"I saw your car outside."

She ignored him and continued to pack.

"I know you hear me, Caiza. What are you doing?"

She couldn't even look him in the eye. He was disgusting to her. "I'm leaving."

He walked forward and sighed as if he were already tired of talking about this. "Kye, please. We need to talk about this. Just let me explain myself. You don't have to go anywhere. We can work this out. I know we can."

She zipped her garment bag around her favorite silk dresses and laid them on her bed. Thinking better of it, she draped them across the chair in the corner. That bedspread was probably one nut away from a biohazard.

"There's nothing to work out, Jacey."

"I know you're mad, baby, but we can get through this. We've had fights before, right?"

"Yes, Jace. We've had plenty of fights. But this? This isn't a fight. It's a breakup."

Jacey was silent a moment before answering. "I know we can still work it out."

Was he kidding? She took three deep breaths and lifted armfuls of shoes into another box. "Jacey, there is no way we could ever work this out."

"That's not true. You know we can get past this. Please, Caiza. I need you, baby."

"Didn't seem like you needed me last night. I think Trina did all right, don't you?"

"She doesn't mean anything to me. You're the one I love, Caiza. I know you know that."

She stopped packing and looked him in the face. "Jacey, are you listening to the words comin' out your mouth? Or are you just sayin' them? Do you really hear yourself right now?"

He looked at her, his face a fat question mark. She shook her head and broke it down.

"We have been together for five years, Jacey. You asked me to marry you around the same time that you start fuckin' Trina. I come home and find you in bed with that nasty slut. Now, flip that and reverse it and tell me if you would stay."

He stood there with his mouth open, eyes rising to the ceiling, as if he was really thinking about it.

"I didn't think so. I'm through with you, you feel me?"

He dropped his hands at his sides. "A'ight. I know I fucked up. I know that. What can I do to make you forgive me?"

She put a hand on her hip. "Can you give me back the last five years of my life that I wasted on you? Can you turn back the clock and think with your brain instead of your dick? Can you do that, Jacey?"

He looked deafeated as his shoulders slumped. "No, I can't."

"Here's what you can do, though. You can burn in hell, a'ight?"

Jacey walked over to her, taking a hold of her hands. "I didn't mean to hurt you. I got caught up trying to get you back for what I thought you did. Was everything a waste, Caiza? We didn't have any good times?"

Caiza sighed hard, weakening at his touch. She made a face like she was concerned with his feelings, then yanked her hands away, snatched up the first of quite a few boxes and dropped the garment bag on top of it. "We did have some good times, Jacey." His face softened. "But that was before you decided you wanted to get me back for something I didn't do. Gotta go."

Caiza couldn't believe this was happening to her. In just two days, her fairytale life was over, and her nightmare was just beginning.

Trina stepped into the salon and tried to ignore the stares. She knew she looked bad. Her right eye had been blackened, she had a large spreading bruise on her left cheek, her lip was busted, and she still had a deep hand mark on her throat.

"Daaaaaaaamn, girl. She whipped your ass!" Peaches cried.

Trina rolled her good eye and stomped into the back. "Shut the fuck up, nigga."

He turned back to his customer, accepting a tip from a girl ready to leave. "Thank you baby. Deena, you see her face?"

"I seen it, baby boy. That right there is what they call a shiner," she whispered, giggling.

Kristina shook up some mousse. "So she did fuck him?"

"Hell yeah. She been fuckin' him. Baby girl just now found out."

"If Trina really was slick, her ass wouldna got caught."

"Well, she ain't, so she did," Adeena said softly.

Trina stuck her head out the door. "I don't wanna hear my name in any of y'all mouths. I ain't got a problem firin' you." She slammed the door behind her.

Adeena smiled and reached out her hand. She slapped five with Peaches.

Myeisha was more than happy to have Caiza as a guest in her home. She knew how hard this breakup was for her. This wasn't some third period Spanish class fling. This was an engagement, a long-term relationship in which Caiza had invested five years. As clearly as the eye could see, Caiza loved Jacey from the very bottom of her heart. For him to think she was cheating and then take so-called proof from someone as unreliable as Trina was a slap in the face. And it hurt bad.

For the next two weeks, Caiza searched for an apartment. After about a dozen loud nos, she settled on a one-bedroom in Harlem, 150th to be exact, right on top of the 1 train station on Broadway. For the first time in her life, she would have to pay rent, but it was a transition she knew she would get used to.

The following week was spent showing the exterminator how to do his job properly. Whoever had lived there before her clearly had no pride in their living space. There were roaches and mouse holes everywhere. After they were killed and the holes patched up, she spent one final week scrubbing everything down with ammonia. With help from My and a friend from her club, it took the three of them two days to move into the new place.

Her neighbors were lovely. The people downstairs didn't go to bed until the sun came up and didn't wake up til it went down. There was a gunfight down the block at least once a week and almost every night, 5-0 was banging on someone's door. Still, she thanked the Good Lord she even had someplace to live. She got used to the new apartment after about a week and a half, and so did Sparkle who spent most of her days sniffing around, trying to find Jacey. She still loved him. Damn traitor.

Caiza credited her survival to Myeisha. My knew exactly how Caiza felt about her man, how much she loved him and how this breakup hurt her. She made sure she took care of her girl, giving her all her love and support. True, she'd told Caiza she was a survivor, but the real truth was, her girl was fragile. Myeisha knew she needed her now more than ever. And she was happy to be there.

Caiza found she was so busy wrapping herself in her work and school that she had no time to grieve for Jacey, so she pushed him to the back of her mind as if "it" had never happened. It was hard, but as the weeks passed, she started to settle back into life as a single woman with her mind on one thing: her goals.

3

And Down Will Come Baby

Caiza had worked at the law offices of Ester and Scarowitz for five years. When she first started working there, it was so she could make enough money to get away from her mother and take care of herself. It had worked, and she took pride in her job, moving from a first floor gofer to a head secretary. She liked her job well enough. It was a relaxed environment and it paid well, not that the money mattered.

After Jacey's real estate business blew up, she continued working because she knew no man liked a lazy woman. Now, she needed to work because she didn't have him to take care of her. Her weekend shopping sprees and expensive trips had ended, and all of a sudden, something came into her life that she had never known when she was with Jacey: bills.

Before, she had a nice setup. He handled all their expenses as long as she bought the groceries. Never before had she paid all the bills on her own. It was hard to do. She didn't save money as she should have and now that she needed it, she didn't really have it.

Friday morning, her boss asked to see her in his office. Caiza practically lived in his office. She was always there making coffee, reading him a memo, or just performing her duties. That day, as soon as she stepped inside, she could feel the negative vibe.

Jon Sapling sat behind the desk in yet another one of his cheap suits.

She didn't understand it. The man made nearly three million dollars a year, and the most he would spring for was a getup from SYMS. Caiza was in no way against bargain hunting, but then again, she wouldn't be caught dead in a Jaguar X-Type with Payless shoes on.

"Good morning, Ms. Bell. Would you have a seat, please?"

She shut the door behind her and did so. "Good morning, sir."

He looked down at his still clasped hands and sighed. "Ms. Bell, you have been with us for, almost five and a half years, correct?"

"Yes, sir," she said. That was she. Humble little slave girl.

"You are aware that we have merged with another major law firm, right? Hawthorne and Label?"

"Yes. It's pretty much the office talk." She smiled, hoping he would get to the point and soon. Hawthorne and Label was the most respected law firm in New York. The only people better at getting you justice was the DA's office. The two men had gone from working cases from two clients in their studio apartment to a multi-million-dollar operation spanning five states, with more than two thousand clients.

He nodded. "We closed the deal earlier this month."

"And I'm very proud of you, sir."

"Thank you." He bowed his head again, then leaned back in his chair "Due to the large volume of workers our team firm is bringing to the table, we are going to need to downsize. While we here at Ester and Scarowitz genuinely appreciate the hard work you have done for us over the years, I must regretfully inform you that we will no longer be needing your services."

Caiza's mind flashed to the movie *Nothin' to Lose*. More specifically, the scene when the mother slapped Martin's character upside the head. That's exactly what she felt like. Like she had been backhanded across the face.

"Ms. Bell?" Sapling asked.

She closed her eyes and took a few deep breaths, feeling light headed. "You-you're firing me?" she whispered. They hadn't even awarded her the decency of a two-week notice. Could they do that?

"I hate to have to be the one to tell you this, Ms. Bell, but it's in the best interest of the company. We have to make room for the employees from the other firm. I assure you that you can come to me at any time for references and help in looking for a new job."

She snapped her eyes open. "When do I need to have my things out?"

"Your last check is already in the mail. But I would appreciate it if you would finish out the rest of the day."

Caiza stood up on wobbly legs and stuck her hand out. "It's been a pleasure working for you, Mr. Sapling."

He shook her hand. "You don't have to leave until five, Ms. Bell."

She was already at the door. It was half open when she turned back to Sapling. "I'd rather leave now, sir. I would hate to stick around and be in the way of the new employees," she answered spitefully.

"Ms. Bell," he started, but she was already gone. Caiza made it as far as the water cooler before she couldn't breathe anymore. Reaching down, she plucked one of the little Dixie cups from the holder and filled it with cold water. It took three refills to slow her heartbeat. Making her way back to her desk, Caiza was sure every eye in the room was on her. Quietly, she turned her back to Denise and picked up her phone.

"Janitor."

"Hey, Wallace? It's Caiza. Do we have any boxes laying around?"

"Like cardboard?"

"Yes."

"Yeah, matter of fact, Moriarty just brought some down. How many you need?"

"Just one, thank you."

"Not a problem. I'll be up in five."

"Thanks, Wallace."

Five minutes later, he appeared off the elevator with a big cardboard box. He placed it on her desk and she thanked him, getting to the task of getting the hell out of there. Denise noticed what she was doing.

"Caiza, where you goin'?"

Caiza fanned her face with one hand, trying not to start crying. She stood and put her free hand on her hip. "Girl, they fired me."

Her eyes widened, and she immediately stood and gave her a hug. "Oh my God! Is it because of the merger?"

She nodded.

"Caiza, I am so sorry."

Caiza didn't want to start bawling in front of Denise, so she went back to packing her things. It would distract her. It took her a while; five years of stuff can pile up. The front desk was spotless; the two women believed in keeping their space clean. Open that desk and it was a whole different story. They kept everything from scrunchies to tampons to condoms to novels down there. Nobody could know from first glance, but when you're a professional, it's all about what the surface looks like.

Caiza said her good-byes to a now teary-eyed Denise and loaded her things into her car. As soon as she slammed the trunk, she looked down at the back tire. A flat. Just fucking great. She opened the trunk again and grabbed the jack and the lug wrench. This grimy job took her about twenty minutes. She just had the last lug tightened when some jackass walked past and asked, "Hey, you need a little help with that?"

Caiza glared at him from where she was crouched. "Do I look like I need help?" she asked. He took this as an invitation to start a conversation. He walked toward her.

"Well, yeah. I think you've got—"

"Get away from me!" she screamed. He hurried on up the block. Caiza straightened up and clutched her sore back. She was not prepared to change a tire during midday traffic in a pencil skirt and three and a half inch heels. Dropping the tools back in her trunk, she left the tire on the sidewalk by the trash, fell into her car and drove home.

Caiza listened to her heels click against the pavement as she walked up the street to her apartment. Passing a trash can, she resisted the urge to throw away everything she carried in her arms. She didn't really want to be reminded of the ugly day.

"Hey, baby girl," shouted one of the corner hustlers. They spoke to her every day. She was the new pretty face on the block, and they were all itching to get a taste of her. Not that any of them would run up and offer to carry her box, oh no.

"Hey," she called back, hurrying inside her building.

Caiza dropped the box on the floor between her legs and reached into her purse for her keys. Fumbling for the mailbox key, Caiza pushed it in the lock only for it to get stuck.

"Today can't possibly get any worse," she mumbled, unaware that it was about to.

The day after Caiza moved in, she realized someone dented the hell out of her mailbox. She didn't know how it happened, but it did. So now she had to bang it just right to get the mail out, but not so hard that her key would break off in the lock. Jingling the key worked this time. Thankfully it swung open, but as soon as she pulled the envelopes out, she wished it hadn't.

Three were from various charities and magazines, and all the rest was the phone bill, the light bill, the rent statement, her cell bill and the cable bill. Never before had all these bills come at the same time. Never. Someone upstairs was *not* looking out.

Caiza rolled her eyes and walked upstairs—an elevator would have been a prayer at that point. Toting herself up those stairs was no joke after the day she'd had. After unlocking and kicking open the front door, Sparkle barreled past her into the hallway, leash in her mouth.

Caiza rolled her eyes again. "Come on, Sparkle. Let me change my clothes, puppy."

Sparkle wagged her tail and barked.

"Come inside. You don't even want to know the day I had."

Sparkle agreed, scratching behind her ear. The dog could care less about the day Caiza had had; she had to pee. Once she relieved herself, she would be more than happy to listen. Sparkle stood her gorund, turning her head toward the stairs. Caiza knew she was beat. She dropped the box in the foyer and locked the door behind her.

When they returned, Caiza's first stop was under the sink. She pulled out a bottle of '85 Merlot and took it straight to the face, wiping her mouth with the back of her hand. She looked around her tiny apartment. She'd just gotten used to the place and was in crisis already. Pulling her hair out of the band, Caiza shook it out over her shoulders. Clutching the bottle, her mind flashed back to the bills in the box in the foyer. She faced the wine again, refusing to think about it.

Myeisha drove over before Caiza even told her what happened. News traveled fast. Apparently, Sapling had blabbed to one of the senior partners who told one of the juniors who told Denise who already knew and called and told My.

"Denise called about ten minutes after you left. She figured you'd need me. They lettin' her go too." That was more bad news. "How you feel?"

She opened her eyes. "Like shit."

Myeisha waited until Caiza's tears slowed to sniffles to put her arms around her friend comfortingly. "Look at me, Kye. Put it this way, you was too good for them a'ight? They had to let you go 'cuz you was puttin' them to shame wit' ya fine ass."

Caiza managed to crack a smile. Behind her smile Myeisha knew there was much more to it than that. Bigger problems were waiting to jump out at her now that she had no job. The plush lifestyle she was used to was over now. She didn't know anything about bills and payments and the like. But she knew she'd better hurry up and find out.

4

From the Top This Time...

Caiza crumpled the receipt in her fingers and threw her head back dramatically as she stormed out of the bank. Exactly seven hundred dollars. That was all she had left after rent and groceries. She hadn't been clothes shopping in nearly a month. She felt like a heroin addict going into withdrawal. Sparkle would need her shots in another couple of months. If she wasn't working by then, she'd be screwed. And to make sure she had enough stress on her back, her mother delivered, right on time.

Caiza was in the middle of a very difficult yoga position when DeLiza Bell called with her bullshit.

"I heard what happened from that nice new girl they hired. Why didn't you call me, Kye? I am still your mother."

"If I told you, Mother, all you would've done was find another way to make me feel awful."

"That is not true, and you know it. I'm trying to be supportive."

"Then support me, Ma," she said.

"Well," she began, trying her best to say the right thing and failing miserably, "I only wish you would listen to your mother more often. I bet things wouldn't be so rough then. How's Jacey?"

Caiza rolled her eyes. "History." Here, the conversation took a U-turn. Her mother hadn't liked Jacey from the day she met him. When things were actually going well between them, she never had a nice word to say about him. Caiza knew her mother would use this occasion to rub it in her face, but it never hurt to give her the benefit of the doubt.

"Really? That comes as no surprise. I knew he was trash the day you brought him home. What happened?"

Caiza didn't want to get into this. "He was with another woman."

"I *knew* it. Low-down dirty dog. Didn't I tell you he was no good? He's been a dog since day one. He was never any good for you. And now you've learned your lesson, I suppose."

"Yes, Ma. You know, I appreciate your sincere sympathy. It's so good to know you're there for me. There is nothing more reassuring than the grating sound of your voice in my ear." Raising her legs over her head, she stood on her hands.

"I hate to say I told you so, dear, but I did."

"As much as I would love to continue this thrilling conversation, I don't need this from you, Ma. I'll call you back."

She sighed heavily. "Go 'head hang up, Caiza."

Caiza clicked the headset off and dropped it on the floor next to her. *There is no way in hell she is going to pin that guilt trip on me,* she thought. It might have worked when she was twelve, but Caiza wasn't stupid anymore. Her mother played too many games. She was an emotional con artist, and Caiza wasn't dumb. She went back to her yoga.

Lowering her legs into a split and raising her arms above her head, Caiza thought about her situation. She had to find a job, bottom line. How long could she last? She found herself in the Pathmark reaching for Ramen noodles and cold cuts and generic dog food. If this was what starving student meant, then she completely understood.

That weekend, Caiza made a date with the *Daily News* classifieds. Her first go round the week before hadn't gone so well. Since she had experience in the office field, she figured any law firm in need of a secretary weould be happy to have her. Wrong. Although she could read tw hundred words a minute and type seventy-five, she had no degree. This was a problem for all five of the firms she called.

So it was back to square one; find a job that pays the bills. Drivers wanted. She could drive, but everybody wanted drivers with at least two years of professional driving experience. She wondered if driving around in the hood counted as professional driving experience.

Accountant wanted, nanny wanted, maid wanted. She could barely count the fingers on her hands, she'd be damned if she'd be some rich white brat's nanny and what the hell kind of self-respecting woman would be a maid? Her mother, that's who. She found a bright spot when her eyes came across a tiny ad under the Adopt-A-Pet section. Someone was looking for a waitress, no experience necessary. That was like a dream come true in New York. The job was for a restaurant in the Village named Heart. She immediately called them up and set up an interview for the following Wednesday.

Caiza was to meet with Charlie, the owner, at nine sharp. She laid out one of her many business suits the night before. Caiza hadn't been shopping in so long, it disturbed her to think about it. Before, she would have gone straight to Neiman's and charged herself a little happy with a new suit. But now she was forced to put on one of her throwback suits. She was so used to living a certain way and now that it was crunch time, she barely knew how to survive. She shook her head and went to meet the man.

Charlie had to be a solid three hundred pounds. He was huge. He looked like an ex-football player—Or an ex-con, your choice. He showed her into the back office and shut the door, sitting across from her behind a desk. He lowered his impressive weight into the chair, glancing at her résumé.

He hadn't said a word from the time they introduced themselves at the front door. The air conditioner behind him was blowing beads of sweat across his bald head. He read very slowly and kept wiping his forehead with the dishtowel over his shoulder. He was wearing a dingy tee, jean shorts and an apron that might have been white in a past life.

Laying the folder on the desk, he crossed his arms over his broad chest. "You seem to have no experience in this business."

She was immediately on her toes. "I'm sorry. The ad said—"

He grunted and interrupted her. "I know what the ad said. I was just hoping you might have had some experience."

"To my defense, Mr.—"

"Charlie."

"Mr. Charlie, you did say experience wasn't necessary. And I'm not retarded in the kitchen. I can boil water, you know," she added, joking.

He didn't share the laugh. He looked at her blankly, wiping his forehead again. Charlie took another glance at the résumé, now rendered irrelevant.

"How do you pronounce your first name?"

"Kye-zah," she said.

"Caiza. Is that African?"

"No. It's a product of my parent's names."

"Which are?"

What the hell did this have to do with the interview? "Cameron and DeLiza."

Charlie shifted his weight again, mopping his forehead. "On paper, you're about as useful to me as a thumbtack on a dark road in a rainstorm."

Her heart sank.

"But I have no reason not to hire an honest, hardworking woman such as yourself."

Caiza breathed a sigh of relief and stood to shake his hand. "Thank you so much, Charlie. I appreciate this. I promise you you'll never regret this."

He wiped again, pointing at her. "Be here Monday at eight. And I'm warning you, if you get one order messed up, you're outta here."

Caiza didn't care if he'd told her to arrive dressed in a monkey suit. She'd be there with bells on. "I won't let you down," she promised.

Monday, he walked her through a brief training. He showed her how to greet the customers, take their orders in short hand and point out the specials. She had to set the tables and keep them clean, refill the condiments, make fresh coffee and take all the breakfast and lunch orders. On occasion, she doubled as the line cook, when Rydell decided he didn't want to show up for work on time.

Rydell Jameson was without question the finest man Caiza had ever seen. He had Jacey by a long shot and Jacey had *GQ* Man of the Year status. The very first minute she saw him, she almost tripped and broke her face. He was as brown as a chocolate Teddy Graham and had a smile that took your panties off and asked what you wanted for breakfast. He had sparkling eyes, and Caiza knew she could just drop him right there in the middle of the store.

Rydell was twenty-five, and he was what she'd describe as a regular guy. He'd done time for an attempted robbery that went bad some years ago and that seemed to follow him around. Charlie was the only person who had given him a chance. But Rydell had a problem with being on time. He was one of those folks that proved the stereotype.

He was a sweetheart and made it clear he was interested in a relationship, but Caiza was still healing from the stab wound Jacey left in her heart. He backed off, stating that he understood, but that he wouldn't give up. She had to smile on the inside. She had to admit that it felt good to have that kind of attention from another man.

After the first month at the restaurant, Caiza saw a little change in the dollar amounts in the bank. It broke her heart when Myeisha started mentioning words like "saving" and "budget" but she knew they were the keys to her survival. She nearly died when she watched the saleslady at Neiman's cut her card in two. Good thing her car was already paid for or it would have been repossessed long ago.

She drew the line when My said she should sell some of her clothes and shoes for a little extra cash. That was not an option. She worked her ass off for her little eight dollars an hour. Although she and Rydell split the tips, it was seven dollars less than what she was used to. More or less, it was a check she desperately needed.

Caiza marked the day of her first full month at Heart on her calendar. She had never worked so hard in her life. Her back was constantly aching, her feet always hurt, and she was sure, one of those days, someone had stabbed her with a fork. Her bed was calling her, and as soon as she shut her apartment door, she made a beeline for her room.

Just as she was ready to get comfortable, Sparkle nudged her leg. Caiza opened her eyes and looked down. Sparkle had her leash in her mouth. Caiza rolled her eyes and stood. "I could kill you, Spark," she said, grabbing her keys. Sparkle practically dragged her down the stairs.

Riverbank State Park was just a few short blocks away from her apartment. Caiza hadn't ever been to the park, but a neighbor had recommended it as a nice place to jog. Being brought up in Brooklyn, she stayed in parks like Irving Square and Maria Hernandez. She was tripping over broken glass and crack vials just to get to the swings. Sparkle liked it well enough, so they went to Riverbank four times a week.

"Sparkle," she shouted as the dog ran ahead of her and almost knocked someone over. That someone happened to be, surprise surprise, Jacey.

Caiza's tongue rolled back up in her mouth, but it was too late. He'd heard her. Bending over, he rubbed Sparkle's back and patted her lovingly on the head. He walked toward Caiza.

"Hi, Caiza," he said, looking awfully guilty.

"Hello, Jacey." She made a mental note to beat the stuffing out of Sparkle when they got upstairs.

"One of my friends said he saw you around here. I've been looking for you. I was hoping we could talk."

She put the leash on Sparkle. Didn't he have a company to run? Why was he hanging around her neighborhood? "What else is there to talk about?"

He looked around. "Could we go somewhere?"

"There's plenty of space in the park."

"No, I meant—"

She wasn't about to let him in her apartment. "Come on. The park's only a few blocks from here."

He put his hands in his pockets and followed. They found a nice bench in the sun. Caiza let Sparkle off the leash, and she bounded away, chasing a group of angry sparrows. The weather had broken and it was looking like it would be a decent spring.

"Well?" she asked.

He looked at her. "Caiza, I've been thinking a lot about what happened…about us. I know what I did was wrong, but every day that goes by, it's crazy knowing you're not going to be there with me. I need you back, baby."

She folded her legs over each other. She had gone over in her mind all the things she would say if she ever saw him again and now she couldn't remember them. "What you did to me was real foul, Jacey. And there's no good explanation. Give me one good reason why I should take you back."

He shook his head. "I don't have one, Kye. All I know is that I'm sorry. I know I hurt you and I'm suffering every day, baby. I really am."

She snorted and turned to him, arms folded. "Really? *You're* suffering? How are you suffering? You proposed to me. That meant you were ready to spend the rest of your life with me. Apparently, you weren't. Who else did you have in our bed, Jacey?"

"There wasn't anyone else."

She stood. "I feel so much better," she replied, her voice dripping with sarcasm.

He tried to follow her. Caiza whistled for Sparkle. The dog came trotting out of some bushes with a stick in her mouth. She dropped it, and Caiza bent to put her leash on.

"Caiza, please. Don't do me like this."

"Do you? Nigga, you're lucky I *didn't* do you." She went to turn, and he grabbed her arm harder than she was used to. He pulled her close to him and whispered angrily.

"I'm not going to let anyone take you away from me. You're mine, and you know this." He glared into her eyes, and Caiza jerked away from him. She rubbed her elbow where he grabbed her. Sparkle growled low in her throat.

Jacey jammed his hands in his pockets and took one last glance at her before walking away. Caiza stood there until she saw him disappear. He'd never acted like that before. She wasn't sure what that threat meant, but if he was trying to scare her, he'd succeeded.

Heart was packed nearly every day for the next few weeks. Caiza had piles of orders to take before she even tied on her apron. That Monday, Rydell was late yet again, so she fired up the grill on her own. Charlie was bitching about something on the phone in the office. Caiza didn't know why he couldn't work the grill himself, but some unknown dilemma kept him in his office on the phone all day.

Pancakes, bacon, eggs, sausages, ham, French toast, buttered toast, cheese toast, hash browns, coffee; she swore if she never saw another breakfast menu again it would be too soon. Her hair was coming out of its ponytail when Charlie finally got off his fat ass and decided to help. He closed his office door and threw his ever-present towel over his shoulder. "Where's Rydell?"

"He'll be here in a few. I've got it covered."

"Sure?"

"I could use a hand with these dishes but beyond that, I'm fine." He nodded.

Caiza wasn't sure but when he walked past, she thought she felt his hand graze her butt. It could have been a harmless accident; Caiza had a very round butt, so she brushed it off and chalked one up for paranoia.

Rydell came through the doors, bringing a blaze of snow and wind in with him. The weather had changed dramatically; overnight a blizzard had sprung up. People barely had enough time to take off their shorts before they were throwing on their sweaters. Rydell took off his things and immediately got to work.

"Third time this week, Rydell," she said, handing him the spatula.

He took it and kissed her cheek. They had grown accustomed to each other in the short time she'd been working there. "Morning, Kye. Don't wanna hear it. What've I got?"

"Grits and cheese, eggs and toast, two big breakfasts, and I'm making a fresh pot right now."

"That's my girl."

After the lunchtime rush, from twelve to three, it was nonstop work, so she didn't get off her feet until she got home. She didn't know how women could be waitresses for years. This job was whipping her ass after only about three months. Standing, bending, twisting, carrying, she felt more like an aerobics instructor than a waitress, and it was starting to take its toll. Caiza wasn't used to heavy work. The most she had to lift at the law firm was a memo, a fax or the phone.

But this wasn't the law firm anymore. Her stable life had been snatched away from her. She looked around her apartment. This was reality. This was what real people did for a living: they worked.

After walking Sparkle, she took a shower, wrapped and set her hair and pulled a pint of Cherry Garcia from the freezer. HBO was showing *Reservoir Dogs*. Caiza held out for as long as she could before her eyes started to cross and Mr. Pink became Mr. White and they both began to swirl across the screen. When Sparkle began to lick the dripping ice cream from her fingers, she turned off the TV, put her ice cream back in the freezer and got into bed.

Once there, she found Caiza couldn't sleep. Her head was a messy swirl of dollar signs, textbooks and past due statements. Her money situation was getting desperate. She was only getting eight dollars an hour from Charlie, and whatever skimpy tips the customers left behind. That was poverty. She did some quick math. Once her rent was paid, she'd have forty dollars.

There was no way she could go a month on forty dollars unless she spent a dollar a day. She shrugged and thought, *If that's what I've gotta do, fine.* The semester she was in now was paid for, but the next two were not. Caiza had a year and a half left until she graduated and not enough money in the bank to cover it.

Caiza knew leaving school wasn't going to happen. If she had to sell everything she owned to make sure she could stay in school, she knew she would have to. That was her first priority, and no one was going to take that away from her. She let her eyes close and pretty soon, she was asleep.

Caiza found it a very strange coincidence that Charlie just happened to make contact with her person every time the two of them came within a foot of each other. It got to the point where she turned around and hugged herself when he walked past, or got as close to Rydell as possible, so he could see it. She hadn't said anything to Rydell—he had other things to worry about—but if she needed a witness, she was hoping she could count on him.

"Rydell, I need a fresh pot when you can, babe," Caiza called as she wiped a table and collected the dirty dishes.

"I'm neckin', ma!" he called back. She smiled, hiding her annoyance as she carried the heavy bucket into the kitchen. Necking meant they were up to their necks with something, that their hands were full and you'd have to get it yourself. Charlie hated the codes, mainly because he couldn't speak the language. Dumping the dishes, she washed out the coffee pots and got two fresh ones started.

The store was busy, and when Caiza looked at the grill, she saw that Rydell was indeed up to his neck. He had the last of breakfast going, as well as three bins of French fries, six burgers, and he had started slicing tomatoes, but abandoned them to tend to half sliced onions. She wiped her hands on her apron and quickly cut up the rest of the tomatoes and lettuce for him, prepping the plates while he finished cooking.

"You're a life saver, Caiza."

"That's what it says on my checks," she sang. Passing out coffee to the necessary tables, she turned on her heel and returned to the kitchen when Rydell rang the bell for pickup. All the tables had been served when the two finally got a chance to rest. Caiza made her rounds, making sure everyone had everything they needed, and then collapsed on a chair just outside the kitchen. Rydell had turned off the grill and they sat at the table closest to the kitchen, waiting for another customer.

"Okay, okay. The roof of my apartment building on New Year's, 1999."

"Are you serious? It was freezing."

He nodded. "I found that out. We ended up stopping after ten minutes and doing it right there in the staircase. You?"

Caiza crossed her legs under the table and pointed at Rydell. "I can top that."

He leaned back. "You think?"

"I know. You ready? The elevator at the Marriott."

He sat forward, his chair hitting the floor with a thump. "Are you being for real? They've got security cameras."

She nodded. "Yeah, *we* found that out. We were in the Bahamas on vacation and drank some crazy smoothie or something. We found out later it was an aphrodisiac. We barely made it to the elevator."

Rydell threw his hands up. "You got me beat. I can't top that."

A couple walked in then, and their break was over. "Back to the grind," she said. He nodded and walked into the kitchen.

Caiza had her pad and pen ready when she walked up to the couple. "Hello. I'm Caiza; I'll be your waitress today. Can I start you off with something to drink?"

The woman ordered hot chocolate, the man a glass of Scotch. That sounded like an idea. While she was pouring his, she made herself one and downed it in a shot. The couple both wanted the clam chowder, so Caiza got busy warming the bread that went with the Soup of the Day. Charlie came out of his office. "How we doin'?"

Rydell was standing over the grill. "Not bad, chief."

He nodded, walking past Caiza. "You alright, lady?"

She shrugged. "Just peachy."

Charlie walked past her and reached into the cabinet for something. As his hands came down, one of them came down a little too hard on her breast. Caiza jumped back, into Rydell.

"What the hell is your problem?" she shouted.

He looked puzzled. "What's wrong wit' you?"

"No, Charlie, what the hell is wrong with you? You got a real issue with keeping your hands to yourself."

Charlie looked to Rydell for help. He shook his head. "Sorry, boss. I saw that too."

He shook his head, walking past her. "I don't know what you're talking about."

Caiza followed him. "Of course you don't. This isn't the first time it's happened."

He rolled his head around, like he was annoyed by her voice. "It was just a little feel. You actin' like I raped you or somethin'."

Caiza couldn't believe her ears. In a rage, she slapped him as hard as she could. Which, as it turns out, was pretty hard. He seemed like he was going to lunge for her, but Rydell stepped in between them.

"Watch it, Chuck," he said in a voice she'd never heard.

"You protectin' her? Only reason you talkin' to the bitch is so you can fuck her," he spat nastily.

"Excuse me?" Caiza said. "You got some real nerve talking to me like that."

"Watch your fuckin' mouth, Charlie," Rydell said, taking a step closer. The two men were in a face-off. Charlie backed down first. Caiza untied her apron and threw it at Charlie's face.

"Please. Is all this really necessary?"

"Yes," she said. "If that's how you think you can treat an employee, or better yet, a human, I'm outta here."

"So that's that? You're gonna leave over something small like this?"

"Yes, Charlie. I quit," she shouted as she burst out of the kitchen. She drove straight home, in a blind fury. There was only one person who could make her day better.

"He said *what*?"

"Mmm-hmm. Said 'it's not like I raped you or somethin'. Homeboy really couldn't understand why I was mad."

"And then what happened?"

"Then Rydell stepped in, and he's like back up out my face. Then Charlie calls me a bitch and says the only reason Rydell is cool with me is 'cuz he wants to hit it."

"Oooh! Drama! What'd Rydell say?"

"Girl, he ain't say nothin'. He ain't even trip. He was like, 'watch your mouth' and Charlie just walked away."

"Now that's the kinda man you need. You *need* to let him hit it."

"Myeisha! Stop it. I just got out of one bad relationship. I'm not trying to jump back into another one."

She made a *pssh* noise. "I ain't wanna say it girl, but he's a step up from Jacey. At least he got a job."

"Jacey does so have a job. How do you think he kept the rent paid?"

"Girl, sellin' dime bags does not count as a job, okay?"

"He stopped doing that long ago, My. You know that."

"Sure he did, Caiza. You go head and believe that if you want to."

The phone beeped, and Caiza flipped it over to see the caller ID. It was Rydell, of all people. "My, let me call you back."

"Uh-huh, who on your line?"

"Rydell."

"Oooh! A'ight, call me in the morning when he leaves."

"Myeisha!"

"Bye, girl." Myeisha giggled, then hung up.

Caiza clicked over. "Hi, Rydell."

"Kye, hey. I was just checking up on you. I wanted to know if you were alright."

She sighed. "I'm okay. I'm glad you called though. Thanks for having my back today."

"You know I couldn't let him talk to you like that in front of me. What are you going to do about work?"

Holy shit. In her haste to make a point and get out of there, she had completely forgotten about her situation. Caiza never even thought that the rent was due in another three days, it was time for Sparkle's shots, and she needed groceries. She resisted the urge to go slam her head in a wall. "I'll think of something."

"Okay. If you need anything—anything at all—you let me know."

"Thanks, Rydell. I appreciate it." Caiza hung up and shoved a pillow over her face, screaming into it as loud as she could. Sparkle took that as a sign that it was time to play, so she jumped on the bed and rolled all over Caiza. Sixty-seven pounds of dog was a lot on her tiny body, so she

shoved Sparkle on the floor, and they wrestled. After a little while, they wound down, and Caiza sat on the floor stroking Sparkle's soft golden fur. "What we gone do, mama?" Caiza asked her out loud.

Like you said, we'll think of something, Sparkle's eyes replied.

5

One More Time

Caiza was back behind a desk.

Two weeks after the mess with Charlie, she applied for a receptionist position at a local day care center. So far, the search that would land her back in a law firm was not going so well. The center seemed desperate because the woman she spoke to informed her she was hired almost as soon she looked at her résumé. Caiza should have known by then that everything in her life had a catch.

Caiza was so happy to be working around real professionals again—or what she thought were real professionals. Halfway into her first day, she knew these people were not normal. There seemed to be certain alliances, as if the staff had formed some kind of clique that she wasn't a part of yet. Like in high school, when you went away for the summer and all the kids bonded in your absence. She kept feeling stares at the back of her neck, and Caiza was sure she was "the talk" at the water cooler. She hoped it would wear off soon, because it was boring.

This job was better than what Charlie had been paying her at Heart. She was getting fifteen dollars an hour to type memos, fax and file, make photocopies and smile when the parents came to sign their children out. It was a joke how easy things were going. She was paid at the end of every two weeks and wisely deposited every check into her bank account, which was now off life support and in the recovery room.

Her budget was working and all her bills may have been late, but they were getting paid. Things were starting to look up. She was still a month behind in rent, so she was backed up to fourteen hundred, but she didn't care. With this job, she could get herself together slowly but surely.

Even though she really couldn't afford it, Caiza treated Myeisha to dinner at the restaurant of her choice on her birthday, a cold wintry day in March. Caiza don't know how Myeisha survived. The girl never did an honest day's work in her life, but she was laced like an NBA wife. She had the power of the pussy and used it to her advantage. Myeisha had a different man paying her rent, her car note, her bills and her other living expenses. She never lifted a finger. Caiza had to hand it to her; her girl was a true hustler. But at the end of the day, she was ghetto as grease on the stove.

"Of all the places we could have possibly gone, we had to come here?" Caiza asked as she parked next to Jimmy's Bronx Café.

My sucked her teeth. "You said wherever I wanted. This is where I want." She had pulled her hair back into a half-updo and under her rabbit fur was rocking an Adidas sweat suit, matching shelltoes, doorknocker earrings and a tee picturing Grand Master Flash. She looked like a relic from the B-Boy era, but she looked good. Caiza was freezing her ass off, so under her old Cavalli jeans she had on thermals, three pairs of socks in her Tims, a scarf under a scully and a sweatshirt with Tupac's face on it, all wrapped in her North Face.

She locked her car and they went inside. Only a few scattered tables were filled—there weren't too many people willing to come out in the freezing weather. A waiter showed them to a table in the corner. He put down two menus and left.

"Damn, no 'hi, how are you' or nothin?" Myeisha said.

Caiza shook her head and laughed. *You do get what you pay for*, she thought.

My settled in, sliding off her coat and velour jacket. "I love this place. It's so homey, you know?"

It sure was homey. *A few blocks in either direction and we're right back in the projects,* Caiza thought. "It's alright," she replied, looking down at her menu. The waiter returned with two drinks neither of them ordered.

"Compliments of the gentlemen in the corner." Caiza and Myeisha turned their heads at the same time. Two of the corniest down-home country bamas waved at them. One of them had a gold tooth that shined when the light hit it and the other was wearing something that looked like it had been dragged from the Karl Kani Collection. She didn't even know people still wore that shit. Caiza could smell the activator and Brut from where she sat. Myeisha smiled and waved them over.

"My! What the hell are you doing!" Caiza shout whispered. Myeisha fluffed her hair and gave Caiza a glance.

"Girl, you better get hip," she muttered back. "It's the end of the month and mama's rent is due." The brothers joined them, one of them sliding in next to her and the other next to Caiza. Oh Christ. Myeisha got the halfway decent one and Caiza got Puff Smokey Smoke.

"How you fine ladies doin' tonight?" Decent asked.

Myeisha smiled her widest and replied, "We're better now that you've joined us."

Caiza took a sip of lemonade. "Speak for yourself."

Smokey got a little too close. "Aw, nah don't tell me you ain't bout ta have a good time?"

She pulled away from the repulsive character. "No actually, we were trying to have a quiet dinner by ourselves."

"It's my birthday," Myeisha said, pointing to herself.

Decent clapped his hands. "Ah, well then. Happy birthday. Hey, Garçon, can we get a bottle of champagne over here?" The waiter nodded. "So what's your name, sweetness?"

"I'm Myeisha, and that's my girl Caiza."

"Caiza," Smokey said. "Kinda like Old Faithful, right?"

"Nah, man, that's *geyser*," Decent said. Caiza put her head in her hands, or else she would've tried to cut her wrists with the closest butter knife. "I'm Steve, and this here is my man Ray Ray."

"Charmed I'm sure," Caiza said from behind her hands. The waiter returned with the champagne. Caiza reached for it and downed three glasses right off the top. Myeisha smiled at her from behind her teeth. "Kye, honey, you wanna save some for the birthday girl?"

Caiza handed it over. She needed something stronger anyway. "Excuse me," she said, getting up from the table. Myeisha grabbed her purse and followed her to the bathroom.

Myeisha went to work on her face in the mirror as soon as the door shut. "Kye, what is your problem?"

"My problem?" she asked, rinsing her hands. "I came out to dinner to celebrate your birthday, not to be entertained by the hip-hop Dalmatians."

Myeisha took the time to smooth her hair around her shoulders. "They're nice guys, Kye. Somethin' you know nothin' about."

She turned away from the sink. "Now what the hell was that supposed to mean?"

"I'm sorry. That was mean." My pouted and knew she would have to beg. "But I wanna have some fun. Please, just this once?"

Caiza sighed and rolled her eyes to the heavens. "My, this is the first and last time."

"Okay. I promise. Thank you, babes." Myeisha kissed her cheek, and they returned to their table.

"We thought you lovely thangs musta got lost," Ray Ray said as his gold tooth clinked against his champagne glass. Caiza bit her lip for My's sake.

"So what do you ladies do for a living?" Steve asked after the appetizers arrived.

Myeisha shifted in her chair. Hi, my name is Myeisha and I'm a gold digger. *Hi Myeisha.* "I'm in between jobs," she said neatly side swiping the question. She wasn't going to tell him she worked at a strip club until it was necessary. By that time, his bankbook would have her name on it. Steve nodded, as if he knew exactly where she was coming from.

"What 'bout you?" Ray Ray asked.

Caiza folded her hands. "I'm a receptionist. And you?"

He offered one of those corny pimp laughs. "I'm a gas station attendant up on 149th. I get the best tips, so me and my man here came out and treated ourselves after a long week."

Myeisha pursed her lips together. "You work together, Steve?" she asked.

"Oh no, I'm a pediatrician." Myeisha smiled, happy that he was a man of status and not a grease monkey. How in the hell did this man get to be friends with Smokey? And even worse was that he was clearly interested in Myeisha. Caiza was stuck with Sir Shit for Brains while My worked her magic and wrapped Steve around her finger.

Dinner went by fairly quickly, with Caiza cringing as Smokey continued to butcher the English language. Steve gave Myeisha his number, and she promised to call him. They walked the girls out to the car. Ray Ray leaned in on Caiza's side of the window. Caiza wondered how long she could drag his body before the cops caught up to her.

"I had a good time wit' you, girl. When we gon' hook up and get together again?"

She turned her head slowly in his direction like her name was Linda Blair. "As soon as you scrape up enough cash to buy a vowel and a clue. Good night." She rolled her eyes and the window up and pulled off.

"That was fun," My said.

"Oh yeah. A real blast," Caiza replied, deadpan.

Myeisha leaned over and flipped the radio dial. "You didn't like Ray? I think he was kinda cute." She settled for the Quiet Storm on WBLS.

"Cute like what, My?" Caiza made a left and got on the Deegan.

"You know, just cute."

"You're only saying that because Steve could spell his own name without the assistance of a bowl of AlphaBits."

Myeisha laughed aloud. "He wasn't *that* bad, girl."

"No, he was worse."

Myeisha spent the night. After they took showers, she climbed into Caiza's bed and lay on her stomach. Sparkle got jealous and joined the girls on the bed. After twenty minutes of relaxed silence, Myeisha spoke up. "What you thinkin' 'bout?"

Caiza shook her head. "I'm a little depressed."

My sat up on one arm. "I know you still ain't thinkin' about that corny fool?"

"Who? Ray?"

"No, Jacey."

"Of course I'm still thinkin' about him, My."

My ran her fingers through her hair. Standing up, she went through the dresser until she found a scarf. She finger wrapped her hair and tied the scarf around her head. "You need to let him go. I held my tongue for five years, but I don't think he needs to occupy any more time in your mind."

Caiza knew she was right. Sparkle nudged her hand, and she absently began to pat her head. "I guess."

"No, you know. You a single, hardworking girl now. He ain't got no place up in there. You think 'bout him too much, you gon' find yourself running back to his triflin' ass. And that's the last thing you need is him back in your life." Myeisha got back in the bed, laid down and stuck her thumb in her mouth. Caiza knew Myeisha was right, as she usually was. And that's why she loved My. She was the voice of reason.

"Ms. Bell, would you please send Mr. Francis up when he gets here?"

"I will," she replied. Her boss, Ms. Louisiana Tate, was the only person on the job who gave her any actual verbal communication. Caiza thought it was because she had to, she was the receptionist. Mr. Francis was helping them with the budget, and he was a member of the senior board of advisors. He'd been back and forth to the center all week.

This job was going fine for her. She was making steady income, and here it was in March and she'd had no problems. She should've figured her luck was about to change.

"Excuse me? Can you tell me where to pick up my daughter?" She looked up and a man she'd had never seen before was standing before her.

"I'm sorry, sir. Who is your child?" He looked puzzled for a moment too long. She knew he didn't have a child there. She was familiar with the face of every parent and child that passed through those doors.

"I think she's in Class Three."

"What is her name?"

At that point, the director of the center, Vanna Fredericks, rounded the corner. The woman had had it in for Caiza since the day she started working there. She was rude and nasty whenever she had the chance and tried to treat Caiza like she was her personal slave. "Hello, Mr. Smith. Are you here for Michelle?"

Smith nodded. All of a sudden the child had a name? "I was trying to get some help from your receptionist here, but she won't tell me what class she's in."

Caiza wasn't a dumb shit. As soon as he said that, she knew this was a setup. She most certainly had not given him a problem, and the fact that the director had shown up at just the right time proved her suspicions. "I was asking Mr. Smith to identify his child because I've never seen him before. I wasn't trying to give him a problem."

Vanna walked over to her and leaned as far over her desk as possible. "Let me tell you something. This isn't the projects, young lady. This is a business. If you want to be ghetto, I'm sure there are plenty of extra shifts open at McDonald's."

Caiza stood, prepared to beat her ass. "Number one, only my mother talks to me like that. Number two, I wasn't giving this gentleman a hard time. I simply asked him what his child's name was. I had no intention of making this a 'ghetto' situation."

Vanna put on a face like she'd been insulted. "How dare you dress me down in front of a parent."

"If you want me to dress you down, I will. Ain't no reason for you to be all in my face." Homegirl should have never got her started.

They went back and forth at it for about ten minutes. She hadn't even noticed the man in the business suit who arrived and was watching the show. Ms. Tate came downstairs.

"What is going on down here? Mr. Francis! Please, this way. Go right on up to my office, and I'll be right with you." She turned back to them, and Caiza knew she was in trouble.

"Ms. Bell here thought it was polite to harass Mr. Smith when all he wanted to do was pick up his child."

"In my defense, I did not harass Mr. Smith. I did what I am paid to do, screen all visitors."

"Mr. Smith?"

"I just wanted to know what class Michelle was in. My wife sent me to pick her up and I forgot which class she was in."

"I'll take it from here," Ms. Tate said. The director smiled evilly behind her back, and Mr. Smith followed her, adding a swagger to his walk. "Ms. Bell, this is not the first complaint I've received about your behavior."

That was news to Caiza. "What?"

"Yes. The other employees have expressed their discomfort with your conduct."

"I have never harassed anyone from the day I stepped foot in here. Everyone was against *me* since day one."

"Beyond that, you disrespected a higher employee in front of a board member and in front of a parent. That is unacceptable. In light of these events, I'm going to have to let you go."

What the hell was she talking about? "Ms. Tate, there is obviously more to this than you know."

She held up her hands. "I'm sorry, Ms. Bell. There's nothing I can do."

Nothing she could do. Caiza couldn't even be mad at her. Her co-workers had clearly conspired against her, and the woman was too blind to see it. So once again, she did the cardboard box tango, dropped her things in her trunk and drove away.

Caiza took twenty dollars out of the bank and bought some takeout and a pint of ice cream. She ate the ice cream with a Snicker bar. She knew it would all go straight to her thighs but she didn't care. She was back to the drawing board.

"Are you sure you're okay?"

"Not really."

"You wanna talk about it?"

Caiza chuckled. "Not really." It had been neary a month since Caiza and Rydell had seen each other and Caiza had to admit, she missed him. He invited her over to his place for dinner. That man could make one hell of a chicken Parmesan. After they cleaned the kitchen, they sat on the couch together with her head on his shoulder talking mostly about her.

"You know I got your back, right? Anything you need, I got you," he said when he dropped her off in front of her apartment.

Caiza put her face down and nodded. She didn't want to drag him into her mess. "I know."

"All right, girl," he said. "Get on upstairs before I turn this car around."

Caiza smiled. She climbed out and waved her good-bye.

"Anything you need," he shouted out the window.

6

And Take Three

"Girl, I really appreciate you hooking me up like this," Denise said, clipping on an earring. Hopping on one foot, she pulled on her other shoe as her children swarmed around her legs. For now, Denise was living off child support and unemployment checks. Her older brother also started sending her a hefty check every week when he heard she was fired, so money wasn't really a problem for her.

Denise wished the best for Caiza, but the best would not feed her. Coincidentally they were both in a bit of a bind. She needed a sitter and Caiza needed some extra cash, so she figured what the hell?

What the fuck was more like it. Caiza didn't know what in the name of red hell she was thinking when she accepted this gig. Denise was offering six dollars per kid per hour for four hours, which landed her ninety-six bucks. It wasn't much but it would cover groceries and a few other expenses for the next few days. That rent was really kicking her ass.

Caiza had a good set-up with Jacey; all she did was grocery shop. That only took a couple of hundred dollars out of her check. The rest she used for clothes shopping. She never thought she'd be alone, so she never saw the need to save money for a rainy day. She could barely afford what she was paying at her place, which was an arm, a leg and her firstborn. Back rent was up to three months, and she couldn't hold off her landlord much longer.

Denise had four badass kids, and they were all in that annoying bastard stage; Tia, the oldest, was six. She had a mouth on her like you wouldn't believe. Couldn't read worth a damn or spell her own name, and somehow, Caiza wasn't surprised that the child knew every word to every song on BET, MTV and Hot 97—even knew where to insert the curses.

Tyrone, four, was a screamer. When she got there, he was running through the house with his Pamper in one hand and a bottle—still couldn't drink out of a cup and still wasn't potty trained—in the other.

Talisha, who looked nothing like her mother, had just turned three. She was quiet, too quiet, and Caiza wished she had a bell to tie around the little girl's neck. She just dragged her limp Bugs Bunny around with her thumb in her mouth and her big droopy eyes surveying the scene. Talisha watched Caiza from the moment she arrived, not saying a word. Caiza wasn't even sure if the little girl could talk.

Finally was Terence, the baby, the youngest at sixteen months. She was one of those babies that you could take or leave; either she was making as much noise as the other two, or she was quietly studying life from her crib.

Denise had apparently had these children one after the other, and from the assortment of pictures on the end table in her shabby living room, Caiza also assumed they all had different fathers. Caiza couldn't imagine having kids with that many different people. She'd never even had sex with that many people.

"Here's my cell number, just in case. If anything crazy happens, just dial 911. I have your number, and I'll call you when I'm on the way back." Denise put her hands on her hips, trying to think whether she'd forgotten anything. Then she held up her hand, dropping her voice to a whisper. "If a guy comes by, and he says his name is Freddie, do *not* let him in."

"Who's Freddie?"

"That's Talisha's father, but I'm not letting him see her until I get me a child support check, you feel me?" she said, nudging her. Caiza smiled and nodded to show she knew what she meant, but on the inside, she was frowning. Number one, Caiza felt that denying a man his paternal rights was wrong, no matter what amount of money he was or was not paying.

Number two, she didn't want to be in the middle of their custody battle. But whatever.

Denise went to the front door and gathered her babies to her. "Come here. Mommy is going out. What are the rules?"

"Behave," said the ones who could talk, meaning Tia and Tyrone. Talisha kept her thumb in her mouth and pouted, while baby Terence playfully swatted her mother's earring. She handed the baby, who already needed a Pamper change, over to Caiza. Denise pulled her purse over her shoulder and blew a kiss. "I love you."

"Mommy," Tyrone wailed, in a failed effort to get her to stay.

"Mommy will be back, okay? I love you. Behave for Caiza, alright?" She waved and quickly fled. As soon as the door shut, all holy hell began.

When the click of Denise's heels could no longer be heard in the hallway, Tyrone stood in the middle of the foyer and began to scream, tears streaming from his eyes as if he were being crucified. Talisha didn't know why her brother was crying, so she sat next to him on the floor and began to cry as well. The baby was fidgeting, squirming, trying to figure out why her mother had disappeared. Caiza lifted her in the air and snatched her head back as the odor of poo hit her in the face. She needed a changing yesterday. Tia was staring at Caiza as if she had a KIDNAPPER stamp on her forehead.

Her first thought was to panic. Of course, she had plenty of experience, she had baby-sat for every mother in the neighborhood by the time she was sixteen, and she was very good with children. But all those mothers had one or two, not four. Caiza let Tyrone and Talisha wail; she figured the neighbors were used to it and wouldn't call the police. Hopefully, Tia was smart enough to keep her eye on them. Walking into the other room, Caiza laid Terence on the changing table. The baby took a page from Tyrone's book and hollered as well.

Caiza had the fresh Pamper on and was lifting the powder when Tia opened her mouth and scared the hell out of her. Caiza squeezed half the bottle on herself, missing Terence completely, choking and coughing as the powder filled her lungs, eyes and nose. She cleared her eyes with a baby wipe, pulling herself together and finishing the diaper.

"Is that a weave?" Tia asked, pointing to her hair.

"No," she replied, tossing her powdery locks over her shoulder. The baby giggled and grabbed at Caiza's hair, clapping her hands like this was some circus attraction.

Tia seemed to be unfazed as her little sister howled with all her might. Damn, that baby could've been the next Aretha if she put her mind to it. She had a serious set of pipes. Tia kept right on talking, as if she heard nothing. She flipped her own plaits this way and that, trying to copy the hair toss.

"My mama said that when I start first grade, I could get my hair any way I want."

Caiza buttoned Terence's one piece and lifted the baby over her shoulder, walking out of the room. Tia followed her. "Oh yeah?"

"Yeah. She said I'm gonna be too cute."

She's already too grown, Caiza thought. *Bet she can't even spell hair.* Caiza walked into the kitchen looking for a bottle, and feeling a headache come on as Terence, Talisha and Tyrone joined in the wailing. He had just quit, but as soon as he heard the baby, he started up again. Caiza thought about putting the bottle in the microwave until she realized there wasn't one. And the kitchen was filthy.

There were dirty dishes everywhere, and roaches. Under the counter were mouse droppings. Disgusting. She found a clean pot, filled it with water and turned the flame on low, not placing the bottle inside just yet. Caiza stepped on a hard toy as she walked into the living room.

"Shit!" Caiza hobbled a bit before kicking the Lego under the couch. It looked like the kids hadn't put their toys away in weeks. Still carrying a now whimpering Terence, she took Tyrone's hand and led him to the living room, motioning for Talisha to follow.

"Now what's the matter? What's with all the crying?"

Tyrone did one of those numbers she remembered from when she was a kid. His chest rose and fell rapidly as he tried to stop crying, giving the impression that he was taking a series of deep sniffs, making his words come out in flashes. "Ma-ma-left-me-here," he managed.

"She comin' back, you baby," Tia said before slapping him in the back of the head and taking off. Tyrone squealed and shouted. "I ain't a baby.!" He ran after her. Talisha, thumb firmly in place, sat down to watch them run around the living room. Caiza set down Terence who was getting a kick out of this, and sat Talisha next to her.

She reached out for Tia, but the little brat kicked her in the leg and darted off into the bathroom. Tyrone followed her lead, kicked Caiza in the other shin and chased her. They locked themselves inside. Caiza hobbled over to the door. "Little bastards," she said under her breath.

She rattled the knob. "Open the door, Tia."

"No!" she shouted.

Caiza was getting impatient. She mentally debated kicking the door in and beating them like their last name was King and their daddy was Rodney. She was used to these kiddy tricks and knew what it took to get them out. She thought she heard the doorbell ring but whoever it was would truly have to wait.

"Will you open the door, *please*?" she asked in her sweetest voice. There was silence for a moment. Then the lock clicked, and the two of them tried to dart out, but she caught one in each arm and hauled them, kicking, into the living room on the couch.

"What did your mother tell you? She said to behave, right? You know I don't want to have to tell her you're acting up." She pulled her cell phone off her hip and made like she was making a phone call.

"No! No! Don't call her," Tia protested. Tyrone's face registered the same fear. Caiza sighed and put her phone back.

"Alright, but you have to promise to behave yourselves, okay? I don't want to call Mommy."

They nodded and agreed. Tia and Tyrone were the troublemakers; it was clear to see. Caiza was so deep into mommy mode that she failed to realize that Talisha was gone, and so was the baby. Her heart dropped when she looked at the front door. It was wide open.

Caiza jumped over the couch and was at the door in an instant, fearing that Terence had fallen down the stairs. When she got out there, a bear of a man was holding Talisha in his arms with tears in his eyes, and Terence was sitting on the floor looking up at them. She panicked and snatched Talisha from the man, sweeping Terence up and kicking the door shut behind her in two smooth motions. Her heart was pumping so fast she could barely breathe.

"Who the hell is this guy?" Caiza muttered, unaware of what to do. Talisha reached out and whimpered.

The doorbell rang. Caiza froze. If that massive meat truck standing out there wanted to, he could certainly break in. She looked through the peephole. "Who are you?" Her question was answered when Talisha reached out again and the only word Caiza ever heard from her escaped her lips.

"Daddy."

Caiza almost dropped them both on the floor. She put Terence down and waved Tia over to her side. Happy to be nosy, she bounded over, her hair bouncing. Caiza put the chain on the door before opening it. Tia waved, her eyes brightening. "Hi, Uncle Freddie."

"You know him?" Caiza whispered.

"Yeah, she know me," his deep voice boomed. "Please open the door." She figured that Tia would not trust this man in her home if he were a messed-up guy. She opened it a little farther, the baby on her hip.

"Who are you?"

"I'm Freddie. Who are you?"

"I'm Caiza, the babysitter. I'm sorry, but Denise said not to let you in."

The man was clearly disturbed. "I know. I know she said that. I called her and told her I was coming because I wanted to see my baby. She says I can't see her until I send her a check. Please, just five minutes. Don't nobody gotta know but us."

Caiza hesitated, shifting Terence on her hip. She looked down at Talisha who had her thumb in her mouth. Tia had lost interest and was back to chasing her brother.

"Please, miss. I ain't gon' bother the other kids. I just wanna see my daughter. I ain't seen her in six months. Please." He looked seconds away from bursting into tears. Caiza couldn't ignore the desperation in his eyes or in his voice. Against her better judgment, she opened the door a little wider and let him in. He scooped Talisha into the air, and she wrapped her arms around his neck. He sat in the hall chair with his child on his lap, and a weight seemed lifted, albeit temporarily, from his shoulders.

Caiza kept a close eye on them, just in case her positive vibes were wrong. He seemed like a nice enough guy. And he was also a man of his word. After five minutes, he handed Talisha over, kissed her, promised he'd see her again and disappeared with a sad glance back.

She shut the door and tried to get the hurt out of her own heart, just as the smoke alarm started blaring. The girls covered their ears, Tyrone began his screaming routine, and Terence buried her head in her shoulder and began to wail. She set the baby down on the couch and darted into the kitchen.

Caiza completely forgot about the water she'd put on to boil. It had long since evaporated and the bottom of the pot was scorched, gray smoke sweeping upward. Snatching a potholder from the side of the refrigerator Caiza tossed the pot in the sink and turned on the cold water. There was a loud hiss, and she jumped back for a second before reaching forward and turning the sink off. That solved that, but she still had to feed the kids somehow and couldn't do it in a dirty kitchen.

Opening the cabinet, Caiza found nothing but a small can of Chef Boyardee. In the fridge were two eggs, butter, a half loaf of white bread and old pancake mix. There might as well have been some hardtack and navy beans. How was she supposed to feed the army of kids on these half rations? Caiza bit her lip and pulled her phone off her hip.

She had just hung up when they started all over again. Tia smacked Tyrone, who in turn began to chase her. Terrence giggled and squealed with glee while Talisha-who could miraculously speak now-shouted "stop it" over and over again. Caiza took a look at her watch and rolled her eyes. Denise owed her big time for this. "Talisha, put—*no*. Put that down. Do not hit him with that." Talisha heard the warning, dropped the toy that she was going to hit her brother in the head with and lifted another.

Terence was clearly getting a kick out of her brother and sister. Caiza shifted the baby back to her hip. "Come here, Tyrone. Come here. She's not going to hit you. No, Tia, cut it out. You're supposed to be the big girl." Tyrone rushed past and Tia stuck her foot out and tripped him. Caiza was about ready to toss them all out of a window one by one. How the hell did Denise do it? This was exactly why she wasn't having kids.

Twenty minutes later, she had the babies sitting down on the floor in the living room eating Chinese takeout and laughing at a *Looney Tunes* rerun. Even Talisha had taken her thumb out long enough to have a few bites of egg roll. Dinner had cost twelve bucks, but it was well spent in her eyes. She warmed a bottle for Terence, keeping her eyes on it this time. She fed the baby while the other kids ate, daydreaming about a hot bath and a foot rub.

When they were done eating, everybody got a bath before they were tucked in. Tia protested at first, but when she was promised a bedtime story, she jumped in the tub. Caiza put Terence in her walker to go crazy for a little while as she watched her sister in the bath. Tyrone went in kicking and screaming, successfully drenching Caiza and her fresh perm in his outburst. She got him in there with the promise of a sound whipping if he didn't behave. Once he had a couple of toy fire trucks and a rubber duck, he was fine. Talisha didn't care what she did one way or another.

"Are you okay?" Caiza asked her, trying to get conversation as she washed the crap out of her hair. These kids were really dirty. She had to get down on her hands and knees and scrub the rings out of the tub after each bath.

Talisha nodded. The thumb never moved.

"You miss your daddy?"

She nodded again, her brown eyes far away. Caiza knew the feeling all too well. She knew what it was like to live without a father. Knowing he was alive and never seeing him was just as bad as not knowing him at all.

"He comes to see you all the time?"

"He comes, but Mama said don't let him in," Tia said from behind her. She stood there in her jammies, leaned against the doorframe. A cigarette in one hand and she could've been Marilyn Monroe. "She's mad at him."

Caiza knew this was dangerous ground but she treaded a little further. "Why?"

Tia scrunched up her nose, as if thinking. "She said he a—a dead feet. No, a dead man. No…"

"A dead beat?" she volunteered.

Tia nodded.

"Listen, don't tell her I let him in, okay?" she told Tia and Talisha, who both nodded.

"This gonna be our secret, okay? Pinkie swears." The girls were too happy to do pinkie swears and share a secret with a grownup. She finished up with Talisha and washed Terence up right afterward.

After she put all the kids off to bed (and Talisha went to sleep after she read *Green Eggs and Ham* seven times), Caiza went through the house and did the expected babysitter cleanup. She put the toys away, fixed up the living room, and cleaned the kitchen. She made sure all their dirty clothes were in hampers, took the garbage out and vacuumed the carpet in the living room.

Denise's place was twice as clean as it was when she got there, and when Caiza collapsed on the couch at eleven, she was bone tired. She wasn't too tired to notice, though, that Denise was an hour late. She needed to get home, feed and walk Sparkle, and get ready for the job hunt the next day. Under certain circumstances they were sweet kids, but there was no way she was ever sitting for the Hell's Angels again.

Denise finally made it in at 12:45. Caiza had long since dozed off. She was half-asleep when she heard the key in the door. Denise tapped her shoulder.

"Hey, girl. I'm back. The kids wore you out, huh?"

"No, they were great," she lied. Caiza could tell Denise knew how "great" they'd been, from the caked powder in her frizzy hair and her clothes to the spots on her jeans and the beat-down, tired look on her face. Denise insisted on paying extra for the overtime and Caiza gratefully accepted, kissing her cheek and promising to call so they could get together sometime.

The twenty-minute drive back to her own home drained what little was left of Caiza's energy. Parking in front of her building, Caiza decided she was too tired to eat, so she didn't bother going over to the take-out spot. Her legs were killing her as she climbed the stairs, and the headache and back pain didn't help things.

When she reached her landing, there was a white envelope stuck in her door. She sighed hard and plucked it, turning her key in the lock. Sparkle met her at the door, as usual. Caiza took her for her quick walk and fed her, dreading the whole time just what was in the envelope. She tossed it on the coffee table and lowered herself onto the living room couch, staring at the envelope before her for over an hour. It took her that long to gather the nerve it would require to open it. The sinking feeling in the pit of her stomach was justified.

As soon as Caiza opened the envelope, she regretted it. Notice of Eviction. Caiza read the whole thing, holding a bottle of Budweiser to her forehead. Nothing she didn't know already, nonpayment of rent. She had until the first of May, her birthday, to come up with the money or the marshal would be coming to get her. It was the fifth of April. She stripped her clothes off, lay in her bed and cried until the sun came up. Then she cried until she fell asleep.

7

What the Hell Am I Supposed to Do?

"Mama, I really don't want to discuss this with you right now. I have enough things going without you on my back."

"I'm just giving it to you straight. If you hadn't bothered to waste so much of your time on that Jacey, you wouldn't be in this situation. I told you so, didn't I? I told you this was going to happen."

"Mother," she started.

"It needs to be said, darling. You think you can get ahead in this life by having a man take care of you? I didn't. I had to take care of myself. No man ever helped me survive."

"I'm broke, Mama. I'm getting evicted at the beginning of the month if I don't come up with some cash. Is that what you want to hear? You want to hear that I'm struggling so you can feel better? Well, forget it, Ma. I'll lay on my back for a living before I scrub some white man's toilets like you did for twenty years," she shouted.

DeLiza lost her mind when she heard that. It was okay for her to trash others, but if someone said one foul thing out of his mouth about how hard she'd worked, DeLiza acted as if someone had spit inside the Sistine Chapel.

"How dare you! How *dare* you? I worked that hard so I could take care of you. That was for your benefit."

Caiza rolled her eyes. "Save it, Ma. You had the talent and the smarts to do anything you wanted to do. But you instead chose to take the low road, just because you thought it'd make me kiss your ass later in life. Guess what? It didn't work. Now I've gotta go."

"Caiza, don't you hang up this phone!" were the last words she heard from her mother that day.

Caiza wasn't really good at working out a situation just sitting still, so she grabbed the leash and took Sparkle for a walk. The dog was happy to be out. It was cool that day and the late spring sun was hiding behind the scattered clouds. They jogged through the park and as her lungs sucked in air greedily, she really put her mind to work.

Her budget currently included her rent, her electricity, her phone bill, gas for the car, her groceries, the rent and the new semester's tuition. All told, her unpaid bills were up to a little over five grand. With just eight hundred in the bank, she had a choice. She could give some of that up for the rent and food, or pay some of the other bills so her utilities could be kept on. Either way, she was robbing Peter to pay Paul.

Caiza's problem was her pride. She was embarrassed to ask for help, but as soon as Myeisha heard the situation, she shelled out enough cash for her landlord to grant her an extension. Now she had until June 1.

Caiza had barely enough food to keep Sparkle alive, much less herself. Every job she called for was either finished interviewing or wasn't looking at the moment. She had nearly no money, very little food and was facing homelessness. For the first time in her life, she would have to miss her birthday. She had never missed her own day before and now instead of a day of pampering, she would be looking for another job.

"Goddamnit, Jacey. This shit is all your fault," she said to herself, stopping to stretch by a tree. Her leg was cramping. Looking up, she saw that she'd run around the park once already. Sparkle dodged back, panting, making sure she was okay. "I'm alright, mama."

"Are you sure?" a familiar voice asked. Caiza turned and looked at Rydell. *Mmm*, she thought. *They do say chocolate is good for you*. He was truly looking good these days. Caiza hadn't seen him since their date at his place, and looking at his fine ass, she realized how much she'd missed him. Despite the sweat, she hugged him as tight as she could.

"Damn, girl. I didn't know you missed me like that."

"I really have. How've you been?"

He rolled his head and his eyes. "It's not like you don't have my number," he said.

"This is true. How are things down at the restaurant?"

He waved his hand as they started walking. "I quit."

"You're kidding?"

Rydell shook his head. "Charlie's got a fat mouth. He said some things he had no business saying." He looked over at her. "You should've told me."

Caiza shrugged and looked down at her Shox. "I thought you two were pretty close, so I figured you wouldn't believe me even if I did tell."

"I thought you know me a little better than that." He took a moment to admire her. "You're lookin' real good," he commented at last.

Caiza stopped walking and modeled her figure. "Oh, well, you know I try. You never know when you'll run into a friend jogging," she joked.

His smiling features got serious for just a second. "I really do want you to consider me a friend, Kye. You can call me anytime if you ever need me."

Caiza kicked a rock, which Sparkle immediately chased. She grew bored and dodged ahead a few steps to chase a butterfly. Rydell could tell she was disturbed. He slowed his pace and put his arm around her shoulder.

"I know I asked you this before, but I want you to be straight this time. What's really going on?"

She sighed. She wanted so bad to tell someone, but what was she going to say? *Let's see, I'll probably be homeless by the end of the month, I'm eating one meal a day to conserve groceries, my dog is going to starve in another week, and I most likely won't be going back to school next semester after all. But the weather's great. How are you?* She played it cool.

"How do you know there's something wrong with me?"

"It's not that hard to read you," was all he said.

"And what is that supposed to mean?"

He held his hands out, gesturing. "Your vibe, babe. Something's gotta be wrong. Your whole vibe is off."

She gave a half smile, keeping his arm around her shoulder. "All this from just three months of working together?"

He shrugged. "It's kinda hard to figure you women out but once you do, you don't forget."

They were coming to her exit of the park. She started to head there, but Rydell pulled her back into another tight embrace. "I know you're going through something. I just don't know what. But when you're ready to tell me, you give me a ring. Remember, day or night." He looked into her eyes and kissed her cheek before turning and jogging away. She watched his tight ass as he trotted off. Hmm, that man was some kinda fine.

Caiza floated until she saw Jacey—could her life get any worse?— standing in front of her building with a bouquet of flowers and his ear shoved up against his phone. She was really not in the mood for him. She crossed the street, hoping he would miss her. Fat chance. Not only did Sparkle race over to greet him; the dog practically snapped her neck getting Jacey to turn and see Caiza coming up the block.

"Baby girl," he said, hanging up the phone. He held his arm out, showing her the flowers. "These are for you, Kye."

She glared at him so hard her eyes began to hurt. "What the hell do you want, Jacey?"

He sucked his teeth. "Caiza, you know what I want. Do we have to play these games? And you're looking so good too." He half-smiled and let his eyes roam up and down her body.

"I still got it, mama," he whispered in her ear.

Caiza jerked her head away, not because he was annoying her, but rather because he was turning her on. She had to get away from him. He put the flowers in her hand.

"Jace, I have a million things to take care of. Thanks for these, but I've gotta go."

He caught her arm, reminding her of what he said in the park that day. "Caiza, I know you're still mad at me, but we really need to have a serious talk. It's important."

"Jacey," she started.

"Five minutes, please, Caiza."

Caiza rolled her eyes and stamped her foot. She knew she was going to regret this, but she figured she should at least hear out "the Pig," as Myeisha had unaffectionately nicknamed him. She held up her free hand. "Five minutes, Jacey."

Caiza didn't even know why she bothered to let him in. Jacey looked around for a few minutes before settling on her Ikea couch. She was pissed as hell that she had to buy that; but the Italian leather couches she sat on with Jacey didn't come with the deal. Caiza poured two glasses of water and brought them out to the living room.

She gave him the water and walked away to put the flowers in a vase, setting them on the kitchen table. It was a lovely bouquet of violets, her favorites.

"This place is nice, Kye."

"The old place was even better." She sat on the other side of the couch, her legs crossed.

"That's what I wanted to talk to you about." He came closer to her. His Tommy cologne wafted into her nostrils, and she felt herself going. "Look, Caiza. I want you back with me. I know what I did to you was foul. I know it was wrong. It should never have happened."

"Damn straight," she agreed, raising her glass.

"But things have changed. The company's doing well, you know that. And I have everything I need except for you. I took advantage of your love and your trust, and I'm so sorry. I can make it up to you a thousand ways. I miss you, and I love you and I think you still love me too."

Caiza hated the hell out of him, but he was the only love she had ever known. Literally. She gave her virginity to Jacey when she was eighteen, and they had been together ever since. That was also another painful piece of the puzzle. She had given Jacey the gift you couldn't get back and he had hit her in the face with his elbow. And it hurt.

Still, she couldn't deny how good it was to see him begging. She didn't ever want to be with Jacey again, because he had broken her trust in ways that she couldn't ever forgive, but she knew getting him back was the only way she'd ever feel any better. Besides, she was heating up in places that only he had ever made her heat up. *Maybe I need to have a little fun and take my mind off things,* she thought.

Caiza slid over a little closer to him. "I need to take a shower, but if you meet me in my room, I'm sure we can work something out," she whispered.

When she came out of the shower fifteen minutes later, she had a towel wrapped around her head and nothing on her body. There were a couple of wet strands hanging out from under the towel. Drops of water slipped down her soft, naked body. She stood in the doorway.

Jacey was already in her bed, watching her. He moved over and made room for her. Caiza rubbed the towel through her hair, drying it as much as she could before she threw it on the chair next to her. Without a word, she climbed into the bed, pulling the sheet back and exposing him in all his fineness.

"I see you don't waste any time," she said softly, looking down at his hardness.

Jacey smiled and reached out for her hand. "It's been a long time. We both miss you."

"So I see."

Jacey wanted foreplay but Caiza wasn't interested. Lifting a leg, she threw it over his hips and straddled him, looking into his eyes as she slid down and let him inside of her.

Jacey closed his eyes and groaned softly as Caiza began to rise and fall on top of him. Caiza had to admit, she truly missed this feeling. Biting her lip, she rode him faster and harder, listening to his moaning and smiling as he called her name. Jacey groaned again and grabbed her hips, burying himself as deep inside her as he could.

"Damn, baby, I'm comin'," he whispered in her ear. Caiza couldn't respond because she was doing the same thing. She exhaled sharply and pulled away from him. Jacey snatched her towel from the bedside chair and shoved it in his lap. Caiza lay back, breathing slowly through her nose. That fifteen minutes of heat made her forget all about everything else.

Needless to say, Jacey broke her in half that night. Five and a half hours of the nasty. It was exactly what she needed, and Caiza really didn't feel bad about using him for her own personal gain. He had used her as a perpetual live-in booty call for five years; she was just returning the favor. If their relationship were based on the sex alone, she would never have left. Jacey was a master at what he did, and he made sure she knew it when she was shouting his name out and carving foreign languages into his spine.

Caiza woke early the next morning, looking at his honey-brown skin, which was now covered in scratches from the night before. The phone rang, and he stirred, rolling on his side.

"Hello?" she whispered. Nine-thirty in the morning. It could only be one person.

"Heyyyyyyy, girl. I gots the hook up."

"What are you talking about?" Caiza asked. She rolled out of the bed and padded to the kitchen to start some coffee. Myeisha never made her point clear when first calling. She preferred to keep you guessing.

"I spoke to my boss the other night. I told her your situation, and she said if you come down and let her get a look at you, she'll see what she can do."

"What?" Caiza was so busy trying not to wake Jacey that she had trouble focusing on the conversation in front of her.

"'Member you said you needed a job real bad before the end of the month? Well, this here is a job and it's almost the end of the month."

Caiza scooped two tablespoons into the Krups, looked back at Jacey and then scooped another two.

"Myeisha, are you kidding me?"

"I'm dead serious. If she likes you, she might hire you right there."

She dropped the spoon. "It's a strip club."

"It ain't church," Myeisha said.

"Myeisha, I am not going to work in a strip club," she shout whispered, peeking again to see if Jacey was awake yet. "Those places are disgusting. What the hell is wrong with you?"

"Ain't nothin' wrong with me, girl. I'm tryna help *you* out. Steve sends me some cash every week. I ain't the one that can't pay my rent."

Caiza narrowed her eyes. "Ouch."

"I'm sorry. But Kye, you ain't got much time left. Tell you what, think about it, okay? For real. Get your rent paid in a week, tops. Promise me you'll think about it."

"Hell no."

"If you feelin' that bad, I'll go in wit' you."

"There's no need for that. I won't be going."

"But Kye, you could get—"

"Bye, Myeisha."

"Caiza!"

"Bye." Caiza hung up. Myeisha had to be crazy, thinking she was going to audition at some strip club. What the hell was wrong with that girl? Caiza wasn't that damn desperate.

8

Push It Real Good

Turned out Caiza was that desperate. After she kicked Jacey out, thanking him graciously for his loving, she took a bath and put her mind on the future. Soaking in peach bubble bath and Merlot, she figured she had three choices. One, she could go back to her mama. There was no way in hell Caiza would ever ask DeLiza for help, and she would never give it without bitching and moaning and her usual "I told you so." She didn't need that.

Two, she could pull a Myeisha and leech off a man. Caiza couldn't picture herself sleeping her way to the top, getting paid for sex like she was a damn hooker. She had just a little bit more class than that. She knew Rydell adored her but she didn't have the heart to take advantage of him. She loved Myeisha, but that girl possessed pussy power she just didn't have.

Or three, she could go for this job. Caiza shuddered thinking about it.

She bit her lip and thought about the grim reality. Everybody kept saying how she looked so good; she'd lost some weight. She'd lost weight because she and Sparkle were sharing food so they wouldn't starve. There was no way she was giving up her baby; that was out of the question. But still, she was anxious. She was exhausted, stressed, near flat broke and hungry. She didn't even have enough money for a full tank of gas. And she had two weeks left to vacate the premises.

Caiza downed the rest of the Merlot, sniffing hard. She was so tired of crying. She was so tired of not having an answer, living day to day without a plan. She barely had enough time to heal from one tragedy before another came and took its place. It seemed this job would be the very last stop on the train of bad luck. It was at least worth a shot. As she stood to let the water out of the tub, the lights flickered.

They flashed, and then went out. Caiza was in the standing there in the dark. She groped in the dark for her towel. She stuck one foot out of the tub gingerly, getting a firm grip on the towel rack. Wrapping her towel around her body she reached for the doorknob. Opening the door, she saw that it wasn't just the bathroom light.

"Oh Christ," she shouted. "Can this shit get any worse?"

Outside, Sparkle was sitting in front of the door. As it was so dark, Caiza tripped over her and fell hard on the floor. "Damnit, Spark. What the hell?" Caiza reached down and felt for her towel. Shaking it off, she wrapped it back around herself. Sparkle acted as her Seeing Eye dog as she moved slowly through the apartment. She made her way to the bedroom and reached for the phone.

"Hello?"

"My, it's me. They cut off my lights."

"What the hell for?"

"I'm going to assume they want their money."

She heard Myeisha move into a quieter room. There was rap blasting behind her. She was still at the club. "How long you ain't pay the bill?"

"Two months," she replied.

Myeisha didn't say anything. Then she whispered into the phone. "Caiza, how broke *are* you?"

She started to cry again.

Caiza finger-brushed her hair in the hall mirror. "I can't believe I'm doing this," she said to her reflection. "This is bullshit." She returned to the mirror four times before she left, making sure she got her image right. Caiza was so embarrassed. Despite having had nothing to drink, she had visited the bathroom four times.

"I'm just going for the cash. That's all I need is the cash." She pulled a black hat over her locks, Alicia Keys style, put on her nicest slacks, and a silver silk shirt whose buttons stopped just at the beginning of her cleavage. There was a loud bang on the door.

"Yeah?" she shouted.

"It's Myeisha, baby. You ready to go? My car is runnin', girl. Hurry up."

"It's open," she shouted back, hopping into the hallway with only one of her heels on as she tried to stick the other one on her foot without falling.

She pushed the door open. "I thought you said you was gon' be ready?"

"Relax. I am ready."

"It's about time. I been downstairs for twenty minutes."

Caiza answered her as she grabbed her purse and locked the front door. "Why the hell didn't you come upstairs?"

"'Cuz you ain't got no elevator in this building, bitch. I love you, but if I ain't stayin', I ain't climbin'."

Myeisha pulled into the parking lot behind the club and found a spot. She looked over at her friend; Caiza's hands were shaking from where they gripped her lap.

"You gon' be alright, Kye. Trust me, baby. Okay?"

Caiza fake smiled through clenched teeth and nodded.

The club, fittingly called House of Sin, was located in Lower Manhattan. It was one of many business ventures owned and operated by Priceless Jones, the queen of New York. Now, that was one fly-ass bitch. Caiza didn't know much about her, but from what she did know, the woman was an urban legend.

According to the ghetto gossip circuit, she owned New York City, all five boroughs, ran the entire East Coast drug circuit and held down the tightest clique in the game without breaking a nail. She was royalty, and Caiza was going for a spot at her club. The positions were coveted, and competition for a slot was fierce. As if she needed the extra pressure.

Following her friend, Caiza stepped into the club and looked around. It was early, but it was packed. There were so many men in there Caiza wasn't sure if it was a club or Rec on Cell Block A. From first sight, she was impressed.

Entering, there was a narrow hall, which held the coat check and the two bathrooms. The hall led forward into the main part of the club. This was the main event, where all the action was taking place. If she didn't see it with her own eyes she wouldn't believe it.

The hallway opened up into a huge floor space, the stage being the center of attention. It spanned the entire length of the back wall, and three platforms stuck out from it, each with a pole at the very end. The one at the center came out the farthest. Three girls were currently working the separate poles, showing off the goods like there was no tomorrow.

On either side of the stage there were two huge red swings hanging from the ceiling and a scantily clad girl graced both of them. One of the girls was standing in her swing, balancing as she unsnapped her bra. She swung forward and back and forward and back, then tossed the bra out into the crowd, grabbing her breasts and laughing. She sat down and hung her head backward and the men pushed forward and put bills in her teeth.

The walls were painted a deep crimson, and every ten feet or so there was a sconce giving off a glow. The odor of marijuana and different colognes and perfumes tinged the air. The red looked good against the gold curtain that shimmered behind the stage. *Whoever decorated this place must have had a lot of time on their hands,* she thought.

Caiza was frozen in time as she looked about and tried to take in the overwhelming surroundings. Everything was alive, moving and so colorful. This place was like nowhere she had ever been before. It was a totally different place than the outside world, and in less than five minutes she had been swept off her feet.

In the back of the room tucked neatly in the corner was the deejay booth, which was next to the bar and an open staircase. From her vantage point, she couldn't see where it led, but Myeisha grabbed her hand and led her forward, so she figured that's where they would be going.

Caiza looked at the stage before she followed Myeisha up the stairs. A pretty girl with blue hair was dancing her ass off to Salt N Pepa's "Push It." She was doing moves Caiza didn't know were possible and was getting cheers and shouts all through the room. A couple of brothers reached out for My as she walked by, still holding Caiza's hand.

"Who's ya friend?" one of them asked over the music, licking his lips.

"Back off. This my girl," she said, giving him a kiss on the cheek. She pulled Caiza toward the stairs, but not before being stopped by a very pretty woman with red streaks in her hair and long crimson-colored nails.

"Where you goin', shorty?"

"Ms. J wants to see her. Caiza, this is Kade. Kade, this is my girl Caiza." Caiza smiled politely.

"Oooh, fresh meat." Kade looked her up and down. She was gorgeous, but Caiza's GayDar was flashing a mile a minute. Kade smiled and walked off.

Walking up the stairs felt like walking the Green Mile. When they reached the top, Myeisha pulled Caiza into the last room at the end of a long hall. She knocked on the door and a voice called, "What?"

"It's Myeisha. I brought my girlfriend with me."

"Come on."

A beautiful, sinister-looking woman sat in one of those crazy expensive Ethan Allen desk chairs, feet up on the desk, smoking a cherry Black and nursing a full bottle of Blue Label. Caiza took one look and felt all her confidence drip out of her body like sweat. The woman hadn't spoken a word to her and somehow she still posed a very intimidating figure. Myeisha stood back and leaned against the wall.

Priceless' sharp green eyes stared at Caiza and scared the hell out of her. "Turn around," she commanded. Caiza did, slowly, coming back to face her. A man sat on the edge of the desk, pulling a blunt out of his mouth, blowing the smoke in the air. He watched her without a word. He turned his face to Priceless, and Caiza watched the two of them have an entire conversation without saying a word. She looked back at her. "Can you dance?"

"Of course," she said.

"Can you dance in heels?"

"Yes."

"How old are you?"

"Twenty-two."

"You're hired," she said, flicking ash into the tray in front of her. She was shocked. "What? Just like that?"

Priceless looked at her. "What's your name?"

"Caiza. Caiza Bell."

"How tall are you? Five-seven? Five-eight?"

"Five-eight."

Priceless nodded, taking a deep puff from her smoke. Caiza wasn't into drugs, but she could respect the smoke the hazel-eyed dude was blowing.

"The pay is one an hour for four hours. You work Monday, Wednesday and Friday."

Caiza wasn't sure she heard right. "A dollar an hour?"

Priceless looked over at Hazel and they began to laugh at the same time. She looked at Caiza's face and realized she was serious. "Honey, that's not even minimum wage. I meant one hundred."

Caiza almost tripped out of the office and died. That would be more than enough to pay her rent and tuition if she saved up. That was forty-eight hundred a month. That was more than she had ever seen, even with Jacey.

Priceless pointed a finger at her. "Be here at seven o'clock on the dot, Monday night. If you're late, don't bother." That was it. She was dismissed as easily as she had been introduced.

Myeisha smiled. "Thanks, girl. She ain't gon' let you down. I promise."

Priceless blew out a smoky ring and pointed at Myeisha. "It'll be your ass if she does. Now get outta here."

The thought of once again having money in her pocket soothed her heart. She was out of the hole for now. Caiza was happy for the moment. It seemed as though her troubles had been briefly put on pause. But somewhere on the inside, she couldn't help thinking she had sold her soul. Her gut feelings and sixth sense were going off at a shocking rate, but she swallowed down fear and hoped the green would shake it off.

Monday night, Caiza was there with bells on. Class ended at ten on Mondays, but she was able to get her schedule switched before it was locked. Her usual schedule was upset, moving her classes to the daytime, but she promised herself it would be worth it.

She got there fifteen minutes early and took a seat in the back, waiting for Priceless to tell her what to do. Long and short, Priceless was not the one to joke with. At seven on the dot, she appeared in the room in a red fedora, a black mini dress and red stilettos, holding a glass of something dark. Caiza didn't know where she was going in that getup, but she looked damned good. The man and Kade appeared at her side, as if out of the shadows.

Priceless made a beeline for Caiza before she got too comfortable. She snatched Caiza by the arm and laid down the law. Whispering in her ear she said, "If you are late, you will be fired. If you give me any lip, you will be fired. If you come up in here actin' like you own somethin' after I was decent enough to give you a job, I will kick your ass, and then you will be fired.

"You get paid every night you work. You don't show; you don't get paid. You keep all the tips you make. Whatever goes in your bra, in your ass, I don't want it. I don't ask for your tittie money. All I ask is that you come to work ready to work. That's Kade, with the nails, and you see him? With the hazel eyes? That's Hearse. Whatever they tell you to do, you do, no questions asked. It came from me. Either that or get the hell out. We clear?"

Caiza nodded, running her hand over her elbow. That woman had a damn death grip, and Caiza knew she wasn't playing. Being that she was a newbie, she wasn't going to dance that night. She wouldn't officially start until Friday because there was a birthday party that Wednesday and only the veterans would be dancing. Priceless preferred that she sit back for one night and watch how it was done.

After three and a half hours of watching naked women twist themselves into the freakiest positions she had ever seen and watching money, drugs and liquor pass through the room like it was nothing, Priceless told her she could go.

"Practice, baby girl," she shouted after her. "Show starts Friday night."

Four days? How was she going to get her shit together in just four days? She knew she'd better learn, because that eviction notice was calling her name.

9

And a One, and a Two

"Thank you for dinner. And the movie. And the flowers. I had fun." Caiza looked down shyly as Rydell walked her to her front door.

"You sure you don't need me to come in and uh, tuck you in?" he asked slyly. Caiza smiled and pushed him back gently. She was feeling the hell out of Rydell, and they had made their relationship official the same day. Caiza knew she only lived once and she also knew she'd be a damn fool if she let a man as good as Rydell go. He leaned in and kissed her lips.

"Call me as soon as you get home," she said.

"Of course I will," he said, leaning in for another kiss. This one lasted a little bit longer than the first. Rydell pulled her close and wrapped his arms around her. When he released her, they both had childish grins on their faces. "Well, now I know I'm definitely going to have a good night."

Caiza giggled and kissed him quickly again before started towards her front door. "I miss you already," she said.

"Me too." He winked, flashed his pearly whites, then he was gone.

Friday came surprisingly quickly. Caiza conveniently evaded discussion about her plans for the weekend; she didn't think Rydell needed to know. He would never let her hear the end of it. She needed to do this on her own, and she couldn't afford to have anyone changing her mind this late in the game.

Caiza was scared as hell as she drove to the club. She had the AC on full blast but she was sweating, and her knuckles were white as she gripped the steering wheel. She found her parking spot outside and took her time getting out. Taking four deep breaths, she rested her head against the steering wheel. There was a sharp rap on her window, and Caiza nearly left her skin behind in her seat. Myeisha. Caiza got out and put on her alarm.

"I had a feeling you was gon' be here early. Good, cuz Priceless wasn't playin' when she said it was gon' be my ass. Come on. You ready?"

"If I don't go in there now, I'm never going in there."

Myeisha nodded and took her hand again. Together they walked into the back of the club. Kade was waiting in the dressing room with a clipboard. She snapped her pink bubble gum and her fingers as the pair walked inside.

"'Bout time. Come on. You gotta get changed."

If Caiza wasn't impressed with the front of the club, she was more than impressed with the back. It was like a dream in there. There were twelve vanity tables, one for each dancer. On the floor was purple carpeting, and the walls were upholstered in golden silk, giving the room a soft, majestic look. Every table was lit, and there was a chandelier in the center of the ceiling. Shit, if Heart looked anything like this, she never would have quit.

Each of the tables had a girl's name on it, in gold script at the very bottom of the mirror. The other girls had pictures, money, hairpieces and a wide assortment of things all over their mirrors. Caiza's was the last table on the left. Her name had been freshly scripted into the mirror, and her table was bare. She figured it would be, so she had stuffed her bag with all her different MAC cosmetics. Undressing in front of other women was no problem for her; she had done it all trhough high school in the locker room. She had stripped was just about to open her mouth and ask when Kade provided her with an outfit.

Caiza held out the hanger and took a look at the piece of fabric Kade just handed her. It looked something like a one-piece bathing suit that had been run through with a pair of scissors. The hot pink halter style getup clipped around the neck with just enough fabric to cover her nipples, and trailing from that was a thin piece of material that went down to her belly and went around the waist, becoming a skirt, which just kissed the bottom of her ass. It came together as a thong underneath. If she were in front of her man, it would have been fine. Instead she was about to drop it like it was hot in front of a bunch of men she had never seen before.

"Kade, where is the rest of this?" Caiza whispered.

Kade snapped her gum again before she smiled and laughed. "Girl, you better get used to it. You in the House now, baby. All we do is sin." She winked and slapped Caiza's bare ass. "And you so fine too."

Before it was time for her to go on, Myeisha introduced her to all the other girls; Kahmes (Lady Snake), Naomi (Candy Rain), Dyannara (Tiger), Shanae (Cherry Pop), and Evelyn (Hershey's Kiss). Only six girls worked a night, and they alternated with the other girls on the other nights. It was just as well. She wasn't in this to make friends.

Kade asked her what she wanted to be called, and the first thing that popped into Caiza's head was La Perla. One, because those happened to be the underwear she had been wearing when she got there and two, because she happened to find that name to be as fly as hell.

Myeisha got off stage and came in the back to give her some words of encouragement before she went on. Caiza got around the fact that she looked like an extra from a BET UnCut video long enough to listen. "Look, mama, just keep your mind on your money and your money on your mind, a'ight? Don't let them niggas scare you. It's only like a hundred of them out there anyway."

"And that's supposed to make me feel better?"

My giggled and put a hand on Caiza's shoulder. "Don't worry, mama. I been doin' this for years. You think I wasn't scared when I got up there for the first time? You got this, boo. Please. You the shit, and you know it."

It seemed like hours that Caiza had to wait for her turn, and when it came, she felt her stomach begin to turn somersaults. Myeisha was right behind her, and she gave her a kiss on the cheek and a little shove out on stage.

"Just roll wit' it," she said to herself, trying to breath as evenly as possible. Her entrance music was "Nice and Slow" by Usher. She cringed. Not exactly her first choice, but there wasn't much she could do about it. She stood behind the curtain, wringing her hands like she was about to do a performance in front of a hundred thousand screaming fans. She said the fastest prayer known to man and crossed herself.

"We've got a new face in the House tonight, another young lady tryna work it right. Brothers, do me a favor, and give it up one time for my girl,

La Perla," said the deejay, Truce, drawing her name out so it sounded like La *Per*-laaaaaaaa.

Nervous as hell, Caiza stuck out her leg first, hoping the flirt thing would work. She heard shouts and cheers, so she brought the rest of her body onto the stage. There were more cheers, claps and whistles as the men got a good look at the "fresh meat." First of all, My had grossly underestimated. There had to be close to about *two* hundred niggas out there. Caiza almost bit down on her heart as it jumped into her throat. She could've sworn the room was smaller on Monday.

Front and center, a brother in a business suit was sitting there practically drooling. She winked at him and shook her hips, slinking over there. When Usher got to "my, my, my, I wish that I," she dropped and shook it slow right in front of his face. They hooted and whistled. She got a couple of fifties for that one. She was slowly, very slowly getting the hang of this thing. The less she thought about it, the less her head hurt. She was still nauseous and ready to barf all over the front row but the soothing smell of dead presidents kept her going.

Turning in a half spin to the left, Caiza locked eyes with Hearse, who was in the back, staring her down as he puffed a blunt. His eyes never left hers, and she was so focused on him that she caught her foot and tripped. But she was prepared. She went with the fall; hitting the stage softly and making it look like she was going into a crawl. More whistles and cheers. Her eyes locked back on Business Suit, who now had a boner that was clearly visible, even in the dark.

Crawling on her hands and knees, Caiza stopped in front of him and pulled at her breasts. She paid attention; they liked that too. The more you touched yourself, the more cash they threw on the stage. Business Suit reached forward and neatly tucked two bills into her chest.

She did not want the rest of them greasy MF's feeling her up, so she teased them, getting just close enough for them to think they could cop a feel. She saw Kade watching her. She motioned for a drink, and Kade nodded. The lyrics had ended but she had the whole front row so ready for more that Truce had just let the record flow.

The room was full of shouts and catcalls now, from the men all the way in the back. Caiza was trying not to vomit as more and more bills came her way. They started shouting "take it off." She didn't have quite enough bills to do that, so she worked the pole and racked up some more green, then slowly reached around to unclip the halter. The whoops came louder and louder, and she ignored them, until she was half naked and her little brown breasts were in full exposure.

Kade walked up to the stage and handed her the glass. Caiza took it to the face and downed it, leaving the glass there. Whatever it was, it burned the black off her. Caiza's mind was gone that quick. *Good lookin' out, Kade.* She was loose now, more comfortable. She decided to give them a big finish. Putting those years of ballet classes to good use, Caiza put her hands firmly on the floor in front of her.

She was still on her knees, so she lifted herself up on her hands and flipped over until she was back on her feet, then ended in a split. She stayed in that position, drawing herself up off the floor like there was a snake charmer in front of her. That brought it home. Money was flying up on the stage faster than she could see it, and she grabbed it all. The lights dimmed as she turned to leave the stage. She took a bow before disappearing behind the curtain. When she was out of sight, she ran into the dressing room and slammed the door behind her.

The return to the dressing room was like getting called to the principal's office the day after you and your best friends carried out the senior prank. You felt justified when you were thinking it up and when you were doing it, but afterward, you felt so unsure that you just confessed your sins right there. Sure, she had made a quick few hundred dollars, but everything had a price.

Caiza rushed past the girls and into the bathroom. She barely made it to the stall before she leaned over the toilet and emptied her guts. She choked and spat, reaching for the roll of toilet paper. She wiped her mouth and stumbled out of the stall. Bending over the sink, Caiza rinsed her mouth out and dried her face with a paper towel. For some reason, throwing up made her feel better. Now all she wanted to do was climb into her bed and fall asleep.

Myeisha found her just as she was coming out of the bathroom. "Are you okay?"

Caiza nodded. She stood there trying to catch her breath. Her eyes widened, and she click-clacked back to the stall. Myeisha half smiled as she heard Caiza vomit. When she returned and repeated the mouth rinse–

face wipe routine, she grabbed the wall to hold herself up. Myeisha rubbed her back.

"Was it really that bad?" she asked.

Caiza began to wring her hands, feeling her kneecaps knocking together. "It was worse. I can't do this again."

Myeisha put a hand on her hip. "You better be joking. I know this is rough. It was rough my first day, too, but you gotta get over it. You got bills to pay, mama."

Caiza nodded, exhaling sharply. Myeisha frowned and took a step back. She left he bathroom and reappeared with a small bottle of Listerine in her hands. "Do us *all* a favor." She managed a small smile as she swished the blue liquid around her mouth. When she pulled herself together, Caiza followed Myeisha upstairs to get her pay.

They got their money in a white unmarked envelope. It was sealed, and Hearse handed them out silently. He hadn't spoken a word to Caiza but she could look in his eyes and feel him burning a hole into her mind. When she reached out for her money, he touched her hand and ran his fingers over hers. She didn't know what that meant, but he bit his lip as she turned away. She knew what *that* meant. Everytime Jacey did it, she ended up walking funny for the next few hours.

Caiza went back to the dressing room to change her clothes. The girl named Kahmes was watching her from where she sat at her table. She was sucking a lollipop suggestively. Caiza was ready to get nervous when the girl parted her lips and spoke.

"What's your name again?" she asked finally.

"Caiza."

"La Perla, right? Kahmes. Nice to meet you," she said, sticking out her free hand.

Caiza was relieved. She thought the girl was going to start something with her. She accepted the soft handshake.

"Where you from?"

"Here. I was born in Brooklyn though."

"For real? Me too. Ain't that something?"

Caiza smiled. "It is."

"What part?"

"Flatbush."

She nodded. "I'm a Bed-Stuy baby myself." Kahmes reached down and tied her sneakers, then lifted a bag over her shoulder. "Well, it was nice to meet you, girl. And welcome to the House."

"Thanks. It was good to meet you too." Caiza watched the door for a little while after Kahmes left, certain that that had been the strangest meeting she'd ever had.

As soon as Caiza got home, she took a long shower, scrubbing the filth off her. She counted the money she'd received that evening. Besides her base pay, she'd made twelve hundred in tips. June 1st wasn't for another week, so if she could make this kind of money again, she'd be back to her regular rent payments in no time. She raced downstairs, face still covered in makeup, and banged on her super's door. He opened it, groggy, and smelling of incense. She shoved all the money in his hands.

"This is half the rent, Mr. Zmirah. I'll have the rest before next week. I promise."

He counted it in front of her, as if she were lying. "How did you come up with it? Where did you get it?" he asked with his thick Middle Eastern accent, wiping his sleepy eyes.

"It doesn't matter," she shouted over her shoulder as she ran back up the stairs. "I'll be back with the rest."

IO

I'm on Top of the World, Baby

Caiza beamed as she watched the PAID IN FULL stamp come down on her tuition receipt. After three short months and a lot of penny pinching, Caiza had successfully paid back all her debts, including what she owed My for taking care of her. There was a glimpse of light at the end of the tunnel she had been stuck in for so long.

It was the end of August, and the summer had been brutal. There was a stretch for two weeks where the temperature never quite made it under ninety-five. Rydell went with her to Sears to pick up an air conditioner, and then insisted on staying to help her install it.

After they took showers to get the sweat off, they sat in her bed and watched old scary movies all night, laughing and joking at the stupid victims. He stayed over and slept in her bed, and the comfort of his body next to hers was more than enough to get Caiza through the night.

Her professors were happy to see her back in their classes. She was on the honor roll and passing all her studies, and it killed her when she told them she didn't know whether she would be back for the summer semester. Now that they knew she was there to stay, they piled on the work. She could care less. Being back in school was more than enough to make her happy.

Caiza settled into life at the House, and to be honest, she was starting to like it. She liked the feeling she was giving those men. She was their fantasy, their home away from home. She was making their wildest dreams come true when she went up there, and for the first time in a long time, Caiza was in a place where she was in control. As soon as they walked through those doors, they belonged to her.

Myeisha had worked for at the House for four and a half years. She didn't really have to, but she chose to, in case her funds were ever cut off. She saw what it was doing to her friend and didn't like it. Caiza's life seemed to revolve around the club. The minute she started getting paid, she seemed to forget that just a few months earlier she didn't want to be there in the first place. She had voiced her opinions in the past few weeks, but Caiza brushed her off. She liked the feeling of money in her pockets.

One day they both had off from work due to "repairs"-that meant Priceless had heavy trafficking to do and couldn't afford to have the public in her club-Myeisha stayed over at Caiza's and raided the kitchen. The pair had been out poer shopping all day and Myeisha need the junk food for energy. She found what she wanted, soda and a bag of chips, as Caiza dropped her bags of clothes and shoes in the bedroom.

It was the first time she had been shopping since she started working at the House, and she knew she deserved it. She hadn't treated herself to anything in the past couple of months. From her fridge she ignored the junk and reached for a bag of carrots and a bottle of water, sliding a coaster under Myeisha's glass of soda. My sucked her teeth.

"I ain't gon' hurt this cheap-ass table."

"It's my cheap-ass table, and I don't want it messed up," she said, huffing. She played back her messages.

"Caiza, it's Rydell. You were supposed to call me, baby. What's up? Let me know if you're busy Sunday, alright? I wanna get together. Just so you know, I got a new cell phone and the number is 646-555-0029. I miss you. Bye."

Caiza blushed as she wrote the number on the refrigerator.

Myeisha wandered into the kitchen and rifled through the cabinets as she watched Caiza write the number. "Did you fuck that nigga yet?" she asked, pulling out the olive jar.

"Myeisha!"

She rolled her eyes and reached under the sink for the gin. "I'm just askin'. I wanna know."

"Ain't none of your business."

Faster than Caiza had ever seen it done Myeisha made two martinis and handed Caiza one. "Since when it ain't my business? You know all my business." Suddenly, she grinned. "You wanna know what Steve did to me last night?"

Caiza hit her in the arm. "Have I ever wanted to know what Steve did to you last night?"

Myeisha giggled and sucked on an olive. "So you didn't, huh?"

"Didn't what?"

She waved one of her fingers in Caiza's face. "If you did, you'd be glowin'. I know the glow anywhere, and you ain't got it yet."

"Why is this such a big deal for you?"

"Because if you banged him, that's a big deal. It means your ass is finally over that triflin' nigga."

"I've been over Jacey."

Myeisha put a hand on her hip.

"Okay, maybe not yet, but I'm not thinking about him. Not since the last time I saw him."

"And when was that?"

Caiza didn't answer.

The machine beeped the next message. "Caiza, give your mother the courtesy of knowing you're still alive, please."

"I'd rather you think I'm dead, Ma. Makes for so much more fun." She erased the message. The next voice startled her.

"Caiza, you played me. I don't like that. I'm not trying to play games with you. Remember what I said. Call me."

She erased it and felt a flash of fear. Did that qualify as a threat? How'd he get her number? What was his deal?

"What the hell was that about?"

"Nothing." She went back into the kitchen, pretending to search for something in the fridge.

"Don't lie to me," Myeisha said, following her. "Why you got that nigga still callin' you?"

"We talked. I guess he thought we was getting back together, or something."

Myeisha put her drink down on the counter and squinted. "Y'all talked? About what? And when was this?"

Caiza giggled and hid her face behind her glass. "We talked about...stuff. Anyway, it was a while ago."

Myeisha gasped, seeing it in her face. "Caiza Vernice Bell. You did not let that man hit it again."

Caiza poked her lips out, right before hiding her face in the open fridge. Myeisha kicked it shut and folded her arms together.

"Well?"

She pulled out a bottle of Dasani water. "He wanted to talk. So we talked. He made some persuasive arguments, but I'm not getting back with him. It was like two months ago."

My lifted the martini to her lips and took a sip. "Uh-huh. What's his idea of a persuasive argument?"

She broke down and gave it to Myeisha straight. "Girl, five hours of the best sex we ever had."

"No. *No*, Caiza. You ain't supposed to let the nigga back in after he done dogged you. He gon' think you easy, and he gon' keep tryna get in. You ain't learned nothin' from me?"

Caiza picked up her drink. Nodding, she said, "He's not comin' back whenever he wants to. He gave me what I needed that night, and I haven't called him since. Yes, I learned from you."

That seemed to make her feel better. "Ooh. You nasty. So you hit it and quit it, huh?"

"You taught me well, mama," she said as Myeisha squealed, holding up her glass for a toast.

Caiza did return Rydell's call, and they went out on Sunday. She was surprised by his choice of date; Caiza found herself walking along the dark cool sand on the beach in Atlantic City. As they strolled along the sand, he took her hand and she let him.

After fifteen minutes of relaxed and comfortable silence, he broke it. "What's up, Caiza?" he asked.

"What?"

"How are you?

She breathed in the salty air. "You know, for the first time in a long time, I am floating on cloud nine."

"Is that so? Well, tell me about it."

Caiza relaxed her shoulders and very slowly told him exactly what had been going on with her, from before the day they met in the park. She started with Jacey, the jobs, the bills, and stopped just before she opened her mouth about the House of Sin. That's all she needed to tell him and she was sure he'd dart down the beach and leave her there. She was surprised he hadn't already asked about her new cash flow.

"So you're okay, now?"

"I'm perfect." She also left out the bit about what happened with her and Jacey the last time she'd seen him.

"That's good. So where's this new job? What's it like?"

Her mind worked at a thousand miles to think something up. "Customer service," she lied. Stripping was technically customer service, if you wanted to put it that way. Caiza suddenly couldn't believe that she had managed to evade this subject for so long. He asked questions and actually cared about the answers. Caiza hoped this one lie wouldn't balloon out of control.

"Really? Where are you stationed?"

"Down in the Village."

"Cool," he said, dropping the question, thank God.

"What about you?" Caiza asked. She was so desperate for him to change the subject she could've died.

"You know I'm doing alright. The handyman job is pretty good. The pay isn't that bad either. Doing mostly bodywork," he said, licking his lips at her.

Caiza cut her eyes at him, but smiled. "Well, you just let me know if you need any new tools."

He laughed, letting his hand wander past the small of her back. "I think you just might come in handy."

Caiza fought the urge to knock him down and have her way with him right there in the sand. She wanted their first time together-her first time with another man-to be special, something they would both remember.

After a long while, they turned around and walked back to where his car was parked. Maybe two hours had gone by as they walked and talked. Caiza was getting closer and closer to him every time they got together.

She was so glad she had taken a chance on him. He was more than worth it.

When they pulled up in front of her building, he reached over and took her hand. "Do I have to leave you?"

Caiza smiled and squeezed his hand. "Yes sir, you do." She leaned over and gave him a kiss. He smiled, and she got out, coasting to her front door. He waved and pulled off. Her high crashed when she saw Jacey leaned against the doorway.

"Who was that?"

"Hello, Jacey? How are you?"

"Why are you playing all these games, Caiza? What the hell is going on with you? And then I come up here to talk to you and I see this?"

"It doesn't really matter what you see because we aren't together anymore, Jace. I'm not a little girl. I don't have to inform you of my whereabouts."

"It's like that? I thought we were trying to get back together."

She laughed at him. "That's what you thought, huh? No, honey. I played you just like you played me. I ain't got no love for you right here," she said, pointing at her chest. "I'm all for me, just like you were when we were together."

His eyes flashed angrily, the same as they had done when he grabbed her the fist time. He took both her arms and pushed her inside the building. Kicking the door shut behind him, he shoved her against the wall.

"I said if I can't have you, nobody could. I wasn't playing. You tell that nigga to step off, and you think about what you're doing to me, Caiza. You don't want it." He released her, gave her the evil eye and pulled the door open, walking out without a glance back.

Caiza stood there catching her breath, scared out of her wits. She was afraid that if she moved, he would charge the door and grab her. Jacey could definitely take her out; he was bigger than her by far. Her heart pounded as she tiptoed up the stairs. She had to get away from Jacey before something went horribly wrong between them.

Caiza was fast becoming the most popular girl at the House. She learned quickly that pride was no factor in this game. Any man who was willing to stuff three hundred dollars in your thong was worth dancing for. They were paying her bills, and she saw nothing wrong with that.

She had been working at the House for some time when Priceless called her into her office for a private meeting. Winter had just set in, and the office was warm and toasty, a welcome feeling after braving the elements to get to work. Caiza had only been in the office once before but as far as she could see nothing had changed.

"Perla," she purred, "have a seat."

Caiza did, closing her legs and folding her hands over her lap. She was still in her stage clothes and felt strangely awkward sitting here half naked. Priceless pulled hard on a cigarette. Caiza don't know how she kept herself looking as good as she did without the help of plastic surgery. The only time Caiza saw her without a drink and a smoke was…well, never. After a solid minute of silence, Priceless spoke.

"How long have you been working for me?"

Caiza counted in her head. "About six months, give or take."

"You like it?"

She shrugged, getting comfortable and leaning back. "It pays the bills."

Priceless cut to the chase quickly, taking a puff before leaning forward. "How'd you like to headline?"

A headline meant she got a select number of days where she was the featured performer. She got a bigger time slot. It also meant bigger money. "It would be nice," Caiza said, not understanding why she was asking.

Priceless saw this in her face as she sat back in her chair and put her feet up.

"You may not know it, mama, but you're in high demand. I get requests for you on all the days you're not here and the niggas is lovin' you. You bring in more money a night than all the other girls. If you get your own spot, you'll make me some extra cash, and I might break you off a little something."

This sounded like a tempting offer. "What's the take?"

"A grand for Friday, Saturday, and Sunday, plus your tips." Caiza already made close to a grand in tips a night, so she'd be taking home four thousand dollars every weekend. At the end of the month, she'd be holding down almost sixteen grand a month. It was more money than Caiza knew what to do with. Much more.

"Sounds like we've got a deal."

"Good," she said. "I'll see you Friday, nine o'clock sharp."

"I'll see you."

The door closed behind her, and Caiza stood in the hallway collecting her thoughts and running the brief conversation over and over in her mind. *I'm rich,* she thought.

II

I'm Untouchable, Baby, Untouchable

Caiza didn't look back as she loaded the last of her things into her trunk. The U-Haul had just departed with the bulk of her furniture, and she was right behind it. She was moving out of that shitkicker apartment and into a duplex on East 65th, closer to work and school. Caiza only had to look around for fifteen minutes before she was sure it was the place for her. They drove back to the real estate office that same day, drew up the papers and two hours later, she signed her John Hancock on the lease.

Caiza's first night as headliner blew her away. It was also the beginning of the downward spiral in her life. As headliner, she had to do three sets, in between each; the other girls would do their thing. And that Friday night, it was on.

Before the show, Priceless pulled her to the side, with her usual cigarette and scotch. "Listen to me," she said, "it's real money out there. You shake ya ass right and you leave outta here wit' more than a much grand tonight. It's more money-makin' muthafuckas than a li'l bit."

Who? Rappers? Actors? "What you mean by money makin'?"

She pursed her lips, obviously annoyed by the lack of knowledge. "You know Arturo?"

"Yeah, why?" Arturo used to sell cocaine in the Bronx, had been muscled out and moved to the West Coast to produce hits for the big rappers with another man named Sledge. Arturo moved out of the New York game completely after Sledge returned to Manhattan and was killed. He still ran drugs, but through Philly instead. He made most of his cash now making music.

She nodded. "He's out there. That nigga came in here to spend some cash. Do *not* fuck this up," she said. Caiza planned to take the advice.

Caiza did it big that night. She had money flying at her from every direction. Big bills too. She came out with a heat in her eyes; two stepping like the ground was on fire. Once again her ballet lessons came in handy. The reason she had a fan base was because she was creative. She could do things with her body that none of the other girls could do. They loved that. Her flexibility was her plus.

As the beat continued, she kept on having fun. At one point, bent over backward, both hands touching the floor, she accepted a hundred with her teeth, like she had seen the girl do the first time she came. Lifting her legs over her head, she put her thighs around the pole. Caiza hated the pole—it was so damn tacky—but they loved it, so she put it in when she could.

Grabbing her legs around the pole, she lifted her upper body and slid down until she was back on the ground with her legs spread again, still dancing with the top half of her body. They went off when she did that, shouting and whistling. Caiza grinned happily up there, knowing she was blowing them away. She was feeding off the crowd's energy, and in that moment it was confirmed that she loved what she did. All the eyes were on her, and there was no better feeling.

Afterward, she took a bow, which the crowd had become used to, and ran back behind the curtains. She had a stack of money thicker than a slice of cake as she burst into the dressing room. Kahmes jumped into her arms, screaming like a wild animal. "Yo, bitch, you tore it up!"

Naomi sat her fat ass in the corner, mad as hell. She was jealous when it came to Caiza. She had been the center of attention before li'l Miss La Perla came along and now she was hating.

"Word, you put it down, baby girl. They love them some you!" Caiza couldn't stop smiling and was about to smile even more as Kade stuck her head in the door.

"Office, now," she said. The girls started a chorus of "oooooh!" Very few times, unless they were getting paid, were the girls allowed in the office. It seemed Caiza was there more than any of them.

"Shut up!" Caiza followed Kade behind the curtain and up to the office. She still had on her stage wear and as Kade guided her to the office, she heard loud cheers from the other side of the room. The man that had been identified as Arturo was standing, whistling, and waving a bottle of Dom. He was fine as hell, but there was a girl sitting as far up under him as she possibly could. She doubted it was his wife so she figured that was his jumpoff. Caiza could care less; she didn't want him.

She waved back and followed Kade upstairs. Priceless was on her phone shouting at someone. She saw them coming and motioned for Kade to shut the door. She did, and they both took a seat. Priceless clicked the phone shut and kicked her feet up on her desk.

"Quite a show you put on out there."

"Thank you."

"You made me fourteen thousand dollars tonight. Half of which is now yours."

"For real?" she asked. That was a hell of a lot of money. There was a two-drink minimum, and a fifty-dollar cover charge, meaning seventy a head. If she made that kind of cash that meant damn near two hundred people had come through tonight. The last time it was that packed was her first night. Caiza made money all the time, but seven grand just to see her dance for an extra hour?

"For real." She slid the bills over.

Caiza stumbled for the words. "All-all this…all this is mine?"

Priceless nodded. "You brought it in, you keep it. Don't get used to that. I'm not that generous."

Caiza flipped through the money. Her mind was blown. She didn't even know what to do with the pile of green in her hands. She was afraid that if she blinked it would disappear, so she stared at her hands until her eyes watered.

"I called in a favor. You know that club Float?"

"Yeah, why?"

"Go enjoy yourself tonight, on me."

That was a pleasant surprise. She had never known Priceless to go out of her way to be nice. But Caiza figured if she were making this much money for the woman, it was the least she could do. Caiza didn't know what else to say so she stood to leave. "I…we-well. Thank you."

Priceless was finished talking, so Caiza returned to the dressing room, but not before being snagged by Arturo. Damn, this cat was smooth. He had a Yankees fitted cap pulled low, down to his eyes, a diamond in each ear, and when he opened his mouth to speak, his clean white teeth shone brighter than the bling. He handed her a sealed bottle of Dom.

"You put it down, baby girl. Me and mine was bout to head over to Speed, get it on. You down?"

Myeisha sidled up to her hip, putting her arm around her waist, probably wondering who the gold mine was. She eyed the girl who was under Arturo's arm, who in turn was eyeing Caiza with daggers. Caiza was still trying to get over the fact that they had come all the way from California to see her.

"I'm going to Float with my girls. You can follow us over there if you want," she said. She was running things tonight. To her surprise he nodded and headed outside. Turning into the dressing room with Myeisha, she went to change her clothes.

Caiza was lacing up her boots when she looked over her shoulder. "Y'all feel like comin' out to Float with us?"

Naomi's foul attitude disappeared. Mention the word *party* and she was instantly down. "Word. I need to do some different kind of dancing."

Evelyn slapped her five. "For real! *Tengo conseguir de la etapa.* You feel me?"

"Don't nobody understand that shit," said Shanae, pulling on a pair of UGG boots.

"It means I gotta get my ass off that stage. I don't know how you do three nights in a row, mami," Evelyn said to Caiza, crossing herself. "I gotta get a break."

She stood and rubbed her fingers together. "It's all about that paper. You comin', Nae?"

Shanae shook her head. "I'ma head on home, if it's all the same to y'all."

Caiza shrugged. "Suit yourself. I'll see you girls," Caiza said, pulling on her gloves, "at the club."

"I'm ridin' wit Perla," Kahmes shouted, grabbing her bag.

"Meet you where?" Naomi shouted at her back.

"Float," she shouted over her shoulder. Then they went out to the parking lot.

Rappers, actors, singers, and paid hustlers came through the House of Sin every night of the week. Lesser-known wallets made it in during the week, but the weekends were strictly bankroll. It meant they were really ready to see a show. In particular, besides Arturo, one of them was there to show her special attention. That man happened to be Bulldog.

Caiza hadn't seen Bulldog since she left the law firm. She remembered seeing him her first night and not quite recognizing him. Outside of the firm, he was much more personal. It was interesting to see him there, under different circumstances. After every show, he sent her a different bottle of liquor.

She had champagnes, schnapps, wines, scotches, cognacs, and rums lining the cabinet in her apartment. He never left a message on them, just the bottle and a white rose. It was odd to her but she liked it. Kade would deliver and say, "This is from Bulldog." And that would be that.

He was a sweet guy, always throwing Caiza a smile when he saw her looking at him from the stage. He could also tip like no other. The nights he came through, she went home with paper out the ass. He always made his homies pay her well too. If not, they'd be immediately dismissed.

It seemed to Caiza that he and Arturo were in competition for her affections. Every time she turned around it was flowers, liquors, a new outfit, new shoes, that kind of thing. They were like two kids fighting over the last cookie in the jar. Each gift one gave, the other felt the need to outdo. If Caiza had to judge by one instance, that night, Dog would've won.

"Yo." Caiza, Myeisha and Kahmes were on their way to Float and had just slammed the back door behind them. Caiza turned her head at the sound of the deep voice while Myeisha and Kahmes made their way to Caiza's Acura. Dog was profiling, leaning against a car as he waited for her to acknowledge his presence.

"Hey, Dog," Caiza answered, smiling brightly, walking over to him. She gave him a hug. She knew him well enough, but shit, he was a paying customer. Any friend of the green founding fathers was a friend of hers. He put his arms around her.

"I been meanin' to get at you. How you been?" he asked.

"I'm chillin'," she said. "And freezing. What's up?" Caiza shoved her gloved hands into her pockets. She started jogging in place to get some warmth into her legs and feet.

Dog lit a cigarette and offered her one. She accepted gratefully, ignoring the look Myeisha threw at her. "I ain't gon' rip you for bein' up in here. I see you doin' your thing."

Caiza took a pull off the smoke, which she couldn't really enjoy in the cold. "You know everybody got bills to pay."

Dog shrugged. "I hear that. I hear that. Anyways, I got a little somethin' for you."

She tossed her hair, angry that she didn't bring a scarf. "Oh yeah? What you got for me?" She was so used to getting gifts from him that she wasn't even surprised anymore.

"Now I know," he started, "Since you got bills to pay and shit, I know you ain't got the kinda time it take to be savin for a ride and all that. So I figure, you do me a few favors and you get to keep this."

He stepped away from the car he had been leaning on. It was a brand spanking new silver Mercedes E430. Caiza had had her eye on that car since the day it rolled off the assemblyline. Dog waved the keys in her face. She dropped the cigarette out of pure shock. Grabbing the keys she shouted, "This is for me?"

He nodded. Caiza screamed. She jumped in the air, and he smiled as he caught her and let her back down.

"This is mine!" she shouted at Kam and My, who were now huddled together trying not to freeze. When she shouted that, Kahmes shouted "What?" and ran over with her eyes and arms wide open. Caiza thanked Dog with a big kiss on the mouth. Before he let her go, he pulled her ear close to his mouth.

"I took care of you, now I'm gonna expect you to take care of me, a'ight?"

Caiza didn't even pay attention to his final remark. She nodded her consent.

"Come to the club wit' us," she said breathlessly.

"Where at?"

"At Float. Come wit' us."

"A'ight," he said and that was that.

"Wait, Caiza," Myeisha began as she climbed in the passenger seat. "Wht you gone do with your other car?"

"I don't know, donate it to charity or something. I'll deal with it in the morning," Caiza replied. She had a one track mind right now. She was ready to get her party on.

As she climbed into the front seat and slammed the door, she saw Arturo spark a cigarette from the rearview mirror. He looked pissed as hell, but made no move to approach her as he got in his car and pulled off behind them. They cruised away from the club, Myeisha and Kam sticking their wild asses out of the moon roof. They were screaming like two teenage porn stars, and they were definitely turning heads. Caiza laughed, switching gears and loving how the Benz responded to her smoothly.

Now this is status, she thought as she turned the radio up. Nelly's "Hot in Herre" was blaring, and the bass was jumping through her speakers. Looking in her mirror, she saw Arturo's Expedition and Bulldog's Range Rover barreling behind them, speakers as loud as her own. They parked down the block from the club, hopping out, making plenty of noise, making sure they were seen. The girls were still laughing when they got to the front door. Caiza had a Diddy-sized entourage behind her, and she felt like a million dollars.

The line was long enough to make one believe that they were giving out unemployment checks inside. *No line for the special people.* Caiza walked straight up to the head of the line, sizing up the bouncer. He was one of those Michael Clarke Duncan–looking cats. "Name?" he asked, as soon as he saw her and the group behind her.

Caiza took a wild guess and answered, "La Perla."

The bouncer nodded and made a note on the pad in front of him. Reaching forward, he unclipped the velvet rope and let them in. Whoever had been standing there before them began to curse and shout. Myeisha stuck her tongue out and smiled as she skipped inside behind her girl. The bouncer gave her a glance as he watched the switch of her backside.

Caiza wasn't exactly sure how Naomi and the girls had made it to the club before them but there they were, tearing up the VIP section like it was reserved for them. There were already three empty bottles of champagne at the corner table, and evidently, Evelyn had had one on her own. She staggered over to Caiza, draping an arm over her shoulder. She'd only been here for fifteen minutes and she was slurring. Damn, this chick was wild.

"Thiz zhit izza bomb, girrrrl! Whoddat?"

"Girl please. You know Arturo. And Bulldog." Arturo nodded his hello. Caiza didn't see the girl he'd been with at the House and didn't miss her. Bulldog didn't even glance her way, just brushed past her and went straight for the bar.

Myeisha took Evelyn's hand. "I think baby done had a little too much to drink. Come on, mama." They walked inside and saw Priceless, Kade, Hearse, and a couple of assorted faces she'd never seen before. She did notice that Priceless was eyeballing the hell out of Arturo the whole time.

Caiza sucked up the attention they were giving her, including the round of applause she received upon entering. Putting on her widest smile, she gave them her best bow. Gassed beyond belief, she headed to the bar. She made good with a glass of champagne. When she grew tired of people introducing themselves to her, she slinked away and joined the other girls at the corner table.

Myeisha tapped her on the shoulder. "Girl, it's some paid niggas out there. I'll be back in a li'l bit."

Caiza knew her girl well. "Go 'head do you, ma," she answered as Myeisha smiled and walked out.

Pulling a clean glass from a nearby table, Caiza popped the cork on a bottle of Cristal and drained a glass, filling Kam's, Evelyn's and Naomi's. No one was touching her Dom so she left it in the car. That was a special gift. She winked at Dyannara who was in the corner, practically in Kade's lap. She watched as Arturo picked up a pool stick and sharpened the tip.

Arturo silently eyed her and tossed her a pool stick. "You game?"

She caught it and nodded. There was something in the air between the two of them, not quite sexual tension, and not quite uncomfortable silence. Caiza wasn't very good at reading people so she didn't know exactly what was going on between them. He was coming over to make a shot when she felt him grab her ass. He leaned over her and stuck his tongue in her ear. Then he turned her around and kissed her hard, pulling her body as close to him as she could get.

"Hey, kids, get a room, hmm?" Kade said as she walked past.

Arturo pulled off her and smiled. She was frozen there on the spot.

Did he just come on to me in the middle of the club? Caiza thought. *Yes, he did.* She waited for him to say something but he didn't, just continued to play the game as if nothing had happened. Caiza won after she sank the eight ball. He raised his champagne and walked away.

Bored now, she sat back down on one of the Italian leather sectionals beside Kam and Evelyn, who were messing around on the table in front of them. She wasn't paying attention. Naomi raised her glass from where she sat on Caiza's left side. "I know I been hatin', girl, but you know you was really puttin' your thing down out there. So cheers to you, bitch."

Caiza giggled and clinked her glass against Naomi's.

"This your party, girl. You need to get up and shake it," Kam said. Evelyn put something in her clutch and Kam handed her a tube. It was green, and it took Caiza a few seconds to recognize it as a dollar bill. Absently, she watched as Kam put her nose to the tube, the tube to the table and a thin white line disappeared into her face. She almost jumped out of her skin, nearly spilling her drink all over the couch.

"What the hell is that?"

Evelyn turned to her. She was already wasted and now she was doing drugs. Her words were running together like the Boston Marathon. "Relags, mija. Iz juz a lilbit a coca."

"Get the hell outta here. You kiddin' me wit' this shit?" She tried to stand and walk away but Naomi pulled her back onto the sofa. Kam laughed, her bright eyes now glassy. "Damn, Caiza. Calm down. Calm down. It's only a line. It'll get you loose. Take one. Just one."

Caiza shook her head. "Don't play wit' me, Kam. This shit ain't funny. I ain't about to be no crackhead."

Kam kicked her with the point on her boot. "You ain't. Look, girl. I'ma take a hit and go home to my kids. You go' be straight. It's just a pick-me-up. Go head."

"No."

"Stop actin' like you fuckin Christian and shit," Kam said. Caiza laughed aloud when she said that. Kahmes was higher than a kite.

"Word," said Evelyn, lifting her face from the table and rubbing her nose. *"Está sobre reaccionar."* She was giggling like mad.

"Peer pressure," Naomi whispered. She laughed in her ear before she sniffed the next line. There was one left. She pressed the tube into Caiza's hand. She stared down at the table, not wanting to look like a bitch but not wanting to get hooked on the shit either. Maybe it wouldn't hurt. And obviously Kam had done it before, and she was okay. She had kids, and she was doing just fine. *Just this once,* Caiza thought. She rolled the bill in between her fingers.

"How you do it?"

"Close up this side," Kahmes replied, placing her thumb on her left nostril, "And sniff. There ain't nothin' to it, girl."

She took one last hesitant look at the group before facing the poison in front of her. Jumping in head first, as usual, she put her face down to the table, held her nose as she'd been shown and sniffed it up. There was an explosion in front of her eyes for just an instant, then a bright light and then her nose felt like it was running.

She rubbed it, and that side of her face went numb. But over the next very slow few seconds, everything around her got mellow, and her body tingled, just once. Then everything was back to normal, except for her numb nose, and she felt like someone had just shaken her awake from a long nap. Caiza was ready to party. "Damn," she said at last.

"Feel better?"

Caiza nodded, rubbing her nose again. Her vision had clouded, but her mind was very clear.

"See? You popped ya cherry, girl." They clapped her on the back and laughed. She accepted her congrats graciously. She was after all, La Perla, the Queen of the House.

Arturo met her outside the club that night. Caiza was having a hard time understanding him as high as she was, so she closed her eyes when he was talking to focus on his words.

"So you got a man?"

"You got one?" she asked.

He chuckled, putting his hands in his coat pockets. "You slick, ma. Nah, I ain't no homo thug. Answer my question."

"Yes, I do."

Although it wasn't the answer he wanted to hear, Arturo figured her man wasn't his problem and there were ways around it. "Well, you know we could just hook up to chill or whatever. I think we might have us a good time."

"Alright." She took down his number, and he did the same.

"I'll call you and we'll hook up, a'ight?" he said as she walked away.

"Sho ya right," she said, not even half believing him.

Caiza was so wasted that night that she couldn't drive home. Kahmes was blasted as well, so she, Caiza and Myeisha split a cab. Myeisha was clearly not amused with their behavior, and she sat in the front of the car pouting. She didn't know Caiza had been sniffing cocaine with Kahmes and the girls. So all this silliness, she blamed on them being drunk. She had no clue that Caiza had at least an ounce and a half of cocaine in her system. They were both too high to hold a conversation.

"And then, and then he saiz…*ha ha*. Stoppit. You mekken me laugh, Kye. He saiz, yo babe, you looken raht." Both girls burst out laughing because neither had any idea what she was talking about. Caiza was laughing so hard that she started drooling. Kahmes caught sight of that, and they fell into stitches again. Myeisha sat in the front seat with her arms crossed, sending them death rays in the rearview mirror.

Caiza leaned against the front seat. "My, I loooooove you, boo." Caiza giggled and that started the laughs up again. The cab stopped in front of Caiza's apartment and Myeisha dug in her purse for some cash.

"Lemme git it," Caiza said, wiping her face. She reached in her purse, then remembered she kept cash in her bra. She pulled out a roll of bills, and they fell into My's hand.

"Caiza, where did you get all this money?"

"Huh? From Priceless."

"For what? Did you rob a bank?"

Caiza looked at Caiza and started crying laughing. Myeisha rolled her eyes and paid the driver. She opened the back door, and Caiza and Kahmes fell out on the ground laughing like two wild hyenas. Caiza tripped over Kahmes and fell again. She crawled into the building. The doorman, Jeffrey, eyed them as they staggered inside, but said nothing.

"Hi, Jeffrey," Caiza slurred.

"Come on, you drunk bitches," My said. She took Caiza's purse and got her keys ready. By this time, Caiza and Kahmes were singing a wildly off key duet of "You Are So Beautiful." They had made it to the elevator and were both seated on the floor in the corner. It stopped on her floor, and Caiza brought herself to her feet; Kahmes was still crawling behind her. Myeisha gave her the keys and pressed DOOR CLOSE.

"My," she moaned, "where you goin'?"

Myeisha didn't break a sweat. "I'm goin' home."

"Whyyyyyyy?" Caiza whined like a baby.

Myeisha stuck her hand out before the doors closed. "Because I am not takin' care of your drunk ass. I got a man waitin' at home for me. You and Mama Crass over there can take care of your own self." She moved her hand and the doors silently slid shut.

Caiza sucked her teeth and fumbled for a good twenty minutes trying to find the right key. When she did, it took another five minutes to get it in the lock. Kahmes rubbed her face and came in behind her, barely walking straight. Caiza stopped to lock the door, and they crashed into each other, starting a new wave of laughs. Caiza's face hurt from laughing so much, and she didn't even remember what was funny.

Sparkle met them at the door, wagging her tail at this new stranger. Kahmes jumped when she saw her.

"Is that a dog?"

"No, it's a cat."

She started laughing again, and that got Caiza started laughing again. She picked up the hall phone and called Jeffrey so he could come walk Sparkle. She was in no state to go back out in the street. He rang the bell five minutes later, and Sparkle was so happy to be going to pee, she didn't care who took her.

Kam's cell phone rang. All of a sudden, she seemed back to normal. They walked into the living room, where she plopped down on the couch. Caiza went upstairs to her room to take off her clothes.

Caiza heard shouting from downstairs. She hung her shirt in the closet and stood behind the door trying to listen in. "What? I said I would be home in the mornin'!" Caiza didn't know who Kahmes was shouting at but she wished she'd stop. It was hurting her head.

"They your kids too, Mannie." she screamed. "So what? And when you leave me wit' them, I don't complain. Whatever." There was a loud crash. Caiza went into the living room in just her underwear.

"What happened?"

Kahmeshrew her hands in the air, digging in her purse for a cigarette.

Gesturing with her hands, she cursed Mannie. "Bastard. 'Oh when you comin' home?'" she mocked. "'I wanna go out. I got shit to do.' Nigga, you ain't got nothin' to do at three in the morning. I been takin' care of them kids all this time. The least you can do is give me a goddamn night off." She lit the cigarette and collapsed on the couch. "Just blew my high." Her phone was in a broken pile on the floor across the room.

Caiza returned to her bedroom and pulled on a silk nightgown. She tossed Kam a pair of sweats and a tee. Kahmes put on the sweats and left the tee on the sofa. She had cut up another line after Caiza went back in the bedroom and was sniffing it on the coffee table. This time, when she offered, Caiza followed through. The doorbell rang. She wiped her face quickly and answered it.

"Thanks, Jeffrey."

"You're very welcome, ma'am. Please enjoy your evening."

"You, too, Jeff." She slipped him a little something and he nodded, walking toward the elevator.

Caiza fell out on the couch, trying to get her head to stop spinning. This feeling was new to her. But she liked it. Kahmes had produced a bottle of champagne from somewhere. Caiza's Dom was on the hall table where she left it when they came in. She didn't touch it, going instead into the kitchen to get a bottle of Captain Morgan. When she saw the Morgan, Kahmes abandoned the champagne. Caiza poured two and flipped the CD player to Deniece Williams' *Greatest Hits*.

Kahmes accepted the rum, lighting two cigarettes. She pulled hard on one and passed the other in Caiza's direction. "Damn, where'd you find this place?"

Caiza rolled her head around on the back of the sofa and tapped her feet to the tune of "Free." "I have the best real estate agent ever."

"What's her name?"

"He. Felix Prescott. Can't dress worth a damn, but he's got an eye for real estate. And he brought it down just so I would buy it. It was eight. I talked him down to five."

"It's so nice," she said, taking another pull and looking around. "I give all my extra money to my kids."

"That's why I'm still single."

Kahmes miled. "I didn't ask for my kids. They happened. But they're a blessing."

"Yes, honey, a blessing I can't afford," Caiza said, knocking back a shot of rum. It burned her throat, but she did it anyway.

Kahmes laughed with her. Pointing with the cigarette, she said, "You'll see. One day you'll be walking around this place with a baby and you'll see then. It's somethin' else." Her face got far away then, as if the sudden talk about her children mellowed her out. Caiza watched her face change and fell silent, just letting the moment pass on its own.

It passed as soon as a thought crossed Caiza's mind. "Yo," she said. "Uh huh."

"Before, Dog was like I could keep the car if I did a few favors for him. What that mean?"

Kahmes shrugged. "It mean do a few favors. Sometimes the guys ask us to do shit for them. They give us nice shit back. Like this one time, you know Sledge? Before he died, he used to have this one girl drive drugs around for him. He broke her off somethin' lovely too. But he died right before I got there."

Caiza nodded absently. She wondered just what kind of favors Dog wanted her to do. More important, she wondered what else he would give her.

The women fell asleep after about three hours of laughing and talking. Caiza floated off in bliss to a place she had never known before, courtesy of the coke. It had done something to her mind. If this was what it felt like to be high, she'd have to do it more often.

Caiza changed her mind the next morning. She woke up with her stomach rumbling. Her first stop was the bathroom. Leaning over the toilet, she vomited up all the liquor from the night before. When she was emptied out, she fell to the floor, clutching her vibrating skull.

Her head throbbed from temple to temple and from her forehead to her neck. Her muscles seemed like jelly, and her mouth was cottony and dry. The room started to spin, and she sat in the middle of the floor holding her face.

"Kam!"

Kahmes appeared as if out of nowhere, still in the sweats from the night before a lit cigarette in her hand. "You alright?"

"No, I'm not alright. What the hell is happening to me?"

She bent down after filling a glass with water. "Don't worry. It's just the after shock. You'll be fine in a couple of minutes. It won't happen again once you get used to it."

Caiza wasn't so sure. She was rocking in the middle of the floor, trying to focus. Kam handed her the glass. After the first sip, she could see clearly again and after the second, the nausea passed. "That's the last time I do that."

"Girl, I said the same thing. I was fine the next day. Don't worry about it."

Caiza rolled her eyes, knowing that was total bullshit. She took another sip of water.

"You want the rest?" Kam asked.

It took her a minute to figure out she was talking about the drugs.

"You don't want it?" Caiza asked, looking up.

Kahmes waved her hand as she got off her knees and sat on the toilet. "Girl, I got so much of that shit lying around. It's gon' cost you though."

"How much?"

"I'll give you the rest for a G."

Caiza frowned. "This ain't Scarface. You ain't got nothin' left from last night?"

She giggled. "I'll give it to you for five."

"Deal." Caiza gave her the money, and Kahmes gave her the drugs. Once again, Caiza leaped in head first, as she seemed to have a habit of doing. Into her drawer went the poison and to Kam went the cash.

Arturo was at the club the following week and the weeks after. And he didn't come empty-handed. He called Caiza every now and then, and they kicked it, but he was more or less a wham-bam-thank-you-ma'am type brother, and she made it clear she wasn't interested in casual sex with him. Whenever they went out, she ended up either getting high or drunk or both. He and his crew carried the best haze Caiza had ever smoked. She was learning all kinds of things about feeling good, and the weed was one of them.

One particular night, he caught her coming out of the dressing room for a drink after her set. "I know you said you ain't into me or whatever, but I got you a little somethin' somethin' anyway."

Caiza leaned back on her heel; giving him a view of the twins through the sheer baby doll she'd thrown on. He made no move to front like he wasn't staring either. She loved that. She could turn him on and off just by standing still.

"Oh, really? What you got for me?"

He motioned with his head. "Come on out to the car. I'll get it for you."

"Let me put some clothes on," she replied.

"A'ight. I'll be right here," he said. "Wit' your fine ass," he muttered under his breath.

Caiza returned, after having pulled on her fur and jeans. Arturo's dark blue Navigator was on the dark side of the parking lot, under a broken streetlamp that seemed to only work when it felt like it. Caiza rarely came to this side of the lot; it was too dark over there. She smiled and shook her head. Every time she saw him, he was driving something else.

Opening the door, Tro reached into the glove compartment, leaning back out a moment later with a black velvet box in his hands. He smiled smoothly and handed it over. Caiza took it, unsure of its contents, and looked up at him.

"What's this?"

"If you open it, you'll find out."

Caiza gave him another shy glance before carefully popping open the hinged case. Her breath caught in her throat. She couldn't see anything but ice. Comfortable on a bed of crushed velvet was a diamond leaf necklace, matching earrings and bracelet, and a huge emerald-cut ring. Caiza knew nothing about being able to tell a diamond size from sight, but this had to be the most expensive set she had ever seen. And the ring was clearly bigger than the one she had received when Jacey proposed.

"That's fifty carats right there, ma," he said, looking awfully pleased with himself.

She pawed at the jewels, having never seen anything this beautiful up close before. She had diamonds, but when the going got tough, she was forced to pawn most of them. Caiza closed her mouth then and held a hand up to her face, almost sure she was drooling. She shut the case and looked in his eyes.

"Tro, I can't take this. This is too much." She tried to hand it back, but he put his hands out.

"That's a gift. I want you to have it, a'ight?"

She tried to pull an excuse out of the air. "But, what about your wife?"

He shrugged. "What about her? She gets shit like that all the time. And another thing." Tro reached back into the car, holding up an envelope, which he handed to her. "You, me, this Sunday."

She reached out and took the envelope. She was scared to open it. What else could he possibly give her? "What are these for?"

"Plane tickets. You, me, Ocho Rios."

Caiza almost fainted right then and there. "I can't go to the Jamaica with you, Tro. You're *married*. I got a man. It just wouldn't be right." She tried to give the jewels back one more time.

Arturo wasn't going down without a fight. He shook his head, laughing. "Listen here, Perla. I'm not really concerned about your man. I don't care what y'all got goin on. I really don't. My wife don't like doin' these type of things. I ain't tryna get in your panties, dang. I just want your company."

Yeah, right. That is the oldest fucking line in the book, she thought. She stepped back and gave him the eye. "Why do you want me to go so bad?"

Taking a step closer, he put his arms around her back and pulled her into him. "'Cuz a nigga that look as good as me need some fine-ass eye candy on his arm." Then he opened her mouth with his tongue, giving her something to think about. She didn't pull away, even when her knees buckled under her. Letting her go, he kissed her cheek cockily and got in his truck. "I'll call you," he said, slamming the door. Caiza stood and watched him as he pulled away. She shook her head and clutched her diamonds to her chest as she jogged back to the House.

He wasn't joking.

Caiza was in economics class when she got the call. Her two-way beeped loudly in her bag, 50 Cent's "P.I.M.P." bouncing around the room. Professor Caine looked at her over his glasses. He was lecturing on consumer price index. She waited until he turned his head to go into her bag. Tro left a text message.

WHEN YOU GET OFF MEET ME AT THE RAMADA AT JFK.

Caiza waited until Caine turned his back again to send of her reply: I

GET OFF AT TWELVE. I'LL MEET YOU THERE. She stuffed the phone back in her bag and went back to her work.

"In conclusion, I want you all to read chapters four, five and six. This will be on the test Wednesday. Now, let's move on to the next…"

Everyone turned when her phone rang again; she was disturbing them. And her choice of ring tone didn't help matters either. There was a wave of giggles across the room. Caiza bit her own lip to keep from laughing aloud. Keeping her eyes in her book, she slowly reached into her bag. Caine removed his glasses and pinched the bridge of his nose.

"Ms. Bell, if there is something more interesting going on in your bag, please feel free to share it with the rest of the class."

She shook her head as the phone continued to play 50 Cent's song. "There's nothing to share." She was still trying to find her phone.

"Then why are you rapping?"

"I'm turning it off, sir." Caiza was relieved as her hand landed on the two-way and she lifted it out and silenced it.

"Please don't let it happen again, Ms. Bell. Now back to the lesson. For Monday, we will be…"

Caiza rolled her eyes as he turned his back and began to write on the chalkboard. She flipped open her two-way and found the message.

WHAT SIZE DO YOU WEAR?

She turned off the ringer and put her phone on vibrate, then returned her answer.

SIX.

AND YOUR FEET?

SEVEN. WHY?

Caiza was dropping it into her lap to take down the assignment when it vibrated again.

DON'T BRING ANYTHING, JUST YOUR PRETTY FACE.

ALRIGHT. I'LL HIT YOU BACK IN A FEW.

Class ended uneventfully, and she called Tro back as soon as she left the building. "You can't call me when I'm in class."

"What, you gon' get in trouble?"

"Yes. Next time I say I'll call you, that's what it means. I'll meet you at the airport."

"A'ight. I'll see you outside."

Dropping her books at home, Caiza took a fast shower and called Priceless.

"What?"

"This is Caiza."

"I didn't ask who it was. I asked what you want."

"I'm not going to be able to make it tonight."

"So I'll see you tomorrow."

"That's the thing. I won't be back into the city until Monday."

There was a slight pause. "Where the hell you goin'?"

"Art—I'm going to Jamaica."

She heard a pouring noise, then a sound like a match being lit, and there was a sharp exhalation of breath. "So you fuckin' wit' baller man now, huh?"

"It's just a vacation. He asked me to come with him," she said, thinking about the diamonds in her top drawer. "I just wanted to tell you that I wouldn't be working this weekend."

"Uh-huh. Alright. Well you know that means you don't get paid this weekend either, right?"

She sighed. "Yes, ma'am."

"Yeah, alright," she said. "Have fun." She hung up. A moment later, her phone rang again.

"Yo, Perla, where you at?" Tro never called her by her real name. It annoyed the hell out of her, but she never called him on it. Shit, with the money he stuffed in her panties, he kept her lights on. Why mess up a good thing?

"I'm on the way to the airport. Why?"

"Damn. I called you like an hour ago. Hurry up, girl. I ain't tryna be waitin' for you all night."

Caiza put a hand on her hip. "Excuse me? Number one, you need to watch who you're talkin' to. I ain't one of them bitches in your videos. Second, I said I was on my way. That means I'm on my way. You best watch your tone."

He was silent for a second, then, "My bad. Lemme know when you just about here, a'ight?"

"Okay." Caiza ended the call and dialed Myeisha's number.

"Hello?"

"Hey, it's Caiza."

"You finally get over that hang over?"

Caiza giggeled. "Are you ever gonna let that go? It was like four months ago. Do me a favor, come watch Sparkle this weekend?"

"Why? Where you goin'?"

"I'm going to Jamaica."

Her tone swerved into the fast lane. "Ooh, I wanna go."

"You're so silly, My. I'll be back on Monday."

"Wait a minute. What you doin' out there?"

"He asked me to come out there with him."

"He who?"

"Tro."

Myeisha sounded suspicious. "Ain't he got a wife?"

"Yes, he does. He told me he already asked her to go and she said no. So, her loss."

"Ooh, I'm tellin' Rydell. I'm gon' tell. You gon' get your ass whipped."

"No you ain't gon' say a damn thing, 'cuz if you do, I will kick your ass. Look, you comin' or not?"

"Yeah, you know I'm comin'. And you ain't gon' kick shit. Better bring me back somethin', trifling bitch."

"I will. Tell Jeff to give you the key to my apartment. I'll tell him you're coming."

"A'ight. See you soon, ho."

"Okay, trick."

Caiza made it to the hotel in record time. She left her Benz in the lot, grabbed her purse and walked across the street. Arturo said he would meet her, and he sure did, reaching out and taking her hand.

"You found the place alright?"

"Yeah, it was cool," she replied. "What we doin' here?"

"I bought you some shit to wear. You just gotta pack it."

"What'd you do that for?"

He pressed the button for the elevator to come down. "It was a nice gesture. I didn't want you to go out there in all your old stuff."

She giggled. "Ain't nothin wrong with my *old* stuff."

He shrugged.

The spread Tro had laid out for her reminded her of the old shopping sprees she had to abandon when she went broke. The bed looked like the dressing room at Neiman's. Caiza squealed like a baby and ran over to the clothes. Arturo smiled when he closed the door behind them.

"What am I supposed to do with all this?" she asked, her eyes glistening like a child on Christmas morning.

"You're supposed to wear it. You think I spent all this for nothing?"

Caiza kissed him and got to packing. Free clothes? You didn't have to tell her twice. This was a rarity, and there was no way she would pass it up.

The flight to Ocho Rios was pleasant. Their private plane left at ten-thirty. Caiza was amazed by how well Tro was received on either coast. The flight attendants were like his personal bitches, and they answered to his every beck and call. "More wine, Mr. Green?" "Can I fluff your pillow, Mr. Green?" It was sickening. Caiza had to remind herself that she was living the lifestyle of the rich and famous now. She would have to get used to the celeb treatment. Caiza was more than sure this was something she could get used to. Arturo raised his glass in a toast.

"To bein' the most fly," he said. She echoed the sentiment and took a sip of the white wine.

"So tell me about you, Miss Perla," he said, leaning back.

She swirled the wine in the glass, staring into the sparkling liquid as if it held the answer to the question. "What do you want to know?"

"You know, where you from, where'd you grow up, what the hell you strippin' for, that kinda thing."

Caiza giggled. "Where'd that come from?" she asked.

He got comfortable, turning his body in her direction. "You know what I thought when I saw you for the first time?"

"I'm sure you'll tell me."

"I thought, well goddamn. That has got to be the single finest woman I have ever laid eyes on."

"Really?" she asked flatly.

"Hell yeah. You got the best body I ever seen. Better than my wife."

What was it with this guy and his wife? Caiza wondered about their love-hate relationship. He was always complaining about her, but he never stopped talking about her. "Thank you for the compliment."

"And you ain't stupid neither, obviously, so I wanna know why the hell you strippin'."

She took another sip of her wine and thanked the stewardess, Tess, as she placed a fruit cocktail in front of her.

"Unlike you, Tro, I didn't have a trust fund growing up. My father left when I was a little girl. The most my mother could afford was ballet. So I took ballet. She didn't think I would ever want to go to college, so she didn't set up a college fund. I got a job right after high school, enough to pay for school, because I wanted to go to college. And I did go.

"Shit happened, I didn't have any money saved, so I had to start hustling. After a few failed connections, my girl—you know Myeisha—she told me I could get all my bills paid if I worked at the House. The rest, as they say, is history."

He never lowered his gaze. "Define 'shit happened.'"

She sighed. "I broke up with my fiancé. After that, I moved out. I thought I could afford another apartment on my salary but right after that, I lost my job."

"What happened to him?"

"Who?"

"Your fiancé?"

She crossed her legs and sipped her wine before answering. "He cheated on me."

Tro didn't say anything to that, only picked a grape out of her fruit cocktail. He changed the subject.

"How high was the rent?"

"Seven fifty."

"And where were you workin'?"

"I was a receptionist at a law firm."

"Straight outta high school?"

"Straight outta high school."

"Your nigga had a job?"

"He runs a real estate company. His real job was to keep me happy. Unfortunately, that came with a price."

"Sorry to hear that. You in school, right? What you goin' for?"

"Business."

"What kinda business?"

"Business. You know, economics, management, that kinda shit."

"No, I don't know what kinda shit. I mean, what do you wanna do?"

"I want a salon. My own salon, from the ground up."

"Hair salon?"

"A little bit of everything. Get a manicure, get a pedicure, get a massage, have yoga. Juice bar and all that shit."

"Interesting. So once again, why are you stripping? There's plenty of jobs out there. If you worked in a law office I know you got a good résumé. You got a diploma, a few years' experience, all that. I know you could find a job if you really wanted to."

She was quickly becoming annoyed at the turn this was taking. It seemed like he was trying to say that it was her fault she didn't have a job. "I needed money fast. It just so happened that the week I started working at the House, I was due for eviction. I would've been on the street. It was a last resort."

He shrugged. "But I know you got something' better goin' for you. This life…this ain't shit, ma."

Caiza finally blew her top, turning to him. "Is that a fact? Well, I ain't see you or none of your niggas complainin' when y'all was shoving dollar bills in my ass. And I don't recall you sittin' next to your wife on this li'l trip. So my life seems to work out fine for you, huh?"

Facing the wine, she turned to gaze out of the window at the black ocean beneath them. Who the hell did he think he was? If memory served correctly, he didn't cough up fifty carats of diamonds with an attitude. After a few minutes of forced silence, she felt him touch her hand.

"Perla," he started, "I'm sorry."

Caiza relaxed, signaling for a glass of water. "No, I'm sorry. It's just…I don't like to be told shit I already know."

"That's my bad. You right. I shouldn't be buttin' in. And you know I love to watch you shake that ass," he said, smiling.

When she heard that, a cash register dinged in her head. She smelled money. Caiza turned back to him. "A'ight now, don't make me have to set it off up in here."

"Go 'head," he said. "Go 'head and set it off."

She didn't need to be told twice. Within a few seconds, she was up out of her seat, giving him a personal dance. Arturo peeled cash out of a gold money clip and pushed it down in her bra, feeling her up, because he couldn't do it when she was on stage. Caiza pulled her shirt back down and sat back in her seat just as Tess appeared around the curtain.

"We'll be making our final descent in a few moments. Please put on your seat belts."

Caiza sat and buckled up, returning to her cocktail. Arturo plucked a cherry out, sucking the juice off and coming close to her lips. She moved toward him, and he kissed her, passing her the cherry and sucking on her bottom lip. He licked her ear before whispering in it.

"Stick by me, mama, and you gon' go places."

They did go places. After three days of partying, drinking and enjoying life, they wound down back at their hotel. They had just come back from a seafood fest on the other side of the island. Both of them were too drunk to hail a cab, so they walked back hand in hand.

"You gon' be a'ight?" he asked, stopping just in front of her door. He put a hand in his pocket and let his eyes roam over her body.

Caiza was having a hard time trying not to swoon. "Yeah. I'm gon' be a'ight."

Leaning her back against the doorframe, he put his hands around her and rested them on the small of her back. Pulling her close to him, he brushed her face gently with his lips. It felt good, but she just couldn't.

"Go," she whispered.

He didn't move. "Are you sure?"

Caiza nodded. She knew deep down inside that she didn't want him to go, but her conscience was bothering her. She wondered in the back of her mind what Rydell was doing right then. Caiza felt a tug at her heart at the realization that she hadn't even called to tell him she'd be going away. Guilt was going to set in and she wanted to run from it while she had the chance. "You know we've both got ties."

Tro put his forehead against hers and pressed his hardness up against her leg. "Ties are meant to be broken," he whispered into her ear, licking just under the lobe. "I won't tell if you won't." His hand went to her side and pulled the zipper down on her sundress.

They were still in the hallway, pressed up against the wall. Tro had the zipper all the way down and stuck his hand in the back of the dress. Caiza jumped and grabbed her purse, which had fallen to the floor.

"You better stop," she said under her breath.

"You don't want me to."

She didn't answer him. Instead, he kissed her again, taking her hand and guiding her across the hall to his room. He dug in his pocket for his key. Finding it, he swiped the plastic card in the door and pushed her inside. Tro let her hand go and switched the Do Not Disturb sign from the inside to the outside handle. He smiled at the couple that walked past and closed the door.

Caiza stood facing him when he turned back to her. She had dropped her purse again. He walked over to her and took her into his arms, placing his face in her neck. She propped her hands on his chest and laid her head on his shoulder. Arturo savored the feeling of Caiza's warm body so close to his own. He kissed her, breathing in her scent.

She smelled so good, like jasmine, and as he slid off her dress, he felt the goosebumps all over soft skin. With his lips still locked to hers, he unhooked her bra and tossed it away. He pulled away from her for a minute and sat down on the bed, looking up at this honey-brown goddess as she stood before him in only a thong.

Tro let his eyes roam up and down Caiza's perfect body. He had seen her when she stripped, but seeing her up close with sexual tension in every atom of the air was a different scenario. He wanted to do things to her that he had never wanted to do to anyone in his life.

"I'm not dancing tonight," she said softly.

"That's fine." Walking forward, Caiza leaned over him and unbuttoned his linen shirt. Standing, Tro took it off. He kicked off his shoes. Caiza looked down at the visible bulge in the pants, and when she grabbed it, he moaned. "Hey. Be gentle with the goods."

Caiza chuckled and unzipped him. "Take those off," she commanded. He did, and stood naked there in all his coffee-brown fineness. Caiza felt nothing romantically for Tro, but she knew there was no way she could get to sleep without him tonight. The only thing going through her mind right now was the words to D'Angelo's "Brown Sugar."

They stood together then, as close as they could, just enjoying the warmth of their bodies together. Tro pulled her close to him again and ran his hands up and down her body as he soul kissed her deeply. If she could testify about how good a kiss could be, she swore she'd be in church that Sunday. He laid her back on the bed.

"What you want from me, baby girl?" he said into her ear. He was grinding on her slowly, teasing her.

"Whatever you wanna give me," she replied.

Whatever definitely meant whatever to him. Arturo pushed the covers back and slid down so that he was face to face with her downstairs. Tro was good at what he did, stretching out the seduction as long as he could. First he touched. He ran his fingers along her inner thighs, then took his index finger and massaged her spot.

Then he kissed her, both sides of her thighs, finally pushing her legs as far apart as he could get them so Caiza was spread eagle in front of his mouth. When he dove in, she gasped loud, then caught a rhythm and grinded against his face. Tro had a long tongue and certainly knew what to do with it. He was very talented. He sucked on her button and stuck his tongue inside of her as far as he could get it. Caiza arched her back, shouted his name and sat almost straight up.

He pushed her back down without moving and kept going. She jerked hard, coming for the third time. Tro groaned and slid his middle finger inside her. She cried out again, moaning and saying his name, which only excited him more. Caiza slammed her knees around his neck.

After twenty minutes when Caiza thought she couldn't take it anymore, Tro lifted his head, his mouth glistening. He wiped his face on the sheet.

"You had enough?" he asked, smiling.

She nodded. Tro climbed back up over her and leaned down, kissing her again. She could taste herself on his lips. His body was so soft and warm. Caiza pulled his body down on top of her. He spread her legs again with his knee. They had closed on their own when he moved his head. Tro took the time to gently bite her neck, her ears, and finally, plant a long, sensuous kiss on her lips.

"You ready?" he asked.

She nodded. Still looking in her eyes, Tro reached down and stroked his hard-on, reaching for her hand.

"Put it in," he whispered.

Caiza gently moved his penis right in front of her walls. He never took his eyes away as he slid in slowly. Caiza had to close her own eyes to keep from crying out loud. He was stretching her out, and he was barely halfway inside her. He smiled when he saw her bite her lip in pain.

He began to pull out. "Am I hurting you?"

Caiza's eyes snapped open and she grabbed his body closer. "No! No, don't stop, Tro. Please don't."

After a little while, the only thing she could feel was the sweet pain as he went in and out of her leisurely. He paid close attention to detail, touching and caressing her in all the right places. It took him a long time to let go, and when he did, he grabbed her to him so tightly she felt like they were melting together. She fell asleep in his arms, knowing she would never feel that way again.

The next day, sunlight streamed through the room and hit Caiza smack in the eyes. She groaned and blinked. Her body hurt bad. Every part of her was sore. She sat up and stretched her arms above her head, yawning. Tro was watching her from the other side of the room. Caiza shook her hair over her body, pulling the sheet up to cover her nakedness. He was in jean shorts and white on whites, bare chested.

"Good morning."

She nodded and smiled. "How long you been up?"

"Couple hours."

"You just been sittin' there watchin' me?"

He nodded and took a sip from the cup he was holding. "Hungry?"

"A little bit." She stood and the sheet fell away from her body. He followed her with his eyes as she walked past him into the bathroom. Before she stepped inside, she ran her hands over his bare chest. "Thank you for last night," she said. "I needed that." He smiled and smacked her naked bottom.

She took a long, hot shower, kneading her sore muscles. Caiza knew she would be counting the night before as a workout. There were parts of her body that hurt, and she didn't remember using them. She knew she would have to do some yoga and stretch. When she got out of the shower, Tro was gone, but his cup was still there, so she assumed he would be back. She stretched for ten minutes then bent over with her head facing the floor, the yoga position known as Downward Facing Dog, to stretch her spine. Clearing her mind and breathing evenly, Caiza was already starting to feel better.

The door opened and she figured it was Tro. She opened her left eye and saw his sneakers. It was hard to talk in that position, and it would break her concentration. She heard him set something down, then heard a sound like metal hitting metal. It didn't click that it was his belt buckle until she felt him slam into her hard from behind. Caiza screamed out and tried to crawl away from him, but he grabbed her hips and plowed in and out of her like she stole something.

Caiza finally gave up trying to get away and just stood there, bent all the way over, getting the life pounded out of her. When he came, he collapsed on the floor and pulled her down on top of his lap. They were both breathing heavily. She sat there in his lap, with her head on his shoulder.

"You know I like you, right?"

"I couldn't tell," she said, smiling, even more sore now than when she woke up.

"So what we gon' do?"

She closed her eyes as he brushed her hair out of her face. "This is strictly physical, Tro."

He reached around her and rubbed her breasts. "It doesn't have to be."

Caiza sat up, and he pushed her hair out of his face. "You know, you seem to be leaving your wife out of this equation."

"She wants a divorce as it is."

"I'm sorry."

"I'm not."

"I've got somebody at home waitin' for me."

"I didn't hear anything about him last night."

She stood up, still naked. "I was drunk. It was a one night thing."

"I'm a one night thing?"

Her shoulders dropped. She didn't mean for him to take it like that. "That's not what I meant, Tro. You're a sweetheart, baby. You really are. But we've gotta be real. This is a sex thing. I've got a man at home that I like. I just might be in love with him. He's a good man. And I can't leave him."

"So why'd you fuck me then?" he asked. He stood as well, pulling up his shorts and climbing on top of the dresser, his legs dangling. Caiza sighed hard, then came and sat next to him.

"It was coming, Tro. If not last night, then next week. It just so happened that there was nothing but space and opportunity last night."

He smiled, as if he finally got it. "One more for the road?" he asked.

She raced him to the bed.

I2

It's About that Time

Caiza Bell was a celebrity.

Her face was known, and it was as good as a MasterCard—accepted everywhere. Caiza tried to get what had happened between her and Tro out of her mind. She finally convinced herself that the past was the past and it wasn't like either of them were running to tell Rydell what happened.

It bit at her that she had to lie, but she knew it would only mess things up with Rydell. Stifling her uncontrollable guilt was the only way she could get over it. She was in love with Rydell, and she was more than sure he felt the same way, so what she had done would devastate him. *What you don't know won't hurt you,* she figured. She didn't tell him about Tro at all, just that some friends had invited her out to Jamaica for the weekend.

Caiza also had a client list. She did private parties and was paid well for them. She was on her way back from a birthday party for some kid's twenty-first birthday party. She had just deposited the money in the bank and was on her way home.

She was happy. She was living the high life, and she loved it. Caiza had everything she needed in her life and everything she wanted. It wasn't just the fact that she had what she wanted; it was the fact that she no longer had to struggle to get it. It came to her easily. She wasn't a prostitute; she was a dancer. She made money off her talents. And she didn't think anyone could knock her for that.

Bulldog had finally made his "favor" known. As she had figured, Dog had illegal activities going on the side. He explained the scenario. Each Friday when she left the club, she was to drive to the South Street Seaport and wait for a man named Nick. According to Dog, Nick would arrive in a black Denali.

Dog gave her a silver briefcase. "I'ma give you one of these every Friday," he told her. "You don't open it or nothin. Just make sure that nigga Nick get it. He gon' call me and let me know he got it and every time I get that call, you get five bones."

"Five hundred dollars to chauffuer a briefcase?"

"That's right."

Caiza saw no problem with the arrangement and pretty soon, she added Dog-and his money-to her private client list.

Caiza thought she was floating on top of the world until she pulled up in front of her building and fell off the flat side. Caiza hadn't seen Jacey in the longest time and here he was, in her lobby, waiting. He had a dozen white roses in his hand. She stopped short, almost falling over. She caught her balance and tried to sneak around him without being seen. His radar went off, and he turned in her direction.

"Caiza," he called softly, "come, come gimme some, girl."

She pretended to be surprised to see him. "Oh, Jacey. Hi. I was just, uh, just checking my mail."

"And avoiding me, I see. I had to come see you because you apparently forgot my phone number."

"I didn't forget it, Jacey. I just haven't called. I felt no need to do so."

He put a hand on his heart. "Don't say that. That hurts, you know. I'm really trying to make all this up to you and you...you're not making it easy for me."

Caiza took off her sunglasses, sighing. "Why do you feel the need to keep harassing me, Jacey? I've moved on. I think you should do the same."

He handed her the flowers. "Can we go upstairs and talk?"

"We tried that already, remember? And how'd you get this address?"

He shrugged. "I've got connections. So what's up? You just gon' treat me like a stranger?" He smoothly changed the subject.

"You have ten minutes to make your point, and then you need to leave."

"Alright. That's all I need."

She led him upstairs. He looked around, astonished by the new digs. "Damn, girl! When you said you moved on, you weren't playing."

Caiza didn't mind using the opportunity to show off. "I've been watching the Style Network." She showed him into the living room. Jacey's gaze took in everything, and he made no effort to show he wasn't jealous.

"Can I offer you something to drink?"

"A soda's cool."

She went into the kitchen and brought him a bottle of Sprite, a glass filled with ice, and a coaster. "I'm gonna use the bathroom. Make yourself comfortable." Turning away, she disappeared into the bathroom. Caiza didn't want him here; she was afraid the events of his last visit would repeat themselves. She reached into the medicine cabinet and found her stash, which she hid in an old Tylenol bottle. Taking a fast hit, she wiped her face and went back out into the living room.

Caiza sat down on one end of the sofa with Jacey far away on the other. "What's up with you, Jacey?"

He looked around, still impressed. "What's it take to live in a place like this?"

She shrugged. "Five grand a month."

He looked back at her. "Where'd you get that kind of money?"

"I started thinkin' with my head. It paid off."

He nodded, studying the bottle of soda. "How's school?"

"It's fine."

"So you're doing alright then?" he asked.

"I sure am."

Jacey ran his fingers over the sofa arm on his side. "I heard a coupla times you're workin' the pole downtown."

Now they were getting somewhere. The whole reason for his visit became evident. He came here to scope her out. "That's what you hear, huh?"

"My nigga Dog says he sees you there every week."

Caiza shifted. She was going to kill that asshole when she saw him.

Here she was hookin' him up and he had the nerve to squeal on her. "That's interesting. I wouldn't know anything about that."

He twirled the soda around. "You sure? He didn't buy you that pretty-ass Benz you're driving?"

"Whether he did or didn't is none of your concern."

He turned his mouth up in a frown. "I know you're not shaking your ass for a living, so I'm just gonna let that go."

Caiza put her arms up on the back of the sofa and crossed her legs. "It's funny how much you care about me now. You didn't seem all that worried when you had Trina workin *your* pole." That was a stab, a low blow, and she knew it.

His attitude changed. "You know I wasn't trying hurt you, Caiza. I said I was sorry, and I meant it." She could hear the gloom in his voice. He looked around again. Taking the rest of the soda down, he put the empty bottle on the table in front of him. He stood up and walked over to the grand piano.

Silently, Jacey tapped out a few unrecognizable notes. The air was heavy with tension as the two of them avoided dialogue for as long as possible. Turning back, he angrily asked, "Why didn't you give me another chance, Caiza?"

Here it was. After all the talking they had gone through, he never asked that question. Had he asked her that before, he would have gotten over her a long time ago.

Caiza reached into her purse and plucked a Newport free. She lit it and smoked for a while before answering. She shifted again. "When I first saw you I was an immature sixteen-year-old. I was a baby. I knew nothing about love. I remember how we snuck around for that first year, denying we were together because my mother wouldn't let me date until I was seventeen. Then my birthday hit and that night…that night I lost my innocence to you.

"I still remember what it felt like the very first time you made love to me, Jacey. It hurt so bad and so good at the same time. I had that feeling in my heart that I loved you and I would never let you go. You promised me that you loved me back. And for five magical years, I believed you. Then you asked me to marry you, and I just knew we were meant to be. I was ready, completely ready, to spend the rest of my life with you."

The glowing, happy sound in her voice fell flat and reality struck. "And then I came home to find you fucking Trina. No matter how much you apologize, how much you say you're sorry, you could never, ever understand how I feel, and you could never, ever make it up to me. Never. You told me you loved me and you didn't mean it."

He stared at her in a silent face-off. Caiza was shocked back into the present when she heard the front door unlock. "Ba-bay," Rydell called. She wiped the back of her hand across her face.

"In here," she said aloud. Rydell entered a few seconds later carrying a few bags. He cast a glance in Jacey's direction that said *you don't belong here*.

"Dell, that's Jacey. Jay, this is Rydell, my boyfriend." They shook hands.

"How you doin', brother?" Rydell knew exactly who Jacey was. And he didn't like him. He didn't know why the man was hanging around.

"A'ight, man. I was just leavin'. Kye, good to see you," he said. Caiza walked him to the door. When he turned to say good-bye, there was nothing in his eyes. "You know that's real fucked up, mama." He tossed her a sweet smile and kissed her face. She had no idea what that meant and was in no hurry to find out.

"What was that about?" Rydell asked. She looked over at him. He looked like a dog whose territory had just been threatened.

"Same old same old. I've heard it all before. He just keeps pushing rewind and play, saying the same shit over again. It's over, and he doesn't seem to understand."

Rydell frowned and stayed silent. He didn't appreciate the disrespect Jacey had just shown him but he held his tongue for her sake. She didn't look like she needed to hear it at the moment.

Caiza counted the bills she made from her last party. "Eleven, twelve, thirteen fourteen, fifteen hundred. Not bad. Some cat name Prince had become a regular at the club and requested her services for his birthday party. Him and his homies had to struggle to come up with it, but they did.

"You really like this dancing shit, hmm?" My asked.

"Better than spendin' my days in a homeless shelter, beggin' for change."

"Ain't that what you do when you shake ya ass? Rydell know about this?"

"I ain't beggin' for change when I dance, they give it to me, number one. Number two, what the hell that gotta do wit' you? Steve know you workin' there?"

"He sure does."

"So what, that makes you feel better?" she asked. "Ain't you the one that said, 'Oh Kye, come on down and get you a job, girl?' Wasn't that you?"

"Yeah, that was me. But that's back when I thought you was just in this for the cash. Now you're getting cars, diamonds, trips. I don't know where your head is at these days." Myeisha shook her head.

"My head is on my shoulders. You're just jealous."

Myeisha smiled and pulled at her ponytail. "Ain't nobody jealous, Caiza. I'm just saying. I think you getting a little too caught up."

Caiza sighed and held out her money-filled hands. "I didn't wanna be doin' this, but as long as I am, I'm gon' be good at it. I can't help it if those horny motherfuckers love me. That's my gift. And if I gotta shake my ass for the rest of my life to pay my rent and live my life, that's what I'm gon' do." She snapped a rubber band around the wad of bills and tossed it on the table.

Myeisha looked like she was sorry she'd brought it up. "I just want you to be careful is all. I don't want you to get too far gone in this, okay?"

She nodded. "I know what you mean, My. You know it's my job to be stubborn." Caiza leaned over and gave her a hug. "I know you just lookin' out for me."

"Sure ya right," My said softly. She eyed Caiza sadly, sure all this was going straight over her head.

"So what you think?"

Kam held her fingers up, blowing smoke out of her nose. "Well, Mannie knows I work here, and he doesn't have a problem with it. And neither does Evelyn's man."

Evelyn nodded. She grabbed her crotch. "He ain't got nada to say about what I do. I got the *cojones* in that house, *comeprende*?"

That made everyone laugh. Caiza had been thinking about what Myeisha told her, and she wanted a second opinion.

One of the weekend girls, Santé, threw in her two cents. "The way I see it, if the nigga got a problem wit' what you doin', tell him to go on then. He liked you before he knew you was strippin', right?"

"Hey," Evelyn said, turning around. "Stay outta grown folks business, mami, si?"

Sante shrugged. Caiza's music came on, and she grabbed the Ziploc bag Evelyn tossed at her.

Truce cut the lights. "My fine brothers, do me a big favor and give me a one time for the innovator, number one booty shaker, our very own heat-bringing baby maker, La Perla!" Caiza had gotten used to taking a hit before she went on stage and this was no different. She wiped her face and gave the baggie back to Ev.

There was Tro in the front row, watching her. She hadn't seen him for a couple of weeks, but somehow, it felt good to have a familiar face watching her. To his left, and a little farther back was Bulldog. And behind them, almost where she couldn't see him was Jacey. Caiza's breath caught in her throat, and she stopped, forgetting where she was for just an instant.

She thanked the Lord that her set went by quickly. After she finished for the night, she dressed, said her good-byes and hurried out to the parking lot. Not only did she have to be at the pier in a half an hour, she had nothing to say. She was busted. *Fuck!* Jacey was standing by her car.

"What the hell are you doing, Kye?"

"Jacey, I just wanna get in my car and go home. I had a long day."

"I would say so."

She tried to get past him, but he wasn't going to let her in the car until she spoke to him. "Jacey, please."

"You gotta promise me you won't ever go back up in there."

"I can't promise you that."

"Why not?"

"How do you think I'm paying my rent?"

He took a step to the side. "This isn't the Caiza I knew. This can't be the same Caiza who told me she'd leave me if I ever stepped in a strip club."

Caiza shifted her bag on her shoulder. "Yes, well times have changed."

"I know we're not together anymore, but if you needed anything, you could have come to me. I leave message after message and you don't never call back."

"Because I don't want anything to do with you, you cheating shit," she said, wailing on him with her bag. "Get away from me," she screamed, near tears and hysterics. He backed away, and she almost ran him over backing out of her parking space. She saw the look on his face as she drove away and knew he had gotten the point at last.

Early the next week, Caiza got home from a very long day to find Myeisha in her apartment looking like heaven had declined her application. "Hey, girl. What time you get here?" Sparkle ran over to greet her, tail wagging. She ran back into the living room and jumped up on the couch, putting her head on My's lap.

"What the hell is this?" she said, showing Caiza the bottle of Tylenol. *Damnit*.

"It's nothing. It's Tylenol."

Myeisha followed her into the kitchen. "You ain't gon' tell me that's nothin', Caiza. If that's cocaine, then you done went off the deep end for sure."

"It nothin', a'ight, My? Damn! Why you goin' through my shit anyway?" Caiza tried to flip it on her.

She began her finger-waving routine. "Don't even go there wit' that shit. We been goin' through each other's shit for years. I came over to hang out, and I got a headache. I go in your shit for a painkiller, and this is what the fuck you got up in there? You ain't just gon' brush this off me. Where'd you get it from?" she shouted, hands on her hips.

Caiza mumbled.

"What?"

"I said I got it from Kam, damn. Why you trippin'? You my mama now?"

"I'm trippin' 'cuz somebody need to be, Caiza. You don't need to be fuckin' wit' this shit, for real. I don't know what you was plannin' to do wit' it, but you need to get rid of it."

"Why is this such a big deal? It's not like I'm usin' it."

Myeisha laughed sarcastically. "What*ever*. So I look stupid? Don't make me hurt you, bitch. I know I got you into this job 'cuz you needed the cash. Fine. Now you got it. But you actin' like them bitches in there is your friends. They ain't gon' hold you down when you get busted for possession, dumb ass."

"Kam *is* my friend."

Myeisha snatched the bottle out of her hand and waved it in her face.

"No, I'm your motherfucking friend. If she were your friend, she wouldn't be givin' you this shit. She got her own kids to take care of, so how smart that make her?"

Caiza snatched the bottle back. "You makin' this bigger than it need to be, Myeisha. It's not like I was gon' use it." Caiza felt that her best bet was to lie. As long as My didn't know for sure whether she was using the drugs, she could deny it.

Myeisha waved her head like oh no you didn't. "You know what, Caiza? I'm tryna look out for you. You wanna know why? 'Cuz I'm scared for you, baby girl. I'm worried that one day somethin' crazy is gon' jump off and I ain't gon' be there to help you up. The Caiza I knew was dancing to take care of herself.

"Now the Caiza I know is fuckin' taking coke. *Cocaine.* You know what that shit does to people? Look at your uncle Chuckie. Look at my mother. You wanna mess your whole shit up, you do it yourself. But it's your funeral. Not mine." She glared Caiza down as she grabbed her purse from the living room.

"Myeisha," Caiza called pathetically, just knowing she'd run right back and tell her she was joking. But when she heard the door slam, she trotted into the hallway. She really was gone. Myeisha was serious. What was the big deal? It was just a little pick-me-up. Right?

Caiza rubbed her hands over her face. She walked out of the kitchen into the living room and clicked the answering machine.

"Caiza, it's been too long since we last spoke. Call your mother." She rolled her eyes and erased the message. Looking down at her nails, she saw she needed to get the paint retouched.

"Hey, Caiza, this is Tori. We have a study group this Wednesday. We havin' it at your place this week. Don't forget. If you can't host it, call us and let us know, a'ight? Peace." The next day was Wednesday. After fighting with her best friend, she didn't feel like having anybody in her house. But she put her name in the hat, and it was her turn to have the study group at her place.

The next message was a hang up. She looked at the caller ID, but it said unavailable.

"I know you know I'm not stupid. I know about the car and I know about the diamonds and Jamaica and all that. You need to do a better job of keeping your business to yourself. You fucked him and you won't even talk to me? You're going to need me one day and I'm not going to be there. I know you better than anybody, Caiza Bell. Don't forget that." *Click.*

Caiza reached for a Newport, her fingers shaking so bad she could barely get the lighter flame to stay lit. She didn't understand why Jacey was acting this way. For someone who claimed he loved her, he sure had a funny way of showing it. She thought about calling Rydell and decided against it. She would have to end up explaining why Jacey was so mad and if he knew what had happened between her and Tro, he would leave her for sure. So she called Myeisha.

The phone rang three times before it went to the machine. Caiza frowned. "Damn. My girl is really mad." Caiza hated fighting with Myeisha. They always made up, but the time they spent not speaking was uncomfortable, beyond unbearable. Oh well. She'd try again in the morning.

"Caiza? Caiza?"

She snapped out of her trance. "Huh?" Sparkle thumped her tail against the floor, turning her eyes like, "Ooh, this is about to get good."

Tori looked at her with a get-it-together frown. "We were asking you the definition of inflation."

"Oh." Caiza opened her notebook and turned to the right page. "Inflation can be described as the rising level of prices in the economy."

"Thank you, mama," she said, shaking her head. She gestured with her French-manicured nails. "Please try to stick with us."

She was obviously interrupting the flow of the study group, and Tori's gaze let her know she didn't appreciate it. Caiza couldn't help it. Her mind was a thousand miles away. She was trying to figure out this Myeisha situation. It wasn't helping that Myeisha was refusing to return her calls. Caiza knew she had messed up this time because My always answered her phone, no matter what they fought about.

The study group ended uneventfully. After everyone was gone, Caiza cleaned up a bit and found herself sitting in front of the phone. It had been silent all day. She wished My would call her so they could finally have a chance to talk. It did ring, some time after one. It was Kahmes.

"Yo girl, you missed it!"

"What happened?"

Kam started talking a mile a minute. "Ay, yo, somebody got popped outside the club! We don't know what happened and shit, all I know is Priceless sent us all home. Five oh was out there and everything. They had news cameras down the block, niggas was crowdin around the body and shit, I ain't get to see nuthin-"

"Wait, slow down," caiza interrupted. She reached over for a cigarette. "Somebody got killed outside *our* club?"

"Ain't that what I just said, ho?"

"Who was it?"

"We ain't find out yet."

"A nigga or a chick?"

"I don't know that neither. I know P was pissed though, cuz she can't afford to have five oh round there like they fuckin' friends and shit."

Caiza sat back, now that the excitement from the announcement had worn off. "I doubt she's concerned. She owns the police."

"Yeah, that's true. It was on the dark side too, where don't none of us park."

Caza shuddered. "By the back door?"

"Yeah. Prolly why ain't nobody hear nothing."

"Damn. That's real fucked up."

"Yeah, I know." They talked for a few more minutes before Caiza heard the beep that indicated she had another caller on the line. But it was not the call she was expecting.

13

When It All Falls Down

Caiza nearly crashed her car trying to park it. She couldn't see within three feet in front of her face. She couldn't get that man's voice out of her head. *We'll need you to identify a body*. She had no time or presence of mind to change her clothes, and Caiza hadn't even put a coat on over her T-shirt and sweats. Her hair was in a wild mess on the top of her head. She raced through the doors to the front desk.

"Miss, is there something I can help you with?"

"Where is she?" Caiza screamed. "Where is she?"

"Okay, calm down, miss. Who are you looking for?"

Her head was spinning. "Brown," she wailed. "Myeisha Brown. Please tell me where she is."

At this point the other nurse stood with a grave look at her face. "I'll take her, Margie," she said. She came around the desk and took Caiza's arm.

"Take me where? Where is she?"

"I'm going to need you to calm down, okay? Are you Ms. Bell?"

"Yes. What's going on? Where is Myeisha?"

A smaller woman, a solemn face and sympathetic blue eyes, took her by the hand and walked her to the elevator. Caiza followed her blindly. When the elevator arrived and they stepped on, the woman spoke.

"My name is Nurse Greene. I need you to calm down, okay?"

Caiza nodded, still not processing the situation. She didn't understand what was going on. Her mind was trying to move in too many directions at once. The elevator came to a stop, and the nurse led her off and into a dark room. The room had two tables in it, one bare and the other covered by a sheet. Nurse Greene gently touched her hand.

"Are you ready?"

Caiza didn't remember nodding, only that Nurse Greene pulled the sheet back gently. She felt her legs buckle and gasped, her breath drawing sharply into her chest. Caiza reached out but seemed not to touch anything but air. This was not her baby girl here. She didn't know who this person was.

Both her eyes were swollen shut. Her jaw had been broken, and there was a large cut above her left eye. Her lip was busted and a handprint was bruised into her neck. Caiza looked farther down. Across her chest and sides was a scattering of black and blue. The body was so battered that Caiza forced herself to believe it was someone else. She shook her head and backed away.

"No, that's not her. Myeisha isn't dead. This can't be her."

Nurse Greene put her hand on her arm. "Ms. Bell, I know this is a hard time for you, but this young woman is dead. I know you don't want to hear it, but I need you to be strong now and tell me if you recognize her."

"It's not her," Caiza shouted, still backing away. "She's not dead."

Nurse Greene lowered her head and bit her lip. "Please, dear. Make sure. Take one last look."

Caiza was trying to stall for as long as she could, not ever wanting to make the positive identification. But her fate was sealed when she caught sight of the shooting star tattoo on Myeisha's hip. Caiza had an identical one on her own thigh. "'Cuz we going places, like shootin' stars," Myeisha had said. Caiza touched her skin, which was cold and clammy, then ran her fingers across her hair, which was still soft. She stood there for a long while and knew this was her best friend.

"Oh, My," she whispered.

Turning around, Caiza doubled over and vomited violently. All she could remember was the sounds of her own screams. Vaguely, she remembered shouting and someone lifting her off the floor. Someone carried her away, and when they set her down, she felt a sharp prick in her arm. She blinked once and then blacked out.

Hours later, Caiza flickered her eyes and blinked, trying to focus. She was in a bed, in a white gown. Where the hell was she? This was not her bed. She breathed in deeply and was rewarded with the sickening sanitary smell of the hospital. Holding her hand next to her was Rydell.

"Hey, baby."

She sat up, her head pounding. "When did you get here? What's going on?"

"I called your cell, and one of the nurses picked up. Greene. She told me what happened." He stroked her hair and a fresh wave of tears brought him into her arms. He whispered, "Shh. It's alright," into her hair more times than she could remember.

After about an hour, Nurse Greene came to check on her. "Is everything okay, Ms. Bell?"

Caiza shook her head.

Nurse Greene gave her a sympathetic look. "You're alright. You stayed overnight, and the doctors gave you a sedative to help you sleep, alright? If you start feeling a little nauseous, it's okay. It's just the medicine working. The police are here to talk to you. Is it alright to send them in?"

Caiza sniffed and nodded. Rydell stayed by her side the whole time, his hands locked into hers. The detectives entered the room; one a tallish, fit-looking man, sort of like a modern-day Dick Tracy, the other a shorter, fatter man, like Carl Winslow from the television show *Family Matters*. Dick stuck out his hand.

"Ms. Bell, I'm Detective Chase Pierce. This is my partner, Evander Scott," he said, pointing to Winslow. Caiza knew them both, by face at least. They were regulars at the club.

"We're here to ask you a few question regarding the death of your friend."

"Her name is Myeisha," she whispered, looking away.

"I'm sorry. I understand this is a hard time for you." He looked down at a notepad. "Ms. Bell, is it?"

"Yes."

He nodded. "I am sorry for your loss. I know what it's like to lose a close friend. But we need to get any details from you while they're still fresh in your mind. When was the last time you saw Ms. Brown?"

"Tuesday. Tuesday night."

"Are you sure?"

"We had a fight. I remember because I kept trying to call her and she wouldn't pick up her phone."

"What did you fight about?" Scott asked.

Caiza knew she couldn't say anything about the cocaine, the real reason for the fight. But she didn't want to lie. So she did the next best thing, something she had become good at over time. She evaded the truth.

"She was concerned that I was letting my job get the best of me."

"Did you all work together?"

"Yes."

"Where?" asked Scott, ready to write it down.

Caiza choked out the words. "At the *House of Sin*." Rydell looked up then, and she saw his eyebrows draw together.

"That's a strip club, correct?"

"Yes."

"Was she a dancer?"

"Yes."

"How long had she worked there?"

"About five or six years."

"What about you?"

Caiza's cover was totally blown. She paused before answering.

"About two years." She felt Rydell's grip on her hand tighten. Caiza turned her head toward him and said, "You wanna wait outside?"

He took the invitation, getting up to leave. When the door shut behind him, the detectives began again.

"Did either of you ever have any problems?"

"No. Myeisha tells me everything. If somebody were messing with her, she'd say so."

Both Pierce and Scott noticed that she mentioned her friend in the present tense. "How long have you been friends?"

"Since we were little girls."

Detective Scott took over at that point. "Ms. Bell, do you know anyone with any animosity toward Ms. Brown?"

Caiza shook her head. "Everybody loves her. I don't understand who would do this to her." She really didn't.

"What was her personal life like? Any scorned lovers? Broken alliances?"

"She never met a man she didn't like," she answered, being as honest as she could without calling her friend a hoe.

"Does that mean she had a lot of sexual partners?"

She frowned. This was taking a turn into a dark alley she didn't want to go down. What the hell were they getting at? "Why is that relevant?"

The detectives took uncomfortable glances at each other before Pierce continued. "We need to ask these questions when dealing with this type of crime."

Caiza tensed. "What type of crime?"

They looked at each other again, seeming hesitant. Caiza sat all the way up, hating the feeling that there was something they were not telling her. "What happened? What type of crime?"

Detective Pierce shifted uncomfortably on his feet. He took a glance at his partner before looking Caiza in the eyes and giving it to her straight.

"Ms. Brown was raped before she was murdered."

Caiza couldn't breathe. She had never had breathing problems before, but she was having them now. She couldn't get any air into her lungs. The harder she tried to breathe, the harder it was. The images in front of her eyes began to cross, and instead of one, Detective Pierce now had three bodies. And they were swirling. A wave of nausea crashed into her like a sack of bricks, and her limbs became like jelly. She fell back against the bed. Scott saw her distress and hollered for help. Nurse Greene came running, took one look at her and went for an oxygen mask.

Within a few seconds, Nurse Greene had returned and snapped the mask on Caiza's face. When she calmed down, the nurse gave Caiza a pink pill to take with water.

"You just had a panic attack, honey, okay? If you're not feeling better within an hour, we're going to keep you overnight for evaluation. You've had a stressful night, and I don't want you to do anything to hurt yourself or someone else."

Caiza nodded. Taking a ragged breath, she turned her head and looked over at Rydell, who had returned. He was angry but he knew this wasn't the time or the place to discuss it. Nurse Greene had ushered the detectives out into the hallway and told them they would have to come back.

With Caiza's permission, she told them to visit her at home within the next few days. She was in no condition to hear anything else.

Caiza found out from the detectives that Myeisha's body had been discovered at about eleven-thirty Tuesday night in the dark corner of the House parking lot—the murder Kahmes had called her about. Two patrons used the back door to get out to their cars and discovered Myeisha. They stayed there until the police arrived. They were questioned and released and the police claimed they had no leads at the time.

Caiza took the next few days off from school to get herself together. In that time, she didn't see or hear from Rydell. He didn't answer her calls. She assumed he wasn't going to call her again, so she tried to fool herself into not thinking about him. As soon as she recovered, her first stop was the club. Caiza stormed inside, looking for Priceless. If anyone knew what was going on, it would be her.

Priceless was in her usual position, shockingly drinking a glass of ice water. "Perla," she said. "I heard. I'm sorry."

Caiza couldn't tell if that were true or not, because Priceless was so good at disguising how she really felt. Besides the fact that cold-blooded animals don't feel warmth anyway.

"She was killed right outside, Priceless. I know you know something."

Priceless looked at her, disinterest painted all over her face. "I don't know anything. All I know is that the jakes ran all through here last night, trying to shake me down." She pointed at Caiza. "I told all you girls to keep your shit to yourselves. I said I ain't want no cops up in here, sniffin' around."

Caiza slammed her hands on the desk. "Do you even care what happened to her? What the hell is the matter with you?"

Priceless looked down at her desk, her eyebrows raised. Reaching for the box of Newports on her desk, she pulled one out and lit it. Blowing a line of smoke in Caiza's direction, she looked her in the eyes and sipped her water. Reaching into her desk, she brought out a bottle. Caiza looked and saw that she wasn't drinking water; she was drinking vodka.

"Listen here, honey. I'm sorry about what happened to your little friend. But I am not her keeper. She came in here around eight on Tuesday. She was pissed about something; I could care less what. She didn't stay long. She told me she wasn't feeling well, then she left. Five-oh rolls up in here like ten o'clock, shakin' me and the girls down, like I know somethin'.

"I didn't even know what happened till yesterday morning. Some DT's came up in here and told me it was her. They didn't even tell me who it was at first. So I'm just as surprised as you, a'ight?"

Caiza could tell she wasn't going to get anything out of her, so she puffed herself up and tried to demand answers. "My best friend *died* right outside your club, Priceless. You gon' sit there and tell me you don't know anything? As rich as you are, no security cameras? No nothing?"

Priceless pointed at her. "I've got security cameras. But you've gotta ask nice."

Caiza's stomach turned. Her best friend had been murdered outside, and the woman was asking her to say please. She was a fucking maniac.

"Please, Priceless. I've done a lot for you and this place. Now can you do something for me?"

Priceless took a long look at her and picked up her phone. Putting the receiver to her ear, she didn't take her eyes off Caiza as she spoke into it. A moment later, Hearse arrived with three jewel cases in his hands. He handed them to her, winked and disappeared.

Priceless pointed a finger at Caiza, her green eyes staring through her skull. "I want those back as soon as you finish. Make a copy if you need to, but bring them back."

"Thank you," she said, genuinely grateful. Caiza got out of there and drove home. In the car, she placed a call to Dog.

"Yo."

"Hey, it's Caiza."

"Oh, what's good, shorty?"

Caiza drove with one hand, the phone tucked under her ear, wiping the tears from her face with the other. "Look, um, you know…abot our situation…"

"What about it?"

"I got some shit that just happened to me-"

"Oh word up, about your girl. Yo, me and the fellas is real sorry about that shit, real talk ma. She was a good girl."

"Thank you. What I wanted to tell you was that I don't think I can work for you anymore."

"Why not?"

"It's just…I'm real fucked up right now. Maybe later we can work something out, but right now," she choked on her tears, "I just can't. I'm confused and shit and I just don't need the extra stress right now."

"Oh, aight. I see."

"I'll give you back all your money, I'll give back the car, whatever."

"Nah, shorty. You keep all that. Those was gifts."

"Thank you, thank you for everything."

"Don't worry about it, ma. You call if you need something, aight?"

"I will." She hung up the phone and flung it away, cryng freely as she drove towards home.

Once there, Caiza fed and walked Sparkle, who seemed to understand that her mama wasn't really feeling well. When they returned, she heard the television. She was nearly sure she hadn't left it on when they left. Rydell was there, flicking through the channels. She dropped Sparkle's leash on the hall table and tiptoed into the living room.

"Hi," she said, keeping her voice low.

Rydell didn't turn to look at her, just kept flicking until he hit ESPN. He put the remote down on the table and put his arms up on the back of the couch. He didn't say anything at first, just kept his eyes forward and pretended to be interested in the highlights.

"Why didn't you tell me?" he said at last.

Sparkle walked over to Rydell and sniffed him, wagging her tail. He patted her head, and she, satisfied, moved on.

"I couldn't tell you, Dell."

He stood. "What do you mean you couldn't tell me? I thought we could trust each other? Don't you love me?" In his eyes was more hurt than she had ever seen. She didn't know she had the power to do that to anyone.

"I do, I do love you. I'm sorry, Rydell. I thought you would be mad at me."

"Did you think lying would make it better?" He turned away from her, walking into the kitchen. She followed him, already scared of the turnout of this argument.

"If I told you, I knew you would have left. I thought you would leave me."

"So you thought lying would help? That makes it worse, Caiza."

He made a drink.

She was getting desperate. If she didn't come up with something fast, she would lose this man. "What was I going to say? That I was stripping for a living?"

He put his hands in the air. "Yes."

She shook her head. "I couldn't tell you that, Rydell. It would have hurt you."

"How do you know that? I mean, at least it would have been the truth."

Caiza didn't even know where to begin. He was making her feel awful. There was so much more to it than 'I strip for a living.' That he would have been able to handle. If she'd told him she was stripping, she would have had to tell him everything else, and she wasn't quite ready to do that yet.

"I know. I know. I'm sorry. It's just that I thought if I told you, you wouldn't want anything else to do with me."

He pulled her close to him, into a hug. "I wish you would have told me, Caiza. I wouldn't have looked at you any different. I just wish I'd been given the chance to make that decision for myself."

She relaxed against his chest; glad that this didn't take the turn she thought it would.

"I'm still mad at you," he said, running his hands over her bottom. "But I think you've got other fish to fry."

She held up her bag. "Priceless gave me the tapes this morning. I'll call you as soon as I know something."

He kissed her forehead and gave her a tight hug. "I've got some thinking to do. I love you, Caiza."

She didn't hesitate as she answered, "I love you too." She smiled soft and let him out, touching the door for just a moment before going back into her living room. The DVDs sat there like a silent warning: stay away. That's exactly what Caiza wanted to do. She wanted to turn and run away, so far into the past that she could reverse time and bring her girl back.

The first disc was from Monday. It was a days worth of nothing. Caiza figured Priceless gave her the extra DVDs so she could see the events leading to and from My's death. Nothing important. Tuesday was the point of interest. Caiza sat up and paid attention. After about five minutes of nothing, she watched as a dark figure walked up and leaned against the back door at about eight o'clock.

He was wearing a black hoodie and hid his face well from the camera. He must have known it was there. He looked at his wrist, clasping his hands together and stretching them out over his head. Caiza saw from the corner of the screen that it was eight nineteen.

The back of the club led directly to the dark side of the parking lot. Caiza remembered how much she hated going over to that side alone. Myeisha came out the back door of the House, slinging her scarf about her neck. She had on a fur coat; Caiza bought it for her as an early birthday present. She was also wearing her favorite knee boots and a pleated miniskirt. She turned her head, meaning the man must have called her name, which meant she knew who it was. She reached up to give him a hug. Caiza leaned in closer, looking at her face. She smiled and the person gestured with his hands. She threw her head back and laughed.

She nodded then, and shook her head immediately after. The person seemed to be trying to get her to tell them something because she put up her hand to wave him away. He threw his hands up. She tried to walk away then, and he grabbed her arm and twisted it, pulling her backward. She began to struggle and then he took her other arm. She opened her mouth in what Caiza thought was a scream. The man clamped a hand down over her mouth, turning her around and pulling her close to his body.

Myeisha began to fight. The man was clearly much stronger than she, even though she was giving him a run for his money. She tried to fight him away. He slapped her hard, and she fell to the ground, holding her face. This was like watching a movie. It couldn't be real. After she fell to the ground, Caiza watched and understood where the bruises on Myeisha's sides had come from. He began to kick her, hard. Myeisha rolled on the ground trying to protect herself, but he never stopped. The kicks became more savage, and Caiza turned her head away for a moment.

When she turned her head back, it looked like Myeisha was unconscious or close to it when he lifted her and carried her body to the hood of her car. Caiza watched, frozen, paralyzed in horrified entrancement as he set her there and lifted her skirt. When his actions became evident, Myeisha tried to struggle again. Again the hand went over her mouth. She fought hard but it was too much for her. The man was choking her. Myeisha kicked her legs wildly but he never stopped what he was doing to her.

Caiza made a whimpering sound in her throat. The man continued to rape Myeisha and watched her struggle. She wanted to cry out, scream, shout, give a warning. But there was nothing she could do. It had already happened, and it was too late. Just when she thought she couldn't take anymore, the man reached out and wrapped his hands around Myeisha's throat.

Myeisha's hands flew to her neck and she continued to kick as the man strangled her. After what seemed like a little while past forever, Myeisha's kicks came less frequently and then not at all. The man fixed his clothing and laid her body out next to her car. He looked around and walked away. The footage ended after a little while. Caiza's eyes stayed glued to the TV, watching the blue screen in a daze.

Caiza was hurt, angry and disgusted by what she had seen. Whoever had done this to Myeisha certainly had to pay. She had to find him. But she didn't even know where to begin looking.

14

Oh, It's On Now

When Steve opened the door, he looked awful. He was in a bathrobe and clearly hadn't shaved in days. His normally neat wavy hair was in a mess on his head, and his eyes were red-rimmed and bloodshot. He let Caiza in without a word. As soon as the front door shut, something happened.

Whatever emotion the both of them had bottled up inside for the past few days came flooding out. They came together in a hug and just rocked each other for the longest time. Their girl was dead, and they were both feeling the pain. He pulled away first, wiped his face and eyes, then took her hand and led her into the living room. They sat on the couch, and he offered her a Scotch. She needed it.

"The police came by here last night. I told them everything I knew, which wasn't much."

"Can you tell me anything?"

"Just a little bit. Them damn cops sniffed around here like I was a murderer or somethin'."

Caiza nodded. "They've just gotta get a profile set up. Just doin' their jobs."

"Yeah. They could've been a little less cold though."

"What do you mean?"

He waved a hand after taking a sip and letting the liquid burn down his throat. "They asked me all sorts of personal questions about her, shit they had no business asking."

"Do you mind?" she asked, touching his hand softly.

"Like whether or not we had rough sex or how often we made love. Things like that. Whose fuckin' business is that?"

"It's their business," she replied, eyes focused on the cover of *Jet* on his coffee table.

"How do you figure that?"

He had no idea. As much as Caiza didn't want to be the bearer of bad news, the parcel was already in her hands. She touched his hand. "Honey, he raped her."

Caiza watched his face change from pain to horror to anger. He stood and paced, waving his hands silently and then turning back to her. "Who? What? When I find that bastard, I'm gonna kill him. Do you hear me? I'm going to kill him." He threw his hand back, and before she knew what was coming next, he punched a sizeable hole in the wall.

Caiza jumped and sat back. She had to calm him down. She knew exactly what was going on in his head. "Don't you think I'm feeling that too, Steve? She was my best friend. If anyone understands, it's me. Now please, just give me what you know."

"She did call me, the night y'all had that fight. She was kinda pissed off wit' you."

"Understandable," she said.

"Yeah. She said she was headin' to the club. She was supposed to come by here when she left. She called me from in the dressing room. I remember one of the girls callin' her name about something. She's like I'll call you back when I'm on my way. I never got that call. I left about three messages on her cell, but after that…" He trailed off, knowing there was no point in stating the obvious.

"When did you see her last before that?"

"Ah, that Saturday. We went out for a few drinks and dancing at the Shadow."

This was of absolutely no use to her. She nodded and made sure the info was still in her head before she stood and gave him a parting hug.

"Um, Caiza?"

"Yes?"

"About the funeral, where, you know," he said sadly.

"I'll give you a call, baby." She didn't even want to be saying the words as they fell out of her mouth. "Just wait for me."

He nodded, and she disappeared out the door. Dark days, these were.

Caiza's first night back at the House was miserable. Priceless wanted her DVDs back, and she was going to get them, but not before she got an earful from Caiza. She stomped into the office, ignoring the shouts from Kade.

"Who watches these cameras?" she demanded, tossing the DVDs on the desk.

"Perla. Good to see you. How's it hanging?"

"I'm going to be hanging you if I don't get some answers."

"Number one," she replied, pouring a generous helping of Remy Martin, "the last person that threatened me is now floating at the bottom of the East River. Number two," she lit a cigarette and sat back, "you got something to say to me you best come correct because I have no problem turning you into an unfortunate accident."

Caiza sat down and composed herself. She didn't know what else to do, where else to turn. She was falling without a parachute, and whatever information anyone had, she truly needed. "I need your help, Priceless. Please."

She nodded. "That's a start. What help?"

"I need to know who watches the security cameras."

"Nobody."

"Nobody?" she cried. "What do you mean?"

Priceless frowned, pulling her features back into a sneer. "You want some cheese and crackers with that whine? Jesus Christ. Nobody watches them because I didn't think I'd have to worry about some chick dyin' outside my club."

"She's not some chick. She's my best friend. If someone were paying any fucking attention, they would have seen her and helped her. Now she's dead," Caiza screamed, borderline hysterical.

"Take a deep breath and relax, sweets. Listen, them cameras are just for show. I put them up to remind people that I'm always watching. Do you really think I'd have somebody sitting there for seven hours a night?

This is my club, and everybody in New York knows better. Whoever killed your girl didn't do it to make *me* upset. They did it so they could get *your* attention."

"What?" This wasn't making any sense.

Leaning over the desk, she blew smoke in her face. "I watched the tape, honey. That nigga wanted you to see what happened. He could have taken your girl anywhere. He raped her and murdered her. In a parking lot. Behind a strip club. He knew I wouldn't be paying attention because I could care less. But you work here. She was your friend. That was a message." She sat back and watched Caiza's features over the edge of her Remy.

Caiza sat back, hypnotized by the logic of her street wisdom. "So…you think…he did it on purpose? He wanted me to see?"

Priceless nodded again. "Wake up, baby girl. She knew who he was. And there's a good chance he knows you too."

That conversation, and more particularly those words, sat on her mind for the next three days. After Caiza received the news the autopsy was complete, she was cleared to set a date for the funeral. Never in her life did she think she would be doing this. Laying her best friend to rest had never once been a part of her future plans.

The burial was a solemn affair. Steve was there, and his friend Ray, all the girls from the club, Caiza's mother, who she managed to avoid the whole day, and surprisingly so was Priceless. Truce came as well, a big hug and fresh flowers on hand. Caiza caught Jacey's eye and almost jumped in the grave behind Myeisha. She didn't want to see him but she knew he'd be there.

Everyone had stood to say a few words, and Rydell nudged Caiza so she could do the same. She stood and made her way slowly to the front of the group, eyes never leaving the silver casket in front of her. She didn't want to believe there was a body in there, the body of a person who had been a living, breathing, laughing thing not just a week ago.

Her voice cracked as she began to speak. "Someone once said you can meet many people who change your life for an instant, but you only meet one person who changes your life forever. When I met Myeisha, I found that to be the truth. Myeisha was the loveliest, most caring, tender and gentle person I have ever had the pleasure of knowing.

"She had the hostility of a hummingbird, and the temper of a flower. I will never, ever meet another person who loved me like she did, and I will never, ever love someone as much as I loved her. Although my very best friend, my heart, was taken away from me, my only joy is coming from knowing she will be looking down on me from heaven like the angel she was here on earth." Silently she made her way back to her seat where she lay against Dell's shoulder. There were no tears left to cry.

Afterward, Jacey approached her, offering a hug. She accepted. Even if he were a dirty rat bastard, if anyone knew how she felt about Myeisha, it was he. His inviting arms were so warm and for less than a second she wished they'd never split.

"I'm sorry, honey," he said, looking at the ground. He looked good, as he always did.

"About the other shit, the phone calls and shit…" he trailed off.

That apology was all she needed. She hadn't asked for it, and he offered it anyway. "Please. Don't worry about it. It's over, right?"

He nodded, twisting his fingers through a handkerchief. "I really am sorry about everything. Are we alright?"

She took a long look at him, and her face and heart softened. She smiled and nodded. "We're alright."

After the funeral, Caiza was on a mission. She leaned on the police department, paying special attention to Detectives Tracy and Winslow. It seemed that ever since they had come to visit her in the hospital, there had been no further investigation into what happened that night. She couldn't rest with this weight on her conscience. Her best friend was dead and no one cared.

Caiza didn't want to go back to the House, but she knew she had to. It was her only source of income, and she had to pay her bills. She had no choice. She had already missed two weeks and had to persuade Priceless to pay her anyway. Priceless knew what she was going through and had let it slide just that one time. Caiza knew it wouldn't happen again.

The week she was back, the first person she laid eyes on was Tro. He had made it to the funeral, but had left before they had a chance to talk. He watched every move she made and she watched him back. He met her in the dressing room after the show. One look from him and all the other girls were out of there.

He didn't speak at first, just shook out a cigarette from the classy silver case he always kept and offered her one. She accepted gratefully. "Thank you."

He nodded. Then, more silence. She sat down at her vanity and started taking off her makeup.

"You weren't even gonna tell me, Caiza?" He startled her when he said that, mainly because he had never used her real name before. He always called her Perla, just like everybody else.

"I didn't think you'd care," she said, knowing she was dead wrong the moment those words came out of her mouth.

He pulled a chair up and sat beside her, looking at her in the mirror. "I think we a little past that, right?"

"Past what? Besides the fact that you and your wife are going through somethin', you have no kids, you come to the club at least twice a week, you can afford a chartered jet, I don't know you at all. And you don't know me."

"That shit don't matter. It woulda been nice to know that your best friend died. Even if I don't know you, I know how close you was to that girl. Shit, everybody knew. You coulda called and told me."

She turned around, her cigarette in her fingers. "And what would you have done, Tro? Sent me some diamonds? Took me on a trip? We only click when you're spendin' money on me."

He seemed hurt that she had spoken to him like that. "You wasn't complainin' when me and my niggas money was payin' your rent."

That was a slap in the face. Caiza sat up and pitched her face forward, hiding it behind her hair. Reality hit her then, and hit her hard. She wasn't a damn celebrity. She was a dancer. She wasn't even a dancer. She was a stripper. Motherfucking eye candy. They didn't give a shit about her. She was their dancing refreshment for a couple of hours an evening, and if they couldn't get their hands on her, they'd get their hands on someone else. She was nothing to them, and even less to them because she stripped. She felt his hand on her shoulder.

"I didn't mean that."

"Yes, yes you did."

He shook his head. "Caiza, I'm sorry, okay? I shouldn't have said that."
She waved at him, the smoke following her hands. "Just go, Tro. Please."

He took one final look at her, then sighed. He stood and kissed her cheek, rubbing her shoulders. Then he disappeared.

"I love you so much, baby. If I could take it back, you know I would. I'd be the first to bring you back. I know this was all my fault. I know that. You tried to warn me, and I didn't listen. And you ended up paying for it. I won't let them get away with this. I swear to God I won't. I love you, baby girl." Caiza kissed her fingers and touched the headstone, laid the flowers down and walked away.

Caiza hated going to Myeisha's grave. Just the very thought that she was dead was just starting to register, and she couldn't handle it. She fought the pain as she walked back to her car. She had skipped her first class to come see Myeisha.

Driving down the road, she turned on the radio to clear her thoughts. Tamia's "Stranger In My House" came on.

The cemetery drive was on a long stretch of private road. It was a pleasant ride, purposefully made that way for quiet reflection to and from the cemetery. Hers was the only car around for a little while until she noticed a black sedan behind her. It was the latest Jaguar, she noticed. She and Myeisha used to joke that they would go half on one when they got older. Those were better times.

She had all but forgotten about the car when the driver began to tailgate. She laid on her horn for a second, annoyed. *Here there is all this room on the road, and you're all up my ass,* she thought. Caiza shook her head when they backed off. "Probably from Jersey," she said aloud. The car got a little too close again, and she sped up.

The sedan sped up.

It was then Caiza realized she wasn't the victim of bad driving. She was being followed. Her only instinct was to keep driving faster, but the sedan matched her speed. At one point it pulled up alongside her. She tried to get a good look at the driver but of course the windows were tinted too deeply. She slowed the car to twenty.

As she did this, the other car slowed as well. Panicking, she sped up again, pushing a hundred. Once again the sedan matched her speed. Caiza was starting to sweat out of fear. She gripped the wheel tighter and pulled her speed back. The sedan rammed her bumper. As if out of nowhere, the sky opened up and a torrent of rain crashed down.

"Just my luck." Flipping on the windshield wipers, she sat forward in her seat, trying to see past the sheeting rain. The car rammed her again, and she pulled back. Caiza couldn't really see the road anymore. If she slowed down, she would get rammed again, if she sped up she would be killed. So she kept the pace at forty. As if reading her mind, the Jaguar hit her again.

Caiza was running out of ideas. She didn't know what to do. She took a fearful glance into her rearview and found that the car had disappeared. She breathed a sigh of relief and tried get out of there. Behind her, the sedan reappeared. Speeding up, the Jag hit her Benz so hard that she lost control and went into a spin.

The skid was like a bad movie. Caiza was whipped into a fast-moving circle while the scenery around her went by faster and faster. She had drawn a complete blank in her mind, sure that she was going to die. She slammed into a tree, hard, on the passenger side. The airbag exploded open. Caiza had her eyes squeezed shut tight, but a tear escaped them anyway. She had stopped moving but her head hadn't. She clutched her hands to the sides of her head to stop the feeling that her brain was spinning in her head.

She pushed open her door and stumbled out, coughing and crying. The rain instantly soaked her from head to toe. The sedan rolled slowly past her, as if surveying the scene. Caiza watched it drive away and shouted after it.

"What do you want from me? What do you want from me?" Caiza shouted. She breathed out as the sedan sped off and disappeared into the driving rain, leaving her there, alone and afraid.

Someone wanted Caiza dead. But she didn't know who and she didn't know why.

15

I Need You

"You can go in now."

Caiza smiled politely and walked into Dick Tracy's office. The resemblance between the fictional character and this detective was scary. He shared the office with Winslow, or Scott, who was MIA at the moment.

"Ms. Bell, please sit down. You sounded a little frantic over the phone. What is it you wanted to talk about?" he asked.

Caiza sat and folded her legs. "Someone tried to kill me."

He leaned back in his chair, already bored. "What makes you think that?"

"I was run off the road in the pouring rain."

Scott openly gaped at her long shapely legs. "You don't think it was just bad driving? Had you been drinking?"

"I don't drink and drive."

"How fast were you going?"

"I tried to speed up, but then it started raining, and I brought it down to about forty."

"Speeding? Over the legal limit?"

She tried to remember. "Well, that road didn't really have a limit."

"How fast were you going?"

"I'm…not really…sure…" Caiza stumbled. "Over sixty?"

She nodded.

"You could have hurt yourself and others."

"I wasn't really concerned about others, detective, I was trying not to be killed."

He stuck the tip of a pen in his mouth, a look on his face like he was thinking about something. Pierce came in then, carrying a bag and a box from Dunkin Donuts. "Toney asked that you not eat up all the doughnuts this time around and…oh. Good morning, Ms. Bell. Am I interrupting something?"

Caiza was going to answer when Scott cut her off. "Ms. Bell was just telling me about her brush with death this weekend. Seems someone tried to run her off the road."

Pierce handed Scott a coffee. "Oh yeah? Why don't you tell us what happened?" It seemed like they were more interested in their breakfast, but she went on anyway. They munched their doughnuts and sipped their coffee, eyes never leaving hers as she related the tale.

"And then you went straight home?"

"Yes."

Pierce held up his hand. "Next time, come straight to the department. If someone really were out to hand it to you, they'd follow you home."

How stupid could I possibly be? Caiza cursed herself out mentally. If the sedan did follow her home, they could get into her apartment. She had so many people over her place that Jeff wouldn't think twice about letting someone up.

"What do you want us to do?"

"I don't know exactly. I just don't know how to go on from here."

"If you see any suspicious activity, report it at once," Scott said drowsily, as if he were reading off a card. "If you have reason to suspect anyone around you of any crimes, please report them immediately. Here's my card."

"And mine," Pierce said, sucking glaze off his fingers and plucking a card out of his back pocket. She accepted them, careful to avoid the spot of sugar from the doughnut. Pierce had his cell number on the back. Scott looked like he couldn't care less.

"What about my friend?" Caiza asked.

Scott had his third doughnut halfway to his mouth. He spoke around it. "The girl from the club?"

"Myeisha Brown," she corrected.

He nodded and sipped the hot coffee, frowning and putting it back on the desk. "We don't have any leads at this point. We've been questioning everyone that works there but at the moment, it seems as if this were a dead end."

Sure. She wasn't a cracker from the high rises. She was a nigger, and that's why there were no leads. Of course it was also because of the "snitches get stitches" mentality of the girls at the House. Even if any of them knew anything, they knew better than to say anything. That was one of the unwritten laws at the House, and no one broke them. You ain't see nothin', so don't say nothin'. Well, someone was gonna say something.

Caiza had to drag herself to and from class at night. She was physically, emotionally and mentally drained, and it was taking a toll on her body and mind. Caiza was so tired. Not to mention that what Detective Pierce told her kept running through her mind. Now adding to her stress, she was paranoid. She parked three blocks from her apartment now, only walked Sparkle for ten minutes at a time and ran all her errands before the sun set. She was rapidly losing weight from her loss of appetite, and her hair was falling out left and right.

She and Rydell were also strained. She was closer to him than ever, but it was hard for them to communicate. He had been upset with her ever since she came home from the hospital. She tried to talk to him but they only ended up fighting. He left after every fight in a blaze of anger.

He called to check on her of course, but the messages were delivered in a voice that meant for her not to call back. He was really tripping. The old Rydell wouldn't have acted like that. In the back of her mind, Caiza wondered if he found out about Tro.

Tro was *another* part of the never-ending saga. He kept sending gifts to apologize. Flowers, cards, love rhymes, all that shit. He and his wife had separated, and he kept saying that she needed to "drop that clown" and get with him. Caiza left a message telling him that Rydell was an honest, hard-working man, not a clown, and she'd appreciate it if he showed some respect. He called back and apologized.

Her mother—part three to this tale of pure hell—was near hysteria when she called. DeLiza continued to blame Caiza for Myeisha's death. She went on and on about how the police called her and told her what happened, and that if she weren't so proud she would have come to her for help. She said she didn't raise her child to be some "dancing whore, but a respectable young woman." Caiza erased the message halfway through, right when DeLiza got to the "ungrateful bitch" part of her tirade.

And those were from last week. Clicking the flashing red button, the automated messenger spoke to her.

"Hello. You have three new messages and two old messages."

Beep.

"Caiza, it's me baby. We need to talk. Gimme a call, a'ight? Love you." She let out a big sigh. She hadn't heard that four-letter word from Rydell in days.

Beep.

"Kye, hey, it's Ev. I'm just callin' to check up on you, chica. I know you goin' through ya shit right now, and I wanna make sure you a'ight. Don't be facin' nothin' 'cuz you feelin' bad, *comprende*?" She was referring to the cocaine. "I'll talk to you *mañana, mi amor.*"

Beep.

The distorted voice was barely recognizable. Caiza had to raise the volume, then play it again.

"Listen, bitch. If you wish to keep living, mind your business. Stay out of it. Or you'll end up in a box next to your friend." *Click.*

Caiza really didn't need this shit. She was already going through enough. It was obviously the same person who tried to run her off the road. She had turned to Rydell, and he had pushed her away. She went to the police, and they were less than interested in her personal safety. She didn't have anywhere else to go. She had to get out of her crib— and now. Sparkle lay in the corner with one eye open, following Caiza's every move.

Caiza grabbed her purse and went down to the club. She didn't feel like being in the house alone. The caller had scared her that badly. She sat in the deejay booth with Truce.

"What's up baby girl? You maintainin'?" he asked, kissing her cheek.

"Just tryna stay alive, my nigga."

He nodded. "I'm 'bout to get into this set, but stay here and I'll talk to you in ten, a'ight?"

"Okay." Caiza took a seat just to his left, giving him enough space to work his magic.

"A'ight, brothers, you know who she is. Melts in your mouth, you melt in her hands, all y'all wanna be her man, give it up for Hershey's Kiss." Caiza couldn't help but giggle at the silly rhymes Truce made up as introductions. He did it for her every week, and she got used to hearing them.

Evelyn winked and blew a kiss when she saw Caiza. Caiza caught it and waved back. She watched Evelyn's performance for about five minutes before catching the nervous jitters and losing interest. She scanned the room, trying to do her own profiling. Who looked suspicious? *Damn near everybody in there, that's who.* She had dealt with so many men since first coming to the House, anybody could have murdered Myeisha. There was literally not one face in there that didn't look suspicious.

"Take a quick break, brothas. Bathroom's in the back, don't get nuthin' on the walls." He spun a dance mix, set his timer and sat next to her. He cracked a Dasani and took a long gulp. "How's it hanging, mama?"

Caiza didn't look at him as she shook her head and answered, "Shit is hectic, Truce, for real."

He cocked his head. "What's hood?"

"Shit, somebody tryna knock me, for real."

Truce didn't want to ask but he did anyway. "You spoke to the police?"

She sucked her teeth. "You already know what the deal is with that, so let's just change the subject right here."

He nodded, sipping again. "I'm feelin' you on that one. It's somebody from here?" Truce looked out for the girls. Priceless saw no need for bouncers because she had no problem coming out of the office and shooting somebody in the head herself.

"I have no idea. They just told me to stop askin' questions and shit, you know, about Myeisha. Trying to scare me into shutting up. I figure it's whoever killed my girl."

Truce frowned. "You know if it's him, you need to get outta your crib. If they wanna come after you, all they need is a phone number."

Caiza's shoulders dropped. How comforting. She shocked herself what just how little she really knew about the world. Other than what she picked up at the club, Caiza had no street smarts whatsoever. He tapped her shoulder as his timer rang. "Time for me to get back to work, mama." She nodded. Just before he put his headphones on, he leaned down and whispered in her ear. "If you need anything at all, you know ole girl upstairs got you. She ain't never gon' say it, but she looks out for you."

Caiza kissed his face and waved to Naomi, who was shaking garter full of bills, accepting money from the men whose faces she had become so used to. Bulldog pulled on her hand as she walked past. She hadn't seen him in a couple of months, mainly because he caught word that she went to Jamaica with Tro. He wasn't happy about that, but she had her own things going on and could really care less. Looking up, Caiza found who she was looking for. Priceless was sitting on the bar, a Black in one hand, a bottle of Jim Beam in the other.

"What you doin' here?"

"Can we talk?"

She took a pull and looked her over, blowing the smoke over her shoulder. "You know it's a two-drink minimum, right?"

This bitch was unbelievable. Frustrated, Caiza slammed a twenty on the bar and grabbed the Beam from Priceless. She pulled down two shot glasses and filled them, downing them one right after the other. Her chest was burning like hell; she didn't know how the hell Priceless could drink bottles of the shit at a time.

"*Now* can we talk?"

Priceless seemed impressed. "Come on." Snatching her bottle back, they went upstairs, and she locked the door behind them. "Any luck so far?" She sat in the guest chair beside Caiza.

"That's why I wanted to talk to you. I need protection."

She frowned and played with a piece of paper on her desk. "What kind of protection?"

"Somebody—someone—wants me dead. Or shut up. One of the two. I don't know who it is, or what else they know about me." Caiza clasped her hands together as her bottom lip trembled. She was about to pour her heart out in desperation.

"Who?"

For the next half hour, Caiza explained as best she could the past month's events, careful not to leave anything out. Priceless' cold green eyes never moved from hers the entire time. When Caiza was done, she sat back in her chair and put a thoughtful look on her face.

"What the fuck you got yourself into, mama?"

"I have no idea."

"I can post somebody outside your crib. They'll tell you who came in and out and make sure nobody gets into your place. Nobody has keys and shit like that, right?"

She shook her head. "No. Rydell is one of the few people whop know where I live."

"A'ight. That's the best I can do. Long as you keep your nose clean and your mouth shut, you'll be alright. That's all I got."

Caiza let go of the breath she'd been holding since she came in the office. "Thanks a lot, Priceless. I owe you one."

"Long as you know," she said softly.

16

Is This the End?

Caiza ran her eyes over her sad-ass transcripts. She was too stressed to study properly, so school was the first thing to suffer. The end of the semester was in two months, and she was barely pulling a C average. She had been at the top of her class for three years and now she was falling apart.

At the moment, her main focus was no longer school. She could take it or leave it. She wanted to know who killed her friend. The guilt and pain were eating away at her when she was awake and haunting her while she slept. What Priceless told her weighed heavy on her mind. Someone was taunting her, playing mind games. She had to have this man put away, and she had to do it before she lost her sanity.

She was losing weight again, making meals out of cocaine, liquor and cigarettes. Her hair was thinning and falling out due to the stress. She couldn't remember the last time she and Rydell had had a coherent conversation. Her cash flow kept going—when she wasn't too drunk or high she did a private party or two. On the outside, she looked fine. The pain, stress and exhaustion was eating away at her from the inside.

Caiza went back to the police station twice before giving up completely. The two detectives were of no use to her. Myeisha's file grew dusty on their desk as they laughed over their doughnuts. She couldn't help feeling like they were laughing in her face.

Meanwhile, back at the House, tensions were high. The girls didn't know what to tell her. They had all seen Myeisha walk out the door but she was on her own after that. They wanted to help, but they didn't know what to do. Even if they did know anything, the code kept their mouths shut. Caiza hated it but she knew that was the way things were. Their safety came first.

She was at a dead end.

Back home, Caiza sat at the kitchen table having a staring contest with a bottle of Remy Martin, one of many liquid gifts from Bulldog. Her mind began to wander again as the thoughts of possible suspects flooded her brain. As much as she wanted to think of other things, this murder still weighed heavily on her mind. Now she could see why some investigations took so long. Just the suspect list was a trip. Caiza rubbed her face in her hands. She looked at her watch and sighed. It was time for her to get to class. Before she left, she placed another call to the police station.

"Ms. Bell, I'm terribly sorry we aren't able to do anything about your friend right now. There are many other investigations pending at this time, and we have to pay at least minimal attention to each case. We're very sorry. But we're doing all we can do."

Caiza shouted and threw the phone across the room in a rage. Caiza slid down the wall and sat there crying until her head pounded. "Why is this happening to me?" she screamed. "Why?"

Sparkle heard the commotion and came to her, wagging her tail with a sad look on her face. Caiza reached out a hand and patted her head. "It's over, baby," she said.

After the better part of an hour, when she tired of crying, she stood and searched for the Tylenol bottle. When she found it, she opened it and spilled it onto the counter, blinded by her wet eyes. Pushing the snow-white powder into lines with her index finger, she desperately searched for something to pull it up with. She didn't find anything and said "fuck it", leaning over and sniffing it up without help.

Pulling her head back from the counter she rubbed her nose and took a deep breath. That was good. She closed her eyes and smiled. After a few seconds, the mellow feeling she had become so used to returned.

Caiza smiled for the first time in weeks. Yes. This was what she needed.

Myeisha was wrong. This wasn't poison. It was medicine. She needed it. Reaching for the bottle of Remy, she took a hard swig. It had taken her too long to reach for the bottle. Caiza usually numbed herself before she could feel the pain. This was all she needed was a little act right. She was feeling better already.

She needed another hit to get her perked up. Still clutching the bottle in her left hand, she helped herself up onto the counter and sniffed down another hit. That one hit her harder than the first one. She felt the familiar euphoria crash over her in waves, and she sank back to the floor, smiling like a circus clown. She lifted the bottle again.

Sparkle barked and ran out of the kitchen when she heard keys out front. Rydell shut and locked the door behind him. His left arm was heavy with groceries. "What's goin' on, Goldilocks?" he asked. Sparkle barked again and looked at the kitchen. He bent over and patted her head, walking in the direction she had just come.

Sparkle began to whimper. "What's the matter, mama? She's at school. Oh it's like that? You don't wanna be here with me? Forget you then."

He almost tripped over her. Rydell tossed the bag on the counter and bent over, touching his fingers to Caiza's neck. She was laid out on the floor, the half-empty bottle of Remy still in her hand. The counter was covered in white powder, as was both of her nostrils. Her eyes were half open as he pulled her into his arms.

"Oh God, Caiza, what the fuck did you do?" he whispered, looking at Sparkle as if she could tell him what had happened. Rydell pried the bottle from her hands. He wasn't exactly sure just how high she was.

"Caiza?"

Her eyes opened and looked around. When she saw him, she smiled, drool sliding out of her mouth. He lifted her forward, where she threw up on the kitchen floor. Rydell cursed and pulled her out of the mess. He carried her into the living room and laid her out on the couch. Running back into the kitchen, he jumped over the foul-smelling bile and wet a rag. He returned to her body and washed her face and hands with it.

She lifted her hand and opened her mouth to speak. "What are you doing here?" It slurred hard as it came out and he tilted his face away from her breath.

"It's a good thing I got here, isn't it? What the hell is wrong with you,

Caiza?"

He didn't even know who to call. Wait. That girl that was always calling there. Carrie, Katrice, Caprice…Kahmes. He found her cell phone and dialed the number.

"Hello?"

"Is this Kahmes?"

"Who's this?"

"This is Rydell."

"Oh, what up, shawty. How you? Where's Caiza?"

Rydell was pacing. "She's on the floor right now. I don't know what's happening to her."

"What? What do you mean?"

Rydell was calmer than he thought he'd be. "I don't know if she's ODing, if she's high or what. I just know that I got her here and she's laid out."

He heard a bunch of rustling in the background. "Is she breathing?"

Rydell was near tears himself. He ran his hands under Caiza's nose and felt a little bit of warmth. "Yeah, yeah. She's breathing."

"A'ight. Feel her head. Is she warm?"

"Yeah."

Kahmes jumped out of her bed and pulled on a pair of sweatpants. Manny, her baby's father, stirred and rolled over. She pulled on a shirt, Nike Shox and went into her closet.

"Put an ice pack on her head. Oh! And milk. Give her milk."

"What's that going to do?"

"I don't know. I saw it on TV once. If her heart didn't stop, the milk will absorb the coke. Or something like that. I don't know, just do it."

Kahmes sucked her teeth. "I knew this shit was gonna happen," she muttered.

"What? Knew what was going to happen?"

"Evelyn said she was gonna fucking OD. And what does the bitch do?   She   ODs." Kahmes sucked her teeth again as she reached for something to tie her hair back with.

Sudden realization dawned on Rydell. "You knew she was on cocaine, didn't you?"

"Honey, we were all on it."

"How could you? How could you do this to her?"

"Look, nigga. Chica didn't tell you what's going on with her, that's not my fault. You called me, remember that."

Rydell needed her. He calmed his tone. "How soon can you get here?"

"I'm already on my way." She hung up.

Rydell tossed the phone on the sofa next to Caiza. He ran and opened her refrigerator, snatching out the quart of milk.

"Here, drink this." Rydell lifted Caiza's head and poured the milk down her throat. As soon as he got it all down, she stood and ran to the bathroom. He heard her hurl again. She came back, using the wall to hold herself up. "I don't feel so good," was all she said.

There was a bang on the door, and Rydell turned long enough to shout out, "Who?"

"Who the fuck you think it is? Open the fucking door."

Rydell let her in and she breezed past, going straight for Caiza. She was laying on the couch now, a bag of peas on her forehead, watching them.

"Caiza? You can hear me?"

"I hear you just fine," she whispered.

"You almost died, mami. What the fuck was you thinking?"

Caiza rubbed a hand over her face. "I'd rather be dead. You shouldn't have bothered," she said, rolling off the couch.

Kahmes stood and put her hands on her hips. "I didn't drive all the way over here to hear you say that."

Rydell's fear turned quickly to anger. "What the hell *were* you thinking? Cocaine? You know what that does to people? And how long have you been on that shit anyway?"

"I don't want to talk about this right now." Caiza stood, wobbling. "Just leave me alone."

Kahmes couldn't believe her ears. "Are you kidding? You almost died, and you want us to leave you alone?"

Caiza stumbled and tripped but got herself upright. She pointed a drunken finger at the both of them. The effects of the drugs hadn't quite worn off yet but she was certainly better than she had been.

"She told me. She told me to slow down. She told me things were going to happen to me. And you know what I told her? I told her not to worry about me. I just knew nothing was going to happen to me. I was just makin' my money, livin' my life.

"She told me something was gon' happen. And it did. But not to me." Caiza cried freely, her words barely audible. She pointed at her chest. "My best friend is dead because I didn't want to listen to her. She told me to slow down, and I didn't want to listen to her."

"Caiza, she's not dead because of you. Someone murdered her. That's not her fault, that's not your fault," Kam said softly.

"It is my fault. I was supposed to look out for her. She was my baby sister. She told me and I didn't listen. Myeisha is dead because of me."

Rydell shook his head. Caiza had to be delusional if she thought her friend was dead because of her actions. "This had nothing to do with you, Caiza. Myeisha loved you and you loved her. You didn't kill her."

"Yes, I did. She's dead because of me."

Rydell took Caiza by the shoulders. "Listen to me, Caiza. Just stop it and listen to me. Stop trying to take the easy way out. Sure it's okay to feel bad over what happened, but it won't change the fact that it happened. Myeisha is dead. You loved her. I loved her. Shit, everybody she met loved her. Some pig raped and murdered her. He deserves all the blame. Not you. You didn't cause it. Stop pity partying and let us help you get yourself together." He was looking into her eyes sternly as he said that.

Caiza covered her mouth with her hands, a single tear finding its way down her cheek. Her face proved that she understood how wrong she had been to take on this burden by herself. It had almost cost Caiza her life. "I need water," she whispered.

Rydell went to go get it.

Caiza pulled Kam close to her, almost taking her arm off.

"Girl, what the hell is wrong with you?"

Kahmes was looking into the face of a sober woman. Something had been said that struck a nerve in this girl because the pain and hurt in her eyes had that quickly been replaced by fear and horror.

"Kam, I never said anything to him about Myeisha getting raped."

Kahmes didn't understand. "Of course, you had to. Didn't he watch the tapes with you?"

"No." Caiza shook her head. "No. He left right before I watched them. And then I took them right back to Priceless. I didn't want anyone to know what happened. It was humiliating."

Kam's face was still twisted in thought. Then suddenly, it seemed as if a lightbulb dinged just over her head. "Caiza, you don't think—"

A glass fell to the floor and broke behind them, splashing water on the floor and on Caiza's bare legs. Caiza jumped and spun around.

"I told you to stay out of it."

Kahmes jumped and yelped when she saw the gun Rydell held in his hand. It was pointed at them, and his face said he wasn't playing. "I gave you a chance, and I told you to stay out of it."

Caiza's breath was falling out of her chest as she tried to take a step backward. Her mind was in no state to handle this. "Rydell? What are you doing?"

"Shut up! Make a move—make a sound—and I'll do you both right here. All you had to do was go to the damn funeral, cry a little bit and let it go. But no—" he walked toward the girls slowly—"no. You wanted to be motherfucking Sherlock Holmes. Here's a mystery for you. How many dumb bitches does it take to dig a grave?"

Caiza was frozen in place. She couldn't believe this was happening to her.

"I sat around and let you treat me like shit. You walked all over me. You think people don't talk? You think I don't fucking know about Jamaica? You lied to me, Caiza. I held out for you and you gave yourself to someone else. What you gotta say about that?"

Sparkle seemed to sense what was going on and stood, ears laid flat back, growling at Rydell. She stood between the two of them and held her ground. Suddenly, without warning, Rydell savagely kicked the dog in the head, and she fell to the floor. Caiza screamed at the sight of her lifetime companion being treated so savagely. Rydell was not interested in her screams, and took no pity on her.

"Answer me, goddamnit!"

Caiza was at a loss for words. How could he have known? Her face burned with shame. "I-I-I don't know what to say. I'm sorry, Rydell. I wasn't trying to hurt you. I'm sorry."

"It's a little late for that now," he answered, cocking the weapon.

Caiza threw her hands up to shield her face. Kahmes shoved Caiza and rushed Rydell, and the gun went off. He pushed her off him and she went down, taking him with her. Someone screamed, none of them was sure who. Kam didn't move from her place on the floor. Rydell rolled her off him and scrambled for the gun, which had fallen out of his hands. Caiza kicked it away from him.

"Bitch," he snarled. He stood and tried to dive for the gun. Before he could, Kahmes stuck out one of her long legs and tripped him. She reached for the gun. "Run, Caiza."

Caiza didn't need another warning. She was almost at the front door when she had an attack of conscience. She couldn't leave Kahmes there alone. She went back and saw Rydell and Kam wrestling for the gun on the living room floor.

Rydell lifted Kam to her feet and punched her in the face. Kam went down hard. Caiza was feeling weak, like another panic attack was coming on. But she gathered all her strength and jumped on Rydell's back. She sank her teeth into his neck, and he howled and clawed at her. His nails raked across her face, just missing her eyes. Kam threw the gun and dragged Caiza off Rydell. She kicked him in the crotch with all her might and ran. Rydell shouted and dropped. Caiza followed Kahmes, who was already down the hall.

"I'm gonna kill you," Rydell shouted from where he was kneeling. Kam had kicked the hell out of him, and he could barely move. He tried to shake off the pain and chase after the girls. He only succeeded in a fast limp. Picking up the gun off the floor, he turned the corner and saw that the front door was wide open. He assumed they wouldn't take the elevator. Rydell limped toward the stairs.

Kahmes was wringing her hands as she pounded on the lobby button. "Come on, hurry up," she muttered.

Caiza's eyes were rolling back in her head. Kahmes saw her slump from the corner of her eye.

"Mami? Mami, what's the matter?" It was when she didn't answer that Kam saw the flower of blood spreading across her left shoulder. "Caiza," she whispered. The elevator stopped at last, and Kam threw Caiza's arm over her shoulder, struggling to carry her weight. Caiza wasn't a heavy girl, but she was dragging now, and her body was turning to dead weight.

Kahmes shouted to Jeffrey. "Help me! Please, help me!"

Jeffrey looked up from the front desk where he was casually flipping through a *Details* magazine. He took one look at Kam's black eye and Caiza's bloody body and lifted the telephone to call the police.

"What the hell is going on?"

Kahmes broke into tears. "It's her boyfriend. He's trying to kill her."

"Caiza!" Rydell shouted from behind them. He let off a shot in Kam's direction. She screamed and pulled Caiza to the ground.

"This doesn't concern you, Kahmes. Let her go. We need to talk."

Jeffrey came from around the desk. "Now, sir, I'm sure we can come to some happy medium here. Just put the gun down."

Rydell's reply was firing two shots into Jeffrey's body. He fell to the floor next to the two girls. Kam screamed again, crying harder. "Stop it! Leave her alone!"

"Shut up," he shouted again.

Kahmes took her eyes off Caiza for just an instant, and then looked over at Jeffrey. He was still alive. She wondered briefly about Caiza's dog. "What do you want? You think it's going to change anything?"

"I want to know why. She lied to me. I loved her. I loved her. You know what it's like to be lied to?"

Caiza was fading, but she wasn't deaf. She lifted her head and spoke to Rydell. "I'm sorry, Rydell." Her voice came out just above a whisper.

"She said she was sorry," Kam choked. She was crying now, afraid for both their lives. "What more do you want?"

"I want her to suffer like I suffered. She's going... You're going to pay for this, Caiza."

Caiza used Kam's body to help herself to her feet. Her shoulder was throbbing like there was no tomorrow, her knees were knocking together, and her stomach was turning, but she had to get Rydell to lower the gun. Kam held her hand as she walked forward.

"But Myeisha... what did she have to do with this?"

"That dirty bitch was the whole reason for this. She covered for you. She was running from man to man, and you were following right behind her. She took you away from me."

Caiza took a wobbly step forward. "Rydell, how could you say those things? Myeisha was my best friend. I loved her. How could you?"

Rydell began to look nervous. "Don't try to guilt trip me. She knew what she was doing. If she were really your friend, she wouldn't have stood by and let you see other men behind my back. You're just as bad as she was."

He steadied his aim on Caiza. If one strained their ears, they could hear very faintly in the background the sound of sirens.

"You women, you demand respect. You demand love. I was good to you, Caiza. I loved you. What did I get in return? You gave me your ass to kiss! Nobody's going to make a fool out of me." He reached forward suddenly and grabbed Caiza. He wrapped his arm around her neck and pointed the gun to her head. "Now we're gonna get out of here, and if you make a move, Kahmes, I swear to God, I'll kill her."

Kahmes was full into the waterworks now. She was crying so hard her eyes were nearly swollen shut. "Please, Rydell," she wailed. "Just let her go. She's sorry. She said she was sorry. Please let her go."

Rydell began to walk Caiza to the door. He had taken three steps when four armed officers burst through the doors.

"Put your hands up."

"Drop the gun."

"No," he shouted back, pointing the gun at Caiza's head.

The seconds passed by too slow for words as the entire scene turned into something out of a movie. Caiza collapsed in his arms. She was losing blood fast. Her heart was pumping overtime, and her breathing was slowing down. Her system was already strained, and the blood loss wasn't helping. He lifted her limp body, the gun still pointed at her head.

Five. "Just get outta here."

Four. "Drop the fucking gun, mister!" the closest officer called. "Nobody has to get hurt here today."

Three. "Let the lady go!"

Two. "You want her?" Rydell screamed. "Take her." He thrust Caiza's body forward. Kahmes dove and caught her, covering her body with her own. Rydell pointed his gun at the police and began to shoot.

One. They fired back.

Shots were fired back and forth, and Rydell's body jerked like a rag doll as the bullets passed through him. Kahmes was clutching Caiza as tight as she could, trying to force the sounds of gunfire out of her own ears. Rydell dropped his gun and staggered backward. He touched a bloody hand to his belly, then looked at Caiza's body on the ground.

He cracked a smile.

"You won, baby girl."

His eyes rolled back in his skull and he fell backward, drawing his last breath as he hit the ground. The officer rushed forward and shouted for an ambulance. Caiza closed her eyes until she could hear the sirens coming to take her away. She was, by the grace of God, still alive.

It was over.

Epilogue

The first person Caiza saw when she entered the House of Sin for the last time was Priceless.

"You workin' tonight?"

Caiza's face twisted up in sudden anger then into a relieved smile when she saw the laugh already formed on her lips.

"You alright?"

Caiza nodded. After she got out of the hospital, she hadn't been able to talk, on account of the trauma. Kahmes had come to stay with her for a few days after her surgery, to make sure she was okay. "I'm alive," she managed to whisper.

Priceless looked her over, taking note of the arm she had in a sling. "Can't ask for nothin' better than that, right?"

Caiza looked away, a far-away look on her face. She didn't want to think about what could have been. If only…

Priceless understood and nodded. "You need a job, you come to me, you hear?"

Caiza shook her head. "I can't come back, Priceless. There's too much…" Caiza let the sentence hang in the air.

"Don't worry about that. You just come see me every now and then, we'll be alright. If you need a job anywhere anytime, I got you. Hear me?"

Caiza's eyes welled with tears for the last time as she accepted a hug. Priceless let her go and smiled softly, her green eyes dancing in the light. This was out of character for her, and it made Caiza wonder what was really on her mind.

"That's never going to happen again, hear that? Now get out of here. Oh and how's that damn dog they said you were bitchin about?"

"Sparkle? She's fine. She's doing real good. The doctor said Rydell didn't break nothin', he just knocked her out."

"Good to hear. Kay, now you can get outta here."

Caiza smiled and headed into the dressing room. The girls were out on stage now, performing a set in Easter Bunny outfits. She emptied the contents of her drawer into the bag, looking at the memories of the past two years with pain and nostalgia. There was one of her with Tro, one with Bulldog, and another with all the girls on her first night headlining, one hand clutching the bottle of Dom Perignon.

Another picture of her and Rydell sat in the upper left hand corner. She frowned and pulled it down, crumpling it. Thinking better of it, she lit a cigarette and threw the burning picture in the trash. The final picture was she and Myeisha hugging each other the night of Myeisha's birthday, the night she met Steve. Myeisha was smiling so wide; she looked so happy.

Caiza dropped the bag on her chair and walked over to Myeisha's old vanity table. The lights had been turned off and a cross had been hung over one of the lights. There was picture of her in the center of the glass. Myeisha was smiling brightly, sitting cross-legged on the bar. Caiza chuckled. That girl always had a smile on her face. The picture said RIP under it and all the girls had signed their names in gold marker around the outside of the mirror. Under RIP, it declared in curly script, *We will always love you*.

Caiza kissed two fingers and touched them to the picture, turning her back. She grabbed her bag and took one last look back at the dressing room. So much had happened here, in what seemed like such a short time. She had learned so much and come so far. But she turned and left the memories where they belonged, in the past.

Caiza stood in front of her car for a few minutes longer than she should have when she made it outside. The big sign meant so much. She remembered briefly what Kade had said her first night there. *You in the House now, baby. All we do is sin.* And sin she had. But Caiza felt she had more than paid for it. Her soul was washed clean. She had made her peace. And now it was time to move on.

Fin

Read an excerpt from

The Desk of Jacki
Simmons:

The Madam

Coming Soon!

The Madam

They say power is the ultimate aphrodisiac.

My girls say its jasmine. The smell fills your body and mind with the most powerful urges. Urges you knew I could satisfy. You looked to me when you wanted something. You called my name. You asked, you begged, you pleaded. And I loved every filthy minute of it.

You tried to fool yourself into believing you could live without me. But you knew you couldn't resist. You were in too deep. Your mind was on me every waking moment and I was the star of all your dreams at night. Your wife and girlfriend no longer caught your eye. She no longer fulfilled your desires or satisfied you. I was your dollar bill, your needle, your pipe. All you had to do was sniff me, shoot me, smoke me. And then I was there in your system until it was time for your next dose. You loved me–no, you were *addicted* to me-and there was nothing you could do about it.

I was any and everything you wanted me to be when and where and how you wanted it. I made your every fantasy come true and I was everything you needed. I was your escape. You ran to me. You told me your problems and I loved them away. You grew attached. Your lovers hated me without even knowing me. They knew there was a force that was pulling your love away. They knew some mystery woman was the reason for your sudden lack of interest. Had they treated you like I treated you, there would be no me.

I've often been asked whether or not I regret it. I would be lying if I said yes. They told me I destroyed lives. I hear it everyday. "Are you happy now? How can you sleep at night? Have you no heart?" I smile at them. I answer, yes I am, on my left side and its right between my lungs like yours. I refuse to feel bad for what I have done. I feel it is my civic duty. It is my job to give back. In the figurative sense, of course.

I would also be lying if I said it wasn't the money. The money was lovely. It poured in not unlike the waters of a rainstorm. It was intoxicating. Once you have it, you only want more. And oh, did I want more. I had never wanted anything more in my life. That had always been my dream to have all the desires I could out of life. And I did what I thought was best to get them. Money and power came hand in hand and there came a time when I no longer knew which I wanted more.

Power is indeed the ultimate aphrodisiac.

One: The Talk

Jade wondered if the fall from the fifth-floor window would be enough to kill her.

She crossed and uncrossed her legs; unaware of what had gone wrong. This had to be some kind of a joke. Any minute now Ashton was going to come out and tell her she'd been Punk'd. Jade scanned the room because she was damn sure she was on Candid Camera.

As the seconds passed and the look on his face didn't change she began to realize how serious this really was. The thought after that was how the hell she was going to get out of here. The door was so close but so far away. There was no way she could make it out before he let off a shot. She couldn't imagine the pain of a bullet in her back and wasn't ready to find out either. So she sat stick straight in the chair, trying her hardest not to betray her emotions with her face.

Clearing her throat she said, "This was not what I had in mind when you said you wanted to talk."

"I knew this was the only way to get your attention."

The loaded .45 in her face had most definitely captured her attention. Jade thought this was the perfect time for someone to enter his office with an urgent message. Any other time his office door would be opening and closing like last call at the Kripsy Kreme. Not a soul. She was assed out as far as help was concerned. Jade shifted her eyes from the gun to his face and back to the gun. She spoke to the weapon.

"Is this at all necessary? Aren't you being a little irrational?"

"I'm not being irrational. You need to learn, Jade, that this is strictly business. I take my business very seriously."

She folded her hands, determined to keep her cool. "I noticed. You're threatening to kill me."

"I didn't threaten you. I gave you a business proposition. Which will not be turned down."

His exact words were "do it or I kill you." That surely sounded like a threat to her.

"A business proposition has two ends. Apparently I have no say in this matter."

"You're finally getting the point."

Jade sighed and studied her fingernails. "You want me to perform an illegal service if I value my life. You want me to run a whore house."

"You're putting words in my mouth."

"Am I?"

"When did you hear the words 'whore house' leave my lips?"

Was he kidding? This *had* to be a joke. Jade was tempted to stand up and bitch slap him. The gun made the thought remain a temptation, not an action.

"I can't do this."

"I didn't ask you whether or not you could do it. I gave you an either or. *Either* you do *or* you die."

"You're going to kill me if you don't get your way. Kind of bratty. How old are you?"

He laughed, a rumbling sound that rose from deep in his chest. He waved the gun. "I like how you put that. Bratty. Well, for lack of a better term, yes."

She exhaled like she was smoking a cigarette. This was ridiculous. She stood to leave.

The gun followed her. "One more step and I will level you, Jade."

Jade shook her head, her curls bouncing. "I'm not doing this."

"We can drag this out as long as you'd like. But the only way you leave this room is working for me," he cocked the gun, "or dead. Your choice."

She slammed her hands on the desk, immediately thinking better of that bad decision. "Really. You're going to kill me? I'm not getting my hands tied up in this. This is your shit, you got yourself into it, it has nothing to do with me." She turned her back.

"I am very serious about this."

She knew he was. Her eyes closed and she bowed her head, biting down on her bottom lip. Silently, Jade laid her cards out on the table. The man had no problem killing her. As tempting as the offer was it was wrong on so many levels. Before she opened her eyes she made a fly-by-the-pants decision, regretting it instantly but knowing it would save her life.

Jade took a deep breath before opening her eyes and turning back around to face him. "Would it be too much to ask that you not point that gun at me?"

"Do we have a deal?"

"Would you lower the gun?"

"Do we have a deal?"

The air was thick with silence and neither of them blinked during the battle of wills. He was going to get what he wanted whether she liked it or not.

"Yes."

He lowered the gun, not before gesturing with it. "Sit down."

She did so, crossing her legs again and folding her hands. She felt completely helpless. In any other situation she was behind the desk pointing the figurative gun, making the threats. Now the tables were turned and he had her trapped in a vise grip. She hated not being the one with power.

He kicked his feet up, sliding a cherry wood box closer to himself. He lifted out a cigar and put it under his nose, savoring the aroma. Producing a cutter from inside his jacket he clipped the end and lit it. Taking a few deep puffs he blew the smoke in her direction. She turned her head ever so slightly and the smoke curled toward the ceiling.

"In your hurry to decline my offer you never heard the perks."

She snorted. "I wasn't sure there were any."

"A salary increase."

"How high?"

"Double, maybe triple in time."

She raised an eyebrow. She was already bringing home bacon high in the six-figure bracket; a couple of extra dollars wouldn't hurt. "And legalities?"

He turned up his face and waved the cigar, the smoke dancing away. "Don't worry about that."

"I am worried about it."

"Don't be."

She exhaled quietly, knowing she would have time to weigh pros and cons later. "How many?"

"Six, maybe seven. If it works out as well as I'm anticipating you can expand."

"What's your part in this?"

"I take half, put it into the company." He clasped his hands together and aimed them at her. "You get to live."

"So let me get this straight. These girls are going to make money on my watch, which you take and use to save yourself from going under?"

"You pick up quick."

Her head was spinning. She rubbed her temples. This was outrageous. "And that's all?"

"That's all."

It was a long while before she answered. "Fine."

"I'm glad we could work this out. You'll be hearing from me." Standing, he waited for Jade to do the same. He stretched his arm out in front of him, indicating her dismissal. He was smiling as if nothing had ever happened.

Jade pulled the door shut behind her. He followed her every move clear down to the elevator. She held her composure as she walked away, head held high. She never once looked back at his office as she waited for the elevator. Stepping off in the lobby, Jade continued to walk at an even pace. Her face was empty, showing nothing. She was no fool, aware of the cameras that tracked her every step.

He was watching her, always watching her. Like fucking Santa Claus. *He sees you when you're sleeping, he knows when you're awake*…He was everywhere. Jade barely slammed her car door before jamming the key into the ignition and speeding off. It was five lights later that her heart finally slowed to a normal pace. Her fingers were shaking as she handled the steering wheel.

At the next red light she slammed her hands on the dashboard. "This is bullshit!" she shouted to herself. The wheels of her mind were still frozen out of shock so thinking her way out of this was out of the question.

Fuck the police. That ain't happenin. I tell them and I'm definitely dead. I don't do this and I'm dead. So I'm screwed. Just keep my mouth shut. I can handle that. It's simple. Nothing to it.

Even as the words ran through her brain Jade was having a hard time convincing herself. She had gotten into some sure shit this time. But she was determined to make it work to her advantage.

The purse skidded across the hall table and hit the floor when it left Jade's hands. She sucked her teeth and locked her door behind her. She kicked the purse as she walked past, letting her hair down with a flick of her wrist. Her jasmine scented locks flooded over her shoulders. Kicking off her heels, she shrugged out of her suit jacket and laid it on the table, promising herself to come back for it and the purse later. Right now she needed to think.

She wanted a cigarette badly. Only problem was that she'd quit that months ago. This was one of few the times she wished she hadn't. The nicotine would have come in handy; she needed to relax. Her mind was reeling and she couldn't get right.

"Baby?"

Jade jumped out of her skin and whirled around ready to fight. She caught sight of the speaker and her heart fell back into its place.

"What the hell are you doing here? You scared the shit out of me."

Cameron noticed. He hadn't seen her in over week and this was not the response he was expecting. He saw how tight her body was and immediately responded to his woman's needs. His big hands made their way to her shoulders. "Why so tense?"

She didn't skip a beat as she replied, "Long day."

His fingers worked a kink out of her neck. "Tell me about it."

Her eyes opened slowly. Was that a question or a statement? She went with the vaguest answer she could muster.

"I'm just glad I'm home."

Cameron seemed satisfied as he walked her into the living room. "You want to talk about it?" He laid her down on the couch and slid her stockings off.

Oh of course my love! Let's see, where do I begin? Well, my boss threatened to kill me today after forcing me to take highly illegal means to save our company from financial distress. I have no choice but to do what he says or else you'll never see me again. Isn't that lovely? "Not really."

"Stay there. I'll be right back." She didn't nod, just watched through half open eyes as he jogged into the kitchen. He was a good man, a man that didn't deserve the hailstorm of shit that was about to come crashing down on his head. Her eyes were closed when he returned. Something cold touched her hand.

"Chardonnay. Relax." He put the bottle on the floor next to the couch.

Jade thanked him and lifted the drink to her lips. She didn't open her eyes, only slowly sipped her wine and thought.

He threatened her life. She wasn't able to move past that point, it was stuck in her mind and every time she thought she could let it go it popped back up. He was serious about this.

Of course, she could go to the police. But she knew the outcome. He wasn't treating this like a game and she didn't expect him to. There were serious decisions to make here, decisions to be weighed out.

One massive pro was the money. It wasn't that she really needed it, her salary as an agent gave her plenty of flexibility and comfort, but she was not going to shake a stick at a little more.

If she looked on the bright side of this thing, she'd be rich and she'd be in. Not that she didn't also have status but much like the money, a little more couldn't hurt. For a few minutes the plan was perfect. As the liquor opened her up and mellowed her out, and Cameron's hands continued to work their magic, her mind wandered into the specifics, namely, the cons.

What he was asking her to do was enough for a lengthy prison sentence. It wasn't her conscience that was bothering her; it was her logic. She saw right through him. He was a moneymaker and he was using her as an amenity. He expected her to keep his clients happy. He didn't care how she did it, only that it got done. The offer wasn't anything to turn her nose up at but the severance package left much to be desired.

What if the money wasn't what he told her it would be? What if she couldn't build up a client list? Who could she trust beside herself? What if it all fell apart? The biggest what if was rubbing her feet at that very moment.

She loved Cameron with all she had. They had been together for seven years, since the day she graduated college. He wanted to marry her, she knew, and he would do anything she asked. She also knew if she did this she would be putting him through hell but she didn't have much of a choice. It was either that or he could kiss his woman goodbye.

She knew her man. If she told Cam that she had been threatened, he'd be on the next thing smoking to the police station. She didn't want to hurt him. Yet at the same time she figured that what he didn't know wouldn't kill him.

"You sure you don't want to talk about it?"

Jade opened her eyes. He had interrupted her train of thought. "What?"

He pointed at her. "Your face is all twisted up."

Because I'm contemplating life and death, baby. She lifted a hand to her cheek.

"Is it? I must be tired."

"You look it."

She playfully kicked him. "Oh thanks. I feel so much better."

He smiled at her and caught her foot. "You're sexy anyway," he said, one hand traveling up her leg.

She smiled when he said that. He returned the sentiment and took it as a sign. Jade sat her glass on the floor and lifted her hips. Cam pulled down her skirt and panties in one motion. Flipping her hair over her shoulder she unbuttoned her shirt. He was already undressed by the time she did so. She tossed her clothes on the floor and climbed in his lap, biting hard on her lip as she lowered herself onto him.

Jade scratched his back with one hand, the other softly holding the back of his head. Cam held on to her hips as she rose and fell on top of him. "I missed you baby," he breathed into her ear. "I missed you so much." He licked her ear then, sending a chill up her spine. Jade moaned softly, biting his neck as gently as she could.

Cameron lifted his hands from her hips and unsnapped her bra, Jade leaned back and slid it off her arms without breaking the rhythm. She kept up the ride as he took one of her small breasts into his mouth. While he massaged and sucked, she continued to moan, digging her nails into his shoulders. Every move they both made turned each other on more and more until both of them were a melted sweaty mess in the middle of the couch.

Jade climbed off of Cam and lay sat back, panting hard. He was breathing hard as well, legs sticky from their exertion. He looked over at Jade and smiled. She returned the smile. They smiled at each other for a long while.

Some inside joke brought on by their eye contact caused them to both laugh aloud. He reached down and grabbed the bottle of wine. Jade held out her glass for a refill. Just when she needed him he always delivered. She loved her some Cam.

That was all she wanted, just to forget every other moment. After the day she had nothing felt better than to clear her mind of everything except her own pleasure.

Two hours later found Jade sitting back on the couch brooding, Cameron's head in her lap. They made love again, on the floor this time, long and slow. He'd been sleeping like a baby since. Since Jade couldn't remember the last time she felt so good, she put off thinking about her situation until just now.

She looked down and rubbed his cheek. He didn't stir so she lifted his head and replaced her lap with a pillow. Tip toeing away, she lifted the phone out of the cradle and went into her bedroom with it, shutting the door behind her.

"*You have reached Marcella Jenkins. I'm either on the phone or away from my desk. Please leave a detailed message and I will return your call as soon as possible. Thank you.*"

Jade rolled her eyes and left her message. "Call me. It's important." She clicked off and let the phone fall back to the bed, knowing it would be a matter of seconds before Marcella called her back. She was right.

"What happened?"

"He has lost his mind."

In her office across town, the late afternoon sun streamed through windows and bathed her office a bright red. Marcella leaned back and lifted her feet up onto her desk. "Yeah?"

"The company is in debt."

"How much?"

"Three and a half million dollars."

Marcella's feet fell off the desk as she shot up. "*What?*"

"He said his artists are leaving and taking their money with them. So he wants me to persuade them to stick around."

"And how do you plan to do that?"

"I don't. He planned it already."

"What's on his mind?"

Jade didn't know how to say it without it coming out wrong. "Using my assets."

Marcella relaxed, returning to her original position. "Money? He wants you to use your money? You've got plenty of that. And you've got pull too. You make a couple of phone calls and he'll be-"

"I'm not talking about money, Marcy. Or pull."

"Okay, well then I'm lost."

Jade sighed, covering her face with a hand, her slender fingers rubbing her forehead. "He wants me to use my *assets*," she repeated.

It took a her moment, but when she figured it out, Marcella shot up again, this time kicking over everything on her desk. "What? He said what?"

"You heard me."

"You're not serious." She didn't want to believe Jade. Leaning backwards, Marcella looked at her calendar. No, it wasn't April 1ˢᵗ, so what kind of prank was Jade trying to play?

"Marcy."

Marcella stood and cradled her phone between her shoulder and chin, sliding her chair out of her way. Reaching into her desk she retrieved a pack of Virginia Slims. Walking behind her desk she flung open her balcony doors, stepping out into the crisp air. She took a deep breath before lighting up and filling her lungs with smoke. Propping the cigarette between her lips, she closed the doors behind her.

"Tell me exactly what he said."

Jade repeated the meat of their conversation. Marcella kept her trained ears open and drank in every word. After a few minutes she shook her head in disbelief. She knew he was running out of money but this was ridiculous. He was asking Jade to do the unthinkable. Marcella scratched the end of her nose and pulled again, asking as she blew out smoke.

"So what are you going to do?"

The line was silent for a while. Marcella thought she'd hung up.

"Jade?"

"I'm here."

"What are you going to do?" she repeated.

Another long silence. Then she heard Jade sigh.

"Do I have much of a choice?"

He saw her coming from down the hall. Her suede coat billowed around her as she stormed in his direction. If he squinted one eye and gave her white hair, she really could have passed for Storm of the *X-Men*. He smiled at the look on her face, amused by her anger. He already knew why she was here; he was well aware of how close she was with Jade. Their conversation had undoubtedly made its way to Marcella's ears.

Marcella flung his door open and filled the room with her presence. He had to hand it to her. The woman knew how to make an entrance. And she was such a beautiful vision, such a lady, so classy-

"You filthy piece of shit," she spat.

He pretended to be unfazed. "Good morning Ms. Jenkins. It's lovely to see you again."

"Don't play games with me, you prick. You know why I'm here."

"I'm quite sure I don't."

"I know what the fuck is going on. You know you're a dog for what you're doing to her."

He clasped his hands together and pointed both indexes at her. "I don't think that's any of your business."

"It damn well is. She is my business."

A nasty visual crossed his mind. He brushed it away. "Are you here to threaten me? Because I'm not moved."

"I'm not here to threaten you. I'm here to get all in your ass. I got my eyes on you, you bastard."

He shifted in his seat and looked past her, out the glass wall. "Marcella, if we're quite finished here I think you should leave."

She narrowed her eyes to snakelike slits and breathed venom in her next words. "You better kill me if you want me to keep my mouth shut. Because there is no way in red hell you're going to make her go through with this." She turned to exit in a blaze of anger. As her hand touched the door he called out to her.

"Ah, Marcella."

She turned.

"You had better keep your mouth shut."

She snickered. "For what?"

"Because if you don't, I *will* kill you."

Wanna get Stripped?

Enter to win a gift certificate
to the
S-Factor
Located in all the major cities
and learn first hand from
professionals
how to
get
STRIPPED

Log onto our web site for details
www.melodramapublishing.com

CONTEST ENDS
JANUARY 31, 2007

WINNER WILL BE ANNOUNCED

FEBRUARY 14, 2007

OCTOBER 2006
SEX, SIN & BROOKLYN
by CRYSTAL LACEY WINSLOW

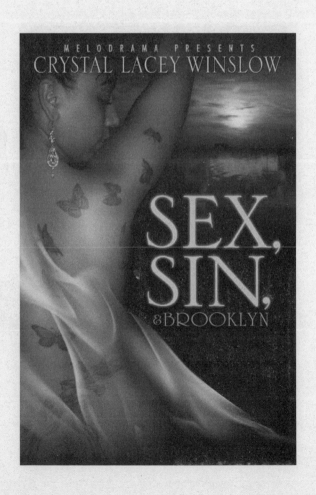

NOVEMBER 2006
IN MY 'HOOD
by ENDY

SEPTEMBER 2006
CROSS ROADS
CARL PATTERSON

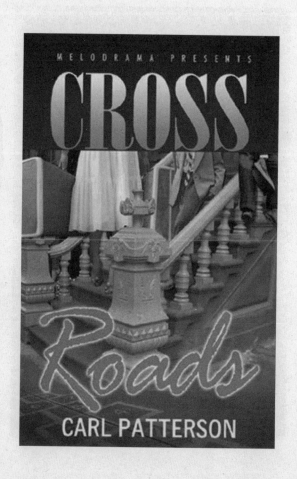

JANUARY 2007
EVA FIRST LADY OF SIN
by STORM

WIFEY
by KIKI SWINSON

#1 ESSENCE MAGAZINE BESTSELLER

I'M STILL WIFEY
by KIKI SWINSON
ESSENCE AND BLACKBOARD MAGAZINE
BESTSELLER

COMING SOON!!!
LIFE AFTER WIFEY (PART 3 OF TRILOGY)

A TWISTED TALE OF KARMA
by AMALEKA G. McCALL

MENACE II SOCIETY
by Al-Saadiq Banks, Mark Anthony, Crystal Lacey Winslow
Isadore Johnson, and JM Benjamin